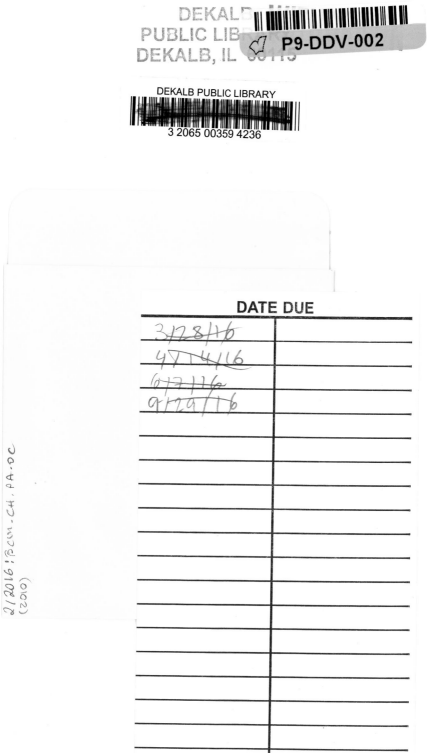

DATE DUE

3/28/16	
4/14/16	
6/7/16	
9/29/16	

| GAYLORD | PRINTED IN U.S.A. |

2/2016 :BCM.CH.PA.OC
(002)

THE WINDSWEPT
FLAME

Center Point
Large Print

Also by Marcia Lynn McClure and available from Center Point Large Print:

Dusty Britches
Weathered Too Young

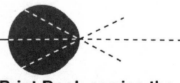

**This Large Print Book carries the
Seal of Approval of N.A.V.H.**

THE WINDSWEPT FLAME

Marcia Lynn McClure

CENTER POINT LARGE PRINT
THORNDIKE, MAINE

The text of this Large Print edition is unabridged.
In other aspects, this book may vary
from the original edition.
Printed in the United States of America
on permanent paper.
Set in 16-point Times New Roman type.

ISBN: 978-1-62899-836-8

Library of Congress Cataloging-in-Publication Data

Names: McClure, Marcia Lynn.
Title: The windswept flame / Marcia Lynn McClure.
Description: Center Point Large Print edition. | Thorndike, Maine :
Center Point Large Print, 2016. | ©2005
Identifiers: LCCN 2015038573 | ISBN 9781628998368
    (hardcover : alk. paper)
Subjects: LCSH: Mothers and daughters—Fiction. | Frontier and pioneer
life—Fiction. | Large type books. | GSAFD: Western stories.
Classification: LCC PS3613.C36 W56 2016 | DDC 813/.6—dc23
LC record available at http://lccn.loc.gov/2015038573

To Sandy,
A continuing story, like ours . . .
And deservedly yours.
A commemoration of twenty-six years of tried
and true "bosom" friendship.
To loyalty, endurance, and two hearts that are
forever melded together.

•   •   •

To "Phil,"
For "the dance" gifted long ago
beneath a warm summer moon . . . in a starlit
field of romance.

•   •   •

To my husband,
My reason to "run for the roses!"

The Windswept Flame

Prologue

Soft pink and warm orange entwined, reaching across the azure of the evening spring sky toward the setting sun. Gentle wisps of clouds floated like phantom feathers fanning across the broad arc of heaven overhead. The scent of new rain still lingered in the air and on the pasture grasses. The cool breeze caused Cedar Dale to shiver, and she pulled her shawl more snugly about her shoulders. Still, it was only a cool breeze, not a cold one—for spring was whispering of warmer weather to come, and winter had grown tired of lingering to listen.

There was no sound, save the quiet whisper of the breeze through the grass, the comforting lowing of cattle in the distance, and the sweet song of some lingering night-trilling bird. Nature's soothing ballad—her lullaby of settling dusk—offered a nearly forgotten solace to Cedar's tired mind and tattered spirit. She closed her eyes and breathed—breathed the fresh evening air of young spring—the scents of renewing life— and she fancied for a moment that her soul had mended.

It was a great relief to Cedar, leaving the city behind—leaving the people she'd known there— the people who had known her. Though her guilt plagued her, she inwardly admitted it was likewise a great relief to leave Logan's grave behind—and even her father's. The tombstones of James Francis Dale and Logan Aaron Davies were daily reminders of tragedy, heartbreak, and loss. Even in that moment, standing in spring's promising evening, Cedar could envision her father's and Logan's tombstones, together in the city's cemetery. There they would ever remain—impervious, lasting reminders of how cruel the world and life itself could be—impervious, lasting reminders of the moment and the losses that had forever changed Cedar and her mother.

Cedar's heart ached for the painful reminiscing, and she fisted the fabric of her shirtwaist in one hand where the pain was most intense. Tears threatened in her eyes, yet she closed them and again inhaled the soft scent of dusk settling over the pastures. The fragrance of evening did calm her, and she opened her eyes in time to see the sky erupt into more brilliant colors than the soft pastels it had worn just a moment before.

It had been Cedar's mother, Flora Dale, who had suggested she and her daughter return to the old house and vast pastures near the small town where Cedar had been born—return to the place where Cedar had thrived during her childhood. The years spent with her father and mother comfortable and loved in the little farmhouse had been the substance of happy contentment—days spent by her mother in baking bread, feeding chickens, and breathing in a life of hard work perhaps, but also of serenity and hope. Those were days when the child Cedar once had frolicked through the surrounding meadows and fields, waded in cool, clear creeks, and captured grasshoppers and caterpillars in chubby, dirt-smudged hands. To Cedar, those had been the days of cheerful play—of lying in the pasture grass and gazing into the bluest sky as the clouds lazily drifted. To Cedar, those had been the days of hope in things that might be—hope in endless happiness and cheer—even hope in love.

The city had never felt like home to Cedar. The city had choked and bound her spirit, in a manner of speaking. Too many houses and city buildings blocked a clear view of the horizon—or even the sky. Too many people bustled about with too many things to drive them to misery and fatigue. And at last, too many fears and anxieties had begun to linger in her dreams.

Yes, Cedar had been more than merely willing and ready to leave the city in search of the tranquility and the promise of blessed isolation—though she was disappointed to find how tightly her trepidation, insecurity, and distrust in mankind still gripped her. Her sleep was yet broken and restless, her anxieties and fears causing her to startle easily. She wondered if the events of almost two years ago would ever release their strangling grasp on her.

Yet now Cedar felt the slightest smile curve her mouth as she watched the sun set in the west. For there she stood, not in the city but in a pasture of cool, moist grass—no tall building to impair her view—no bitter scents of the city causing her nose to wrinkle in displeasure—no tombstones erected nearby to remind her of the horrors that had befallen her and her mother. Furthermore, it was a testament to her father's true nature and longing, his having never sold the farm. Cedar was somewhat comforted in knowing that if she could not have her father, she could at least linger in the place where her family had been most happy. There was no comfort in having lost Logan—none that she had been able to find as yet. Still, she fancied that even her heart's aching for Logan's loss was not quite so brutal as she stood there in the pasture—a night bird's sweet trilling and the subtle fragrance of spring rain still lingering at sunset.

Tom Evans dropped his saddlebags to the floor and collapsed into the chair that had once been his mother's favorite. The house was quiet—hauntingly so—and he sighed with the weight of fatigue. The two days' ride back to the ranch had seemed longer than usual, probably for the sake that he'd been hammered by spring rain for most of it. He sighed as he pulled off his boots and socks and dropped them next to his saddlebag. Tom stretched his long legs out in front of him, removing his hat and tossing it to the sofa nearby.

Raking a hand over his head and through his brown hair, he thought that he should've had his sister-in-law, Lark, trim it up for him while he was up helping to raise the new barn. Now he'd have to ride into town and have the barber cut it for him. The thought caused his feelings of fatigue to increase. He shook his head and chuckled, thinking how very like his older brother he was—all the way down to feeling his age.

It seemed like only yesterday that Lark Lawrence had shown up on the front porch and melted his brother's Slater's cold, hard heart. Truth was, it had been months, not days, and now Slater and Lark were settled on the new ranch up north, with a new barn to boot. Tom rubbed at his sore shoulder—a reminder that he'd helped raise it.

Closing his eyes for a moment, he let his mind wander back a bit—back to the day he'd opened the door and found Lark standing on the porch, to the moment he'd known she'd managed to pierce Slater's leathery old hide and plunge into his soul. He thought of Katherine and the children— of the warm, loving Christmas they'd all spent together. He smiled when he remembered how happy Katherine had looked on her wedding day only the month before—when Eldon Pickering had slid that gold band on her finger and hauled her and the children out to the old Cathcart place Eldon had managed to purchase. Tom had feared Kate would never get over her husband John's death. Fact was, he knew she wouldn't—how could she? Still, he and Slater had both hoped Kate would at least be able to move on one day, find love again, and she had with Eldon Pickering.

Shaking his head, he mumbled, "Who woulda thunk it? Kate and ol' Eldon." He chuckled, delighted by imagining his and Slater's old ranch hand Eldon Pickering married to their beloved cousin Katherine and having three children to wrangle as well as his own herd.

For a moment, Tom's smile faded as the memory of the cowhand they'd lost the day the outlaw Samson Kane had come gunning for Slater washed over him. Grady James had been a good hand. Tom's guilt over Grady's death was thick and heavy, even for the fact he owned no blame for it. Fact was, he even felt guilty over Chet Leigh's jumping over the fence to be an outlaw and getting himself killed too. Tom certainly owned no blame for Chet's sad end either, but he still felt bad about it.

Tom exhaled another heavy sigh, tucked his hands behind his head, and stretched. He hoped the two new hands he'd hired before leaving to help out Slater and Lark had kept the ranch in check. Ray Kirby was an older horseman, experienced, and seemed as responsible as ever Eldon had been. And though Pete LaRue was young, he could break a horse near as fast as Tom could.

A whiff of worry and anxiety flittered through Tom's mind a moment. What was he thinking by giving up raising cattle to breed horses? Yet his daddy had always said Tom had more horse in him than bovine. His daddy swore Tom took after his mother's side of the family. Tom knew he was meant for horses. So he forced his fatigue-borne worry to the back of his mind and reminded himself how handsome the new thoroughbred stallion he'd brought home all the way from Kentucky two months before was. The sleek, chestnut stallion had cost him nearly his entire share of the money he and Slater had gotten from Reno Garrett when they'd sold him half the ranch. But it didn't matter. Tom knew the new stud would help make Tom Evans the best horse breeder this side of Kentucky. Furthermore, he still had the money Slater had insisted on paying him for his share of the herd.

Tom silently assured himself that their parents would be happy knowing that Slater was running cattle up north on his own place and Tom was breeding horses on what was now his. Still, all at once, Tom felt a strange sense of lonesomeness creeping around at the back of his neck. Slater was gone, Lark, even Kate and the children. Tom had never thought such quiet and solitude would unsettle him, but it did. He chuckled, figuring it was just what he deserved for not having any empathy for his brother over the years. He'd plumb lost patience with the attitude of agedness Slater had harbored before Lark came along to save him. But now—now as he sat all alone in the house, his shoulder aching from the exertion of the barn raising, his hind quarters aching from the hard, long ride home—he thought maybe he could've owned a little more sympathy for his brother at times.

Groaning, Tom stood up. Unfastening his shirt, he tossed it to the sofa. Pushing his blue jeans down to his ankles, he simply stepped out of them, leaving them in a heap on the floor next to his boots and saddlebags as he headed for the stairs. He was careless of leaving his clothes strewn in the parlor. After all, what did it matter? No one was there to see them anymore.

Chapter One

Spring had blessed the morning with bright, warm sunshine. The long-absent calls of meadowlarks echoed through the crisp morning air, lending a nearly tangible melody of hope to the onset of more congenial weather. From the kitchen window, Cedar Dale watched a robin tug a worm from the moist earth and was again glad it had been rain that had fallen in the days before instead of snow. There was bound to be more snow to come before winter released spring to make way for summer. Yet, for the time being, the sun shone brightly, and a variety of early spring flowers were pushing tender green heads up through the soil in the flowerbeds.

Cedar would much have preferred to linger at the kitchen window in gazing at the evidences of spring's approach, but she knew an unexpected storm in the days to come might find her and her mother without certain necessities. Furthermore, her mother hadn't pressed her to speak to anyone—to even see anyone—for over a week. Cedar knew her mother was concerned about Cedar's reclusive state, and if one trip to town for supplies lessened her mother's anxieties for another week, then it would be worth braving her own misgivings.

Determining then that a brisk walk would contribute to good health, Cedar retrieved her coat from the wall hook near the front door and slipped her arms into the sleeves. Fastening the top button, she then pulled a pair of woolen gloves from one pocket and put them on. She sighed, knowing she would more than likely have to carry the coat home along with the supplies her mother was sending her to retrieve. The morning was cool yet, but she knew the sun would be brilliant on her return trip and wished her mother would allow her to leave her coat behind. Still, Flora Dale was nothing if not protective of her daughter's well-being—especially since her father's and Logan's deaths.

Smoothing a loose strand of chestnut-colored hair into her braid, Cedar loosely bowed the ties of her bonnet beneath her chin. She hoped to look as plain and inconspicuous as possible. Perhaps then she could simply slip into the general store unnoticed, purchase the things her mother needed, and return without so much as one word to anyone other than Mrs. Gunderson. Mrs. Gunderson would, no doubt, engage Cedar in conversation. Yet Mrs. Gunderson, proprietress of the general store, was a kind and pleasant woman. She had not as yet tried to draw Cedar into conversation with any other patron that might be lingering in the store. Thus, if Cedar could walk to town, escape notice by anyone other than Mrs. Gunderson, and return home, then perhaps the day would not be too taxing.

She could only hope Lucas Pratt wasn't tarrying in town. Any attention from Lucas would entirely unnerve her. She'd simply avoid Tillman Pratt's drama house—walk the boardwalk across the street from the theater Lucas's father owned until she needed to cross to the general store. If Cedar owned any luck at all, Lucas would be far too busy flirting with the new actress on the playbill at Mr. Pratt's theater to be watching for Cedar.

Cedar closed her eyes for a moment and inhaled a deep breath, attempting to rally her courage.

"To town and back," she whispered to herself. "Just simply walk to town and home. That's all it will be . . . a walk."

Opening her eyes, she called over her shoulder to her mother. "I'll be back as quick as I can, Mama." She retrieved a basket from a nearby shelf, again considering slipping out of the house without her coat.

"Do you have your coat, sweetheart?" her mother called from the kitchen, however.

Cedar felt an amused grin spread across her face. "Here it comes now," she whispered to herself. She well knew the story that her mother was about to relate to her for at least the hundredth time.

"I'll never forget the winter you were three," her mother began, "when all those children were caught in that early spring blizzard coming home from school with not a coat or a blanket between them."

"Frozen to the bone!" Cedar whispered in unison with her mother's familiar warning.

"I've got my coat, Mama," Cedar said. "I'll be home soon."

"Now, you take your time, sweetie," her mother called. "No need to hurry. You get all the news from Mrs. Gunderson for me. All right?"

"Yes, ma'am," Cedar said.

For Cedar, there *was* a need to hurry, for facing anyone in town, even Mrs. Gunderson, was a harsh challenge for her. Fear had beaten her, scarred her—and the scars of fear and loss took time to heal. Some never did. Cedar Dale faced her fears each and every time she left the small farmhouse she shared with her widowed mother. Oh, people in town were friendly enough—tried to be understanding. Still, she knew whispers followed in her wake—knew she would never feel completely safe and secure again, not with what happened to her father and Logan still haunting her dreams. And it made any sort of contact with people all the more difficult.

Yet Cedar and her mother did need supplies, especially with the weather as unpredictable as it was in spring. And the only way to acquire the supplies they needed was to venture into the terrifying reality of the township.

Thus, with great trepidation—her hands beginning to tremble with her own anxiety—Cedar stepped out of the farmhouse and into the world. She closed her eyes for a moment, attempting to steady her nerves, reminding herself most of the people in town had known her since she was a small child—that no one had been cruel to her since she and her mother returned three weeks before. In fact, everyone had been very welcoming and kind—sympathetic. Thus, Cedar drew another breath of resolve in bravery and set out.

The breeze was cool on her cheeks as Cedar made her way toward town. Inwardly she admitted that her mother was right. It was good she'd worn her coat, whether or not the weather warmed later. She hoped the weather did warm later, for something in Cedar was tired of being cold. She fancied that she'd felt cold for a very long time—that even the summer sun hadn't been able to warm her completely since the tragedy that had so altered her mother's life and hers. Still, Cedar was hopeful, for the sun shone brighter in the west—warmer. Surely the brilliance of the western sun and sky would finally warm her body—and her heart.

As she walked, Cedar had a notion to begin humming. Still, the notion passed quickly—as it always did. She kicked at a rock in the road—watched it go tumbling into the grass to one side.

She smiled when she saw the line of purple crocus near one wagon rut. They were blooming already, bright and happy and hopeful, and the sight made her smile. They hadn't been in bloom two days before when Cedar had taken a short walk. But now—now they seemed to nod a welcome greeting as the breeze played among them.

Cedar glanced up toward town, once again astonished at how it had grown. When she was a child—before her father had moved the family to St. Louis—there had been perhaps half the buildings in town that now marked the horizon. Before there had been only the general store, the livery stable and blacksmith, the land grant office, the telegraph station and post office, and the saloon. Now there stood with them Tillman Pratt's drama house, Mrs. Jenkins's dress shop, a small barber's building, a boardinghouse, a hotel, and a restaurant. Cedar mused that it wouldn't be long before what was once just a small town grew into a full city.

Still, this was farming and ranching land, and Cedar hoped it would be many, many more years before too much growth changed the face of things. As always, the thought of ranching caused Cedar to gaze to the west. Certainly there was nothing but open pasture as far as she could see. Yet she knew farther off than she could see was a ranch—a cattle ranch—or at least what had once been a cattle ranch. Mrs. Gunderson had explained to Cedar and her mother upon their arrival (as she'd been spilling out as much information and gossip as she could in a short time) that Vernon Evans and his wife, Ada, had both passed away since Cedar's family had moved, leaving the Evans ranch to their two sons, Slater and Tom. Slater and Tom Evans had sold off their best grazing lands to a man named Reno Garrett, a cattle rancher from Texas who had lately settled nearby—for Slater Evans had recently wed and moved the bulk of the Evans cattle to a ranch farther north. His younger brother, Tom, retained the horse stock. It seemed Tom Evans meant to leap from raising cattle to breeding horses, and folks in town were sure he'd be wildly successful. Tom Evans had always known horses better than cattle.

Mrs. Gunderson had explained that Tom Evans had never married—not yet. The Evans brothers had always worked too hard to have time for courting or marriage—until the girl that had managed to steal Slater Evans's heart had arrived.

Mrs. Gunderson had been interrupted in her tales of the Evans brothers that day by other patrons of the general store. Cedar had been far more disappointed than she consciously wanted to admit, and she wondered if perhaps this fresh spring day would find Mrs. Gunderson talkative about the Evans brothers again—about Tom Evans.

She felt the discomfort of her heart fluttering in her bosom at the thought of Tom Evans. She wondered if he were still as handsome as he'd been ten years before. She wondered if he would even remember the Dale family that had once lived just outside of town. She wondered if he'd remember the little Dale girl—if he'd remember her.

Shaking her head, disgusted at her own ridiculous musings, Cedar turned her attention back toward town. She was nearly there. Just a short distance and she would be stepping onto the boardwalk. Instantly her heart began racing with trepidation. She glanced to Tillman Pratt's drama house and did not see Lucas Pratt standing outside the front doors as he usually did. This relieved her somewhat, and she hurried her step—desperate to reach the general store before Lucas Pratt or anyone else noticed her.

Several of the townsfolk nodded and smiled at Cedar as she stepped up onto the boardwalk, however.

"Mornin', ma'am," one young cowboy greeted, touching the brim of his hat as she approached the boardinghouse.

"Good morning," Cedar managed to respond. She recognized the cowboy—Hadley Jacobson. According to Mrs. Gunderson, Hadley had hired on with Reno Garrett after Reno had purchased a portion of the Evanses' ranch property.

Everyone in town was glad Hadley was riding for Reno Garrett's brand, for Hadley had been able to verify to everyone that Reno was a good, hard-working man. Townsfolk were always wary of strangers. Thus, Hadley's reassurance had made everyone more willing to take to Reno Garrett.

"It looks to be workin' up to a mighty fine day," Hadley added.

"Yes," Cedar said.

Hadley Jacobson sauntered past, and Cedar exhaled the breath she hadn't even realized she'd been holding. She was proud of herself for having managed not only a response but a friendly smile.

Cedar glanced across the street to Tillman Pratt's drama house. Lucas was still nowhere to be seen, and Cedar hurried on. A mere one hundred feet and she would be inside the general store. As she quickened her step, Cedar thought of the young, carefree girl she'd been not so long ago. She missed that girl—the one who would've stopped and talked to Hadley Jacobson awhile, the one who would've been happy in lingering in conversation with just about anyone. In her most secret thoughts, Cedar feared the girl she'd once been was lost forever the day her father and Logan had been lost. There were moments she felt the struggling deep within her own soul—the struggle to overcome the fist of fear and doubt that horrible day had gripped her in. Yet even now she was frightened—startling when she heard someone shout from the boardwalk across the street to Hadley Jacobson. She glanced back to see Hadley chuckle and cross the street toward the man who had shouted to him. Both men smiled and struck hands, yet Cedar still trembled from the unsettling start the unexpected noise had caused in her.

As she stepped into the general store—sighing with ridiculous relief—Cedar knew the carefree, happy girl she'd once been was gone forever. Furthermore, she wondered if even the hot sun of a western summer sky could warm her. Would she ever be warm again? Would she ever feel happy deep inside—happy, fresh, and hopeful like the purple crocus of spring? Or would she continue to feel withered, dark, and cold like old leaves under snow in winter?

"Well, good mornin', Cedar!" Mrs. Gunderson cheerfully greeted. "How's yer mama?"

Cedar couldn't help but smile as she met Mrs. Gunderson's merry countenance. Mrs. Gunderson and her husband were the proprietors of the general store—a jolly elderly couple, each ever smiling and with eyes always twinkling with delight.

"She's fine," Cedar answered.

"That's good to hear," Mrs. Gunderson said. "What can I do for ya today, honey?"

"We're needing just a few things . . . in case the weather comes in and keeps us out at the house awhile," Cedar answered.

"Indeed!" Mrs. Gunderson said with an emphatic nod. "And you two definitely want to stay in if there's snow. I remember all those years ago . . . it's gotta be goin' on sixteen years, in fact . . . sixteen years since we lost those children in that spring blizzard."

Cedar nodded, her smile broadening. "Mama told me about that. It must've been awful."

Mrs. Gunderson shook her head, clicking her tongue with affirmation.

"Oh, it was! Just awful . . . terrible!" she said. "I don't even like to think on it! It just makes me tear up somethin' dreadful."

"Mama always makes sure I don't leave the house without my coat because of those poor children," Cedar said.

"And well she should," Mrs. Gunderson confirmed, wagging a scolding index finger at Cedar. "She's your mama, after all . . . and she wouldn't be a good one if she didn't see to your bein' bundled up properly." Mrs. Gunderson smiled, and Cedar did not miss the mischief in her eyes. "Of course, someday you'll have a man to make sure you're kept warm. But until then . . . it's your mama's place."

Cedar forced the smile to stay on her face—even though Mrs. Gunderson's innocent teasing had torn through her heart like the sharp blade of a knife.

Mrs. Gunderson was a good woman, however, and Cedar saw the expression of instant realization and regret wash over her face.

"Oh, honey!" the kind woman gasped, placing a plump hand over her ample bosom. "I'm so sorry! I wasn't thinkin'! I swear, sometimes things just shoot right out of my silly mouth before I have a chance to catch 'em."

But Cedar was touched by the woman's sensitivity and quickly shook her head. "It's fine, Mrs. Gunderson. You're so sweet. Mother and I so greatly appreciate your kindness to us . . . and your understanding."

Mrs. Gunderson's cheeks were still pink with humiliation and self-scolding, however.

"Now, what can I get for you and your dear mama, honey?" she asked Cedar.

Cedar was disappointed in the woman's obvious change in demeanor, no matter how slight. She'd enjoyed Mrs. Gunderson's teasing—more than she could've imagined she would—and she didn't want her to feel uncomfortable.

"Well, we're needing some thread, witch hazel, a few potatoes if you have them, and we're nearly out of sugar too. And do you have any eggs? We haven't been able to get over to the Perkins place to purchase any laying hens yet."

"Nearly out of sugar? No eggs?" Mrs. Gunderson

exclaimed. "Well, we can't have that, now can we?"

"No, we can't have that," Cedar agreed. She smiled and added, "And I wouldn't mind a bit of news . . . if you have any." She missed the look of delight that had been on Mrs. Gunderson's face a moment before. She knew the opportunity to share any new information she'd recently gleaned would most likely perk the old woman right back up.

Instantly, Mrs. Gunderson's face brightened— her smile broadening with pure, delicious glee.

"News?" Mrs. Gunderson nearly giggled. "Honey, I've got so much news bottled up inside me it's near to spillin' right outta my ears!"

Cedar giggled, surprised by the feeling of delight that tickled her heart for a moment.

"First let me get them taters for ya," Mrs. Gunderson said, bustling out from behind the counter and going to a big barrel nearby. "Mr. Bartley brung these in just yesterday. Nice big ones too," she said. "Ain't nothin' like a nice warm tater all slathered over in butter."

"Nothing like it in the world," Cedar giggled. Mrs. Gunderson always made Cedar feel better, more hopeful in humanity—and Cedar was beginning to love her for it.

"First off, I hear tell Lucas Pratt's got his eye on ya," the woman said as she placed four large potatoes in the basket Cedar had set on the counter.

Cedar's stomach immediately began to twist into knots at the mention of Lucas Pratt. He certainly had become very attentive to her over the last few weeks. Though she'd only seen him on a handful of occasions, the handful had been enough to cause her anxieties to fester. Lucas owned his mother's easy manner and his father's handsome good looks. Yet Cedar had no wish to hold his interest.

"Has he . . . has he come courtin' yet?" Mrs. Gunderson tentatively ventured.

The woman was sensitive now, worried in knowing that Cedar wasn't ready for a man to court her—might never be ready for a man to ever court her again.

"No, he hasn't," Cedar answered. "And to be honest, Mrs. Gunderson . . . I-I . . ."

Mrs. Gunderson smiled with compassion and said, "Don't ya worry, sweetie. Hearts do heal. May take some time yet, but you'll be fine . . . someday."

Cedar nodded and tried to keep the tears from escaping her eyes. She felt guilty for the fact her tears were for herself—for the sake of her own fears and insecurities—rather than for Logan or her father.

"Now," Mrs. Gunderson chirped, tossing a spool of white thread into Cedar's basket, "there's certainly more goin' on in these parts than Lucas Pratt."

Cedar smiled, captured by the woman's good nature.

"Such as?" she asked.

"Such as Hadley Jacobson told me not ten minutes ago that Reno Garrett—the man who bought the acreage off the Evans ranch—that Reno's never been married . . . not in all his life!" Mrs. Gunderson had lowered her voice, and Cedar leaned toward her, amused by the woman's expression of conspiracy.

"Never?" Cedar asked, baiting the funny old gossip.

"Never!" Mrs. Gunderson whispered, her eyes widening to near the size of supper plates. "Seems he cowboyed for a good part of his life and just never met a woman who could capture his heart." Mrs. Gunderson's eyes narrowed. "He's as handsome as heaven. I swear if I weren't twenty years the man's senior and already so happily married to my dear Theodore . . . I'd have myself a go at that Reno Garrett."

Cedar giggled. "Mrs. Gunderson!" she exclaimed in a whisper.

Mrs. Gunderson chuckled. "I know, I know! I'm as sinful as a preacher swimmin' in a whiskey barrel . . . but I'm just speakin' my mind."

"What else?" Cedar urged. Mrs. Gunderson was amusing, and her stories kept Cedar from worrying about other people happening into the store.

31

"Cora Perkins was in this mornin'," she began, "and told me her daughter saw Tom Evans ridin' through town last evenin'. I guess he's back from helpin' Slater and Lark with raisin' their new barn."

At the mention of Tom Evans's name, Cedar could've sworn her heart leapt into her throat.

"Cora's daughter Amelia is sweeter on Tom Evans than ants are to sugar!" Mrs. Gunderson exclaimed. "It's shameful the way she flirts with him whenever he's in town."

Cedar felt a frown pucker her brow, and though she was familiar with anxiety, the anxiety filling her in that moment was new—a strange sort of sickening disappointment she hadn't known for a long, long time.

"I mean, I encourage flirtin' between men and women," Mrs. Gunderson continued. "Married folks oughta flirt with their spouse . . . and unmarried folks oughta flirt with other unmarried folks." She paused to shake her head. "But Amelia Perkins . . . she's plumb embarrassin' to me sometimes." The woman sighed, still shaking her head. "Still, there's one in every town, it seems—some woman or man who don't know what's proper and what's not where flirtin' is concerned. And in this town . . . it's Amelia Perkins."

"I'm afraid I haven't had the pleasure of seeing Amelia," Cedar said.

Mrs. Gunderson frowned. "Well, count your

blessin's, honey," she said, shaking her head again. " 'Cause meetin' Amelia Perkins is certainly somethin' that a body can wait for."

Cedar smiled again. Mrs. Gunderson was more entertaining than anyone Cedar could ever remember meeting.

"So we've got Reno Garrett . . . the handsome, never-been-married rancher out west of the Evans place. Tom Evans is back home, and word is his new stud stallion is gonna make him famous. What else . . . what else . . ."

Cedar watched as Mrs. Gunderson carefully wrapped half a dozen eggs in an old flour sack and placed them in the basket.

"Oh! I knew there was somethin' else!" she exclaimed. Leaning forward, she lowered her voice and whispered, "I'm pretty certain Esther Burnes is expectin' another baby."

"Esther Burnes?" Cedar asked in a whisper. "Doesn't she already have seven children?"

"Eight!" Mrs. Gunderson corrected. "If ya ask me . . . seems like Clarence and Esther Burnes do an excessive amount of flirtin' with one another."

"Mrs. Gunderson!" Cedar exclaimed as the vermilion of a heated blush warmed her cheeks.

"Well, I'm sorry, Cedar," Mrs. Gunderson said, arching her brows in exaggerated astonishment. "But they've only been married twelve years.

Eight children eleven and under? She'll end up in the insane home if she's not careful." Mrs. Gunderson's expression softened almost instantly, however. "Still, them Burnes children . . . they're about the sweetest, most adorable children I've ever seen! I swear, Esther's babies look just like little cherubs." Mrs. Gunderson smiled. "I guess the world can never have too many cherubs . . . even if they all do come from the same poor mother."

"No," Cedar said, smiling. "There can never be too many cherubs in the world."

She felt happy in that moment—amused, delighted, and happy. She liked to imagine an entire family of chubby-cheeked cherubs. She liked to imagine the handsome bachelor Reno Garrett living nearby, all the women curious about his past. And she certainly liked to imagine Tom Evans—anything about Tom Evans. Mrs. Gunderson wasn't so different from Christmas morning with its sense of wonder and joy.

"Oh! I almost forgot the witch hazel!" Mrs. Gunderson chirped.

Cedar watched as the woman bent down behind the counter and then popped up with a small bottle of the liquid.

"There ya go, honey," Mrs. Gunderson said. "Now you tell your mama I said hello. Tell her to come in for a visit this week . . . if the weather don't turn ugly."

"I will," Cedar said. "Thank you, Mrs. Gunderson."

"Oh! One more thing," Mrs. Gunderson began.

"Yes?" Cedar asked. She'd turned to leave but paused when the woman addressed her once more.

"Does your mama still crochet them pretty little gloves she used to when you all lived here before?" she asked.

Cedar smiled, pleased that Mrs. Gunderson would remember her mother's skill.

"Yes, ma'am . . . she does," she answered.

Mrs. Gunderson smiled. "Well, that's just dandy! Do you think she might be willing work a few pair and let us sell them here in the store? We'd pay her for them, of course."

Cedar felt her smile fade a little. There it was—the pity. She quickly tried to convince herself that Mrs. Gunderson truly thought Flora Dale's crocheted gloves would please some patrons of the general store—silently tried to tell herself that the sweet old lady wasn't merely trying to find a way to charitably contribute to the Widow Dale's income.

"I'll ask her," Cedar answered.

"Please do," Mrs. Gunderson said. The old woman's eyes twinkled then. "And let me know any news you might hear that I might find interesting. Will you?"

Cedar's heart softened once more, and she

nodded. Mrs. Gunderson was a kind and caring woman. She meant no offense or harm, and in that moment, Cedar was determined to visit her again soon—whether or not her fears campaigned to keep her from doing so.

Chapter Two

Tom Evans reined in his horse, dismounted, and wrapped the reins loosely around the hitching post in front of the livery stables.

"Mornin', Tom," Clarence Burnes greeted from across the street.

"Mornin' there, Clarence," Tom called in return.

The day was pleasant enough, and surprisingly, Tom was glad to be back near town. He'd enjoyed the past weeks out at Slater and Lark's house, helping to raise the new barn and build the fence. Still, even for the solitary loneliness out at his place, he was glad to be settled back in his own space.

Tom smiled at the thought of his elder brother and his young bride. What a handsome couple they were—and so lost in their love for one another. It was good to finally see Slater so happy.

Stepping up onto the boardwalk, Tom removed his hat, running his fingers through his tousled brown hair—glad he'd stopped in to see the barber before anything else. He plopped his hat back on his head, nodded, and smiled as June Bartley walked past him, blushing under his gaze. He chuckled and shook his head, amazed at how little girls grew up into young women and wives so quickly. Furthermore, in that moment, he saw things a little more through Slater's eyes—more than he ever had before. It seemed like yesterday June Bartley was no higher than his waist—playing at mud pies and sneaking around to spy on him and Slater bathing in the creek. Now she was a grown-up woman, married, and with two little boys of her own.

Tom had never considered himself to be old and weathered the way Slater always did. Tom's life hadn't been as hard as his elder brother's; he hadn't carried the same scrapes and bruises on his soul that Slater had. But now—now he had a bit more empathy for what his brother had been feeling before Lark had salvaged him. Seeing June Bartley all grown up the way she was—well, it did make him feel a might more aged than he had felt a moment before. Still, he smiled—for the way June looked back at him, giggled, and blushed—well, he couldn't be all that worn out, now could he?

Tom strode across the street to the boardwalk in front of the general store. He glanced up when he heard the doves frequenting the roof take flight, simultaneously feeling an all-too-familiar, moist splatter on his trouser leg just above his knee.

"Dammit," he grumbled, looking to the white bird mess now drizzling down his pant leg. "Somebody oughta shoot them dang . . ."

Someone bumped into him then—and with enough force that it sent him stumbling back a few steps. Tom looked up to see a young woman stumble backward, lose her footing, and end up flat on her sitter on the boardwalk. Immediately the expression on the young woman's face—the expression of startled shock—caused a chuckle to rise in Tom's throat. He choked it back, however, and managed to allow only an amused smile to spread across his face.

"I'm sorry, miss," he said, offering a hand to the young woman. "Some doggone bird just give me cause to have to do some more washin'."

The pretty young woman looked up to him. Her blue eyes widened as her perfectly arched brows rose in surprise. Instead of blushing, however, Tom fancied the pink drained completely from her lovely cheeks as she tentatively took his offered hand.

"Tommy Evans?" she whispered as he assisted her to standing once more.

Tom's smile broadened, even as a puzzled expression puckered his strong brow.

"Tommy?" he repeated. "Ain't nobody called me Tommy in years," he said. "Do I know ya, miss? Surely I'd remember meetin' up with such a purty little filly as you."

In truth, the girl was akin to an angel where her pretty face was concerned. He could see light nut-brown hair peeking out from under her bonnet, her face rather heart-shaped with the softest complexion. He quickly surmised her figure was far more than merely pleasing as well, even for the coat she wore. Surely he'd remember if he'd ever come across such an attractive young woman before. Still, as he studied her a moment, something in her did seem familiar.

Cedar swallowed the lump in her throat. She tried to breathe normally—but it was Tom Evans standing before her. Truly it was Tom Evans—and what woman could breathe normally with Tom Evans looking at her? Oh, he was ever so handsome! More so even than he had been ten years before. He was taller, she thought—his shoulders broader—the brown of his eyes deeper—and his smile all the more mesmerizing. Even so, Cedar recognized him as the man she'd so thoroughly adored during her childhood.

"I-I'm Cedar Dale," she stammered, unable to keep herself from staring at him. "You probably don't remember me, but my family used to—"

"Jim and Flora's little girl?" Tom Evans asked. His smile broadened, and Cedar felt her heart swell—overjoyed at his remembering her existence. He chuckled, studied her from head to toe for a moment, and then said, "Well, you certainly grew up, now didn't ya? You weren't more than eight or nine years old when I seen ya last."

Cedar nodded, her delight expanding. Still, in

the next moment, she was thoroughly embarrassed as well—embarrassed that he remembered
her—for if he remembered her, then he remembered the way she'd shamelessly chased after
him as a child. Oh, she'd chased after Tom Evans
something awful! Often she literally skipped
along behind him like a lovesick puppy. No
doubt he hadn't forgotten. How could he have
forgotten? She must've driven him nearly mad!

"How's yer daddy and mama?" he asked. "Have
y'all moved back out this way? I know yer daddy
never did sell the place."

Cedar fought the tears threatening to brim in
her eyes. Her heart was pounding so hard it was
rattling her entire body!

"My mama's fine, thank you," she managed to
respond. "But . . . daddy was killed two years
back. It's just Mama and me . . . but we have
moved back out to the old place."

Cedar was moved by the sympathetic frown
that puckered Tom Evans's handsome brow. Oh,
he was ever so much more handsome than even
he had been! She could hardly take in the truth of
it.

"Killed?" he asked. "Why, I can't believe that.
I'm so sorry. Yer daddy was a fine man."

Cedar nodded, accepting his sincere con-
dolences. "Thank you," she whispered.

Cedar held her breath as he reached out, placing
a strong hand on her shoulder. His touch was

warm, powerful, reassuring, and entirely affecting.

"If you and yer mama need anythin'," he began, "anythin' at all . . . you just give me a holler. Okeydokey?"

Cedar nodded and forced a smile. "Thank you," she managed.

"I mean it now," he said. "If you two need somethin' . . . just let me know."

"Of course we will," Cedar lied.

Tom Evans nodded, apparently convinced she was telling the truth.

"You tell yer mama I'll drop in on her one of these days," he said, "to pay my respects and see if there's anything I can do for her."

Cedar nodded, terrified by the thought that he actually might stay true to his word and visit her and her mother. He smiled—chuckled a moment—the warm brown of his eyes sending a thrill through her the like she'd not known for years.

"And . . . I hope yer sitter ain't too sore," he said. "I guess I need to pay more attention to where I'm goin'."

Cedar smiled—a sincerely delighted smile. Not only was Tom Evans even more handsome than she remembered but also even far more charming.

"Oh, it was nothing to speak of," she said.

"Well, that's mighty kind of ya to be so forgivin', Miss Dale," he chuckled.

"There's nothing to forgive," she added. She was

feeling warm—overly warm—near to nauseous. She knew it was her coat. It was overheating her, and she needed to remove it.

"Leastways you didn't drop your basket," he said, nodding toward the basket she still held with one arm.

"Oh, yes," she said—only then remembering that she held anything at all.

"Well, you have a nice day, ma'am," Tom Evans said.

"And you too, M-Mr. Evans," she stammered. In her own mind, she could still hear herself as a child, calling after Tom Evans, begging for his attention.

All at once, her child's voice resonated through her. *Tommy Evans, Tommy Evans! Sent to me straight from the heavens!* her own young voice echoed in her mind. She blushed at the memory of the time he'd turned the corner to find her playing in the mud down by the creek near her home and singing her silly song at the top of her lungs.

Tom Evans touched the brim of his hat, smiled, nodded, and moved past her into the general store.

"Well, good mornin', Tom Evans!" she heard Mrs. Gunderson exclaim. "Now ain't you a sight for sore, tired eyes. Then again . . . you're a sight for any eyes!"

Cedar heard Tom chuckle. "Well, hey there,

Elvira," she heard him greet. "And yer lookin' good enough to eat this mornin' yerself!"

Cedar could feel him—feel herself moving away from him as she walked down the boardwalk. Even for the lingering cool of the morning, she felt warm—hot all over as if she'd broken into a fever. Tom Evans! It was only then she silently admitted to herself how she'd longed to see him. Ever since she and her mother had returned, she'd dreamt of such a reunion. Still, for some reason, she'd never really believed it would happen. Tom Evans! He'd been standing right there—right before her. They'd shared the same air—the same sunshine. For the first time in two years, Cedar had known a moment without fear—a moment filled with true delight. Yet it was only a moment—only meant to be a moment—and as all her anxieties returned, Cedar Dale hurried home, glad she hadn't dropped her basket when she'd bumped into Tom Evans.

"That there Dale girl . . . was she just in here, Elvira?" Tom asked as he leaned back on the counter in the general store, gazing out the door after Cedar Dale. Elvira Gunderson immediately leaned sideways, following his gaze down the boardwalk to where Cedar Dale was crossing the street.

"Yep," Elvira said. "She just come in for a few

things. It's so hard for her to leave the house, you know. Poor little thing."

Tom frowned. He looked back to the sweet old woman as she shook her head with a heavy sigh.

"Poor little thing? Why's that?" he asked. "'Cause her daddy was killed?"

"Well . . . that too," Elvira answered. "But it's more 'cause she's just plumb terrified of people, I think," she explained. "I'm sure it's because of everything that happened. Ya do know how her daddy died, don't ya, Tom? The circumstances . . . and what else she lost?"

"Elvira Gunderson," Tom said, smiling at his friend, "you know darn well I've been up at Slater and Lark's place for near to a month." He chuckled, reached out, and tweaked her nose as if she were just a young thing he was considering on courting. "How am I suppose to know anything when I ain't been here for you to tell me?"

He chuckled, pleased by the old woman's pinked-up cheeks.

"You're a shameless flirt, Tom Evans," Elvira scolded. "Why . . . I'm a married woman! You know that."

"I know it, Elvira . . . but I just can't help myself," he teased.

Elvira Gunderson placed a plump little hand on Tom's arm. Lowering her voice, she began, "You see, Cedar was engaged to a fine young man up in St. Louis."

Tom felt his brow pucker—sensed the story Elvira was about to tell him wasn't as light-hearted as usual.

"Mm-hm," he mumbled, urging her on.

"Well, Cedar and her feller was all ready to get married . . . when one night, Cedar and her folks and that young man of hers were strollin' 'round the city after supper. All of a sudden, a couple of drunk gamblers come a-stumblin' out of some drinkin' establishment or another . . . and the way Flora tells it . . . well, one of the drunks said somethin' terrible to Cedar. Something vile and awful inappropriate. Cedar's young man started into arguin' with the drunkard. Pretty soon Jim Dale was involved too. And before Flora and Cedar could think what to do . . . Jim Dale and Cedar's young man were dead . . . both shot clean through and lyin' in puddles of blood right there in the middle of the city street at their feet!"

"Surely not, Elvira. Surely not!" Tom exclaimed.

"Well, that's the tale . . . straight from Flora Dale herself," Elvira assured him. She sighed, the pink caused by Tom's flirting completely gone—only sympathy and concern on her face in its place. "Now, Tom, that kind of a thing . . . it can really scar up a woman's heart and soul for life. Ya know what I mean?"

Tom nodded and mumbled, "Yep."

"Anyway," Elvira continued, "Cedar has been in here four or five times . . . needin' just a few things here and there . . . duckin' under her bonnet like she'd be just as happy to be plumb invisible. Lucas Pratt's got his eye on her, but she don't want nothin' to do with him. I don't know if it's Lucas himself . . . or if them losses she's known have just clean broke her heart for good."

Tom watched the girl walk down the boardwalk until she stepped off and turned the bend. He frowned and exhaled a heavy sigh. What sad and miserable circumstances for Flora Dale and her daughter. He well remembered Cedar as a child—such a confident, happy little girl. In fact, she'd nearly pestered him to death when she'd lived near town before—always running after him, tugging on his pant leg, and begging for his attention. It was disturbing to see her so changed—so fearful and unhappy. Though in the same moment, Tom thought it was not so disturbing to see the beautiful young woman she'd become.

"Well, that's a darn shame. That's just awful," Tom said. "All of it. Jim Dale was a good man. I hired out to him one summer when I was a boy. Mrs. Dale was always kind to me. And that little Cedar . . . she was always so full of mischief and giggles."

"She's a pretty little thing, don't ya think, Tom?" Elvira asked. "The right man could heal her heart and have a nice little wife for his own."

"Well, I know I can trust you to agreein' with

me that Lucas Pratt ain't the right man," he said.

"No indeed!" Elvira said, shaking her head. She stared at him a moment then—and Tom recognized the naughty twinkle in her eye.

Tom shook his head and smiled. Elvira Gunderson had been trying to marry him off to every pretty young girl in the territory for years. Furthermore, ever since his older brother, Slater, had swept his own pretty little wife away to marital bliss, Elvira had exhausted even more effort on Tom's behalf.

"Now, Elvira," Tom began.

But the woman was undaunted. "That Amelia Perkins ain't for you, boy," the woman told him. "I know she's latched onto you like crumbs on a baker's beard . . . but she ain't for you."

Tom chuckled. "She's a darn sight closer to my own age than Flora Dale's little girl," he reminded her.

"Flora Dale ain't got herself a little girl, Tom," Elvira needlessly pointed out. "She's got herself a beautiful young woman . . . in need of a good, carin' man who can protect her."

"But you forget, Elvira," Tom said, "Slater's already married."

Elvira sighed and scoldingly smacked Tom on one shoulder.

"You know darn well I wasn't thinkin' on Slater," she told him. "Which reminds me," she continued, "Cedar forgot to put the sugar she

48

come in for in her basket. Do you think you could drop it by to Flora for me on yer way out of town, Tom?"

Tom smiled, shaking his head again with disbelief at Elvira Gunderson's infinite attempts at matchmaking. "The Dale place ain't on my way out of town, Elvira. And you know it," he said.

"Oh, please, Tom," she cooed. "I wouldn't want that poor girl to have to come all the way back for it . . . knowin' how shy she is and all. And besides, the weather might turn on us . . . and then those poor women would be all alone out there with no sugar to get them by."

Tom smiled, entirely amused by the old woman's tricks. How could he possibly tell her no? And besides, it wouldn't hurt to drop in on Flora and see if there was anything he could do for her. Tom's own mother had always taught her boys to look after orphans, widows, and old people. If Flora and her daughter had moved back to the old farmhouse, chances were there were some things needing doing.

"Oh, all right, ya little she-devil," Tom agreed. "Far be it from me to deprive two women livin' alone of their sugar."

Elvira smiled and pinched his cheek as if he were some tousle-haired schoolboy.

"Oh, thank ya, Tom!" she exclaimed, going to the counter and retrieving a sugar sack. "Here it is. You remember where the Dale place is, don't ya?"

"Yes, ma'am. I do," Tom confirmed.

Elvira followed Tom out of the store, shading her eyes from the sun's rays as she watched him walk to his horse across the way.

"Now, you go on and linger as long as ya like, Tom," she called as Tom put the sack of sugar in one saddlebag and mounted his horse. "Them ladies could use some company."

"I'll see they get the sugar, Elvira," Tom told her. "Then I gotta get on back to my place. I'm a month behind on everything needin' doin'."

Two trots down the road, Tom grimaced with self-disgust. Between the bird mess, the pretty Dale girl, and Elvira Gunderson, he'd plumb forgot to get the ten pounds of flour he'd come into town to get for himself.

"Go on, ol' Fred," he said to his horse, clicking his tongue to urge the animal on. He'd come back for the flour later. Best get the sugar to that poor Dale girl before she turned around to head back.

"Cedar!" Flora Dale exclaimed as her daughter hurried into the house, slamming the door behind her. "What on earth?"

Stripping off her coat, Cedar rushed into the kitchen and began working the pump. She pulled off her bonnet, splashing the cool water on her crimson cheeks.

"Whatever are you up to? Did you run all the way home?"

Cedar drew an apron from its hook nearby, dabbing the water from her face.

Quickly she loosened the braid holding her hair, letting chestnut locks cascade in soft curls over her shoulders. She ran her fingers up through her hair, reveling in the feel of the cool air on her neck and head. She was so overly warm she thought she might have to lie down a moment. Swishing her hair this way and that, she sighed—soothed by the cooling effect.

"You'll never guess who I saw in town not ten minutes ago," Cedar breathed. Her heart was still racing, but not from the exertion of the walk home—rather from the residual excitement of having seen Tom Evans.

"Who?" her mother asked.

"I thought I was dreaming at first," Cedar said, running her fingers through her hair once more. Her entire scalp had begun to tingle when she'd found herself face-to-face with Tom Evans. And it hadn't quit yet!

"Who?" Flora asked again. "Who did you see?"

Several firm knocks on the front door caused both women to gasp before Cedar could answer, however.

Cedar's heart began to hammer with anxiety as her mother mumbled, "Whoever could that be?"

"Probably Mrs. Gunderson," Cedar said. "I forgot

to pick the sugar sack up off the counter. I'm sure she's brought it over for us." Quickly Cedar moved past her mother toward the door.

"But, Cedar," Flora began, "you haven't told me what has you hopping around like a toad in a skillet. Who did you see?"

"Let's thank Mrs. Gunderson first, Mama. Then I'll tell you everything . . . I promise," Cedar said as she opened the door—fully expecting to see Mrs. Gunderson's smiling face on the other side.

Instead, her jaw dropped, her mouth gaping open in astonishment.

She stood awed—simply astonished to silence as she heard her mother exclaim, "Why, bless my soul! Tom Evans! Is that you?"

Chapter Three

Cedar stared at Tom Evans as he stood in the doorway.

"Miss Dale," he greeted, touching the brim of his hat. He looked beyond her to her mother then. "Yes, ma'am, Mrs. Dale . . . it is me," he chuckled.

Cedar was too stunned to respond. She'd only just left town. Certainly she'd walked very quickly, but when Tom Evans had said he would drop in on her mother, she hadn't expected he meant to do it directly on her heels. She wondered briefly if he'd followed her home—seen her nearly running all the way back from town. Oh, how she hoped not! It couldn't possibly have appeared to be very ladylike, her nearly wild pace. Though she thought it impossible, her heart began to beat even faster. Her mouth grew dry, and she felt a slight trembling begin to overtake her.

"Oh, it's wonderful to see you again, Tom!" her mother chirped. "Do come in and sit for a spell." She watched as Tom stepped across the threshold and into the house—as her mother took his arm and led him toward the parlor. "What brings you out this way?" Flora asked.

Tom Evans removed his hat, raking strong

fingers through tousled brown hair. What a handsome man he was! Cedar heard a sigh escape her lungs and immediately gasped, holding her breath and hoping Tom Evans hadn't heard the evidence of her admiration. He glanced to Cedar and smiled, sending a delightful, comforting sort of warmth washing through her.

"It seems Miss Dale left a bag of sugar on the counter at the general store. Elvira asked me to run it on out to ya," he answered. "Thought I'd bring it out, say howdy, and see if there's anythin' I can do for you two ladies."

Cedar was somewhat disheartened—not for having forgotten the sugar and thereby causing inconvenience for Mrs. Gunderson and Tom Evans, but rather for the fact he'd only come to offer his charitable help to the poor Widow Dale and her daughter. Of course, what other reason could he have possibly had for paying a visit? Yet it was a good man who thought of the needs of the unfortunate.

"Well, that's so kind of you, Tom," Flora said. "You always were the nicest young man in town."

"I'm afraid I ain't so young anymore, Mrs. Dale," Tom chuckled.

"Call me Flora," she said. "And you aren't so old either." Flora motioned for Tom to have a seat in one of the large parlor chairs. She then sat down on the sofa herself, patting the seat next to her to indicate Cedar should join her.

"I heard tell Slater got married not too long ago," Flora said.

"Yes, ma'am," Tom confirmed with a nod. "He married a purty little thing named Lark. We sold off half our place to Reno Garrett. I kept the rest of it. Slater and Lark bought their own place about sixty miles north. I just come back from helpin' raise their new barn up there."

"Well, I am so glad to hear he's finally settled," Flora said, smiling. "I'm sure your mama and daddy are smilin' down from heaven on seein' that."

"Yes, ma'am," Tom agreed.

Cedar gasped—blushed when Tom looked at her then. His smile broadened, and he winked as he said, "Yer little girl sure grew up mighty fine, Mrs. Dale. Mighty fine indeed. I couldn't hardly believe it was the same little girl when she told me who she was in town just now."

Cedar felt her eyes widen and her cheeks burn vermilion at the compliment. Again the tempo of her heartbeat increased. She wondered how it could beat so wildly and not quit. She was certain Tom could see how ruffled she was in his presence.

Flora laughed. "Oh, they do grow up fast, Tom. It'll break your heart when you have children of your own and have to watch them change so quickly."

"I can imagine it will," Tom said, still smiling at Cedar.

She wanted to jump up and bolt from the room. Why on earth did he keep staring at her? Why on earth did he keep smiling? Yet she remembered that Tom Evans was nothing if not perpetually jovial. It was one of the things that had always drawn her to him when she'd been a little girl—his appearance of constant amusement and mischief. There was no doubt in her mind that he was amused in that very moment—no doubt in her mind that he was thinking back on what a pest she'd been as a child. Suddenly, the entire situation was nearly mortifying. Cedar was blushing so thoroughly that her cheeks actually hurt!

"I guess you know we lost Jim," Flora said.

Immediately, Tom's smile faded. He returned his attention to Cedar's mother, nodding with affirmation that he had heard of their loss.

"Miss Dale told me when I seen her in town this mornin'," he said. "I am so sorry, Mrs. Dale. Jim was a fine man . . . a fine man."

"Yes, he was," Flora sighed. "That's why I brought Cedar back here. We wanted to get away from that city . . . that place. We need to try to find some peace," Flora explained. "The house is a little run down," she said, glancing around the room. "But it's still comfortable and sturdy. We'll get a garden going in a few weeks, and . . . and things will be fine."

Cedar forced a smile as her mother reached over, placing a reassuring hand on her daughter's knee. She knew her mother wasn't as certain things would be fine as she tried to appear. Though they had some money left from her father's business ventures, it was by no means a fortune. Her mother had explained that they would have to live far more than thriftily if they were to stretch the little money they did have.

"Well, I'd be glad to come on out and till up your garden space for ya, if you like, Mrs. Dale," Tom offered. "And I noticed a weak spot or two in yer roof when I rode up. Thought I'd come on out in a day or two and patch it up, if that's all right with you."

Cedar wanted to shrivel into a corner. How humiliating! It was just as she thought. He'd come out to tend to the poor widow and her pitiful daughter. Secretly she'd hoped their meeting in town—her having grown up since last he saw her—had sparked something in him, an interest in her of some sort. Now she was certain, however, that it was only his kind heart or sense of responsibility to widows and orphans that found him in their parlor.

For a moment, Cedar did marvel. The fact was she and her mother had had more offers of help and consoling over the past three weeks since they'd returned to the old place than they'd had in two years of lingering in the city after the death of her father. Still, she'd secretly wished Tom Evans's interest in paying them a visit had to do with more than just charity.

In the next breath, however, Cedar was silently scolding herself. Had she lost her wits? What about Logan's memory? What about the fact she never wanted to care for anyone other than her mother ever again? Still, she'd cared for Tom before tragedy had changed her heart—long before.

"That's very kind of you, Tom," Flora began, drawing Cedar's attention back to the conversation at hand, "but you don't have to do all that. We'll be fine."

"Nobody has to do nothin' they don't choose to, Mrs. Dale," he said. "But I think two lovely young ladies such as yerselves deserve a little pamperin' here and there. And the fact is . . . I got too much free time on my hands since Slater and Lark set off on their own. It'll give me somethin' to break up my days."

Cedar smiled. She was certain Tom was plenty busy with his own place. She remembered how well known the Evans boys were for their hardworking ways. Furthermore, without his brother to help—and considering the fact that Mrs. Gunderson had said Tom was leaping from running cattle to breeding horses—she was sure he truly had less time to spare than ever before. He was a good man—a rare and great man—just as he'd always been.

"Looky there, Mrs. Dale," Tom chuckled. "I got a smile out of yer daughter."

Cedar blushed as her smile broadened. She glanced away from him, uncomfortable and shy under his handsome gaze.

"But I guess she lost her voice somewhere between town and here. She ain't said a word since I walked through the door," he said. "Are you still cross with me for knockin' ya down in front of the general store, Miss Cedar?" he asked.

A perplexed frown puckered Flora's brow. "What?" she asked, looking to Cedar.

Tom winked at Cedar again, and a delightful shiver ran up her spine.

"I'm afraid I wasn't watching where I was going when I was coming out of the general store this morning," Cedar explained. "I bumped into Mr. Evans."

"It was my fault, Mrs. Dale," Tom countered. "One of them dang doves roostin' on the roof got me with bird mess, and I was busy fussin' about it. I didn't see Miss Cedar comin', and I plowed right into her. Knocked her down hard too."

Flora covered her mouth with a dainty hand for a moment as she giggled with amusement.

"Well, what a reunion that was!" Flora said.

Cedar wrapped a long strand of her hair around her finger, twisting and untwisting it mercilessly. She was so unsettled! For Pete's sake, she could feel goose bumps breaking over her arms as she looked to see Tom smiling at her again. His eyes fairly twinkled with merriment, and she knew he must be again remembering what a pestering little parasite she'd been as a child.

"I 'spect that's why she's so quiet now," Tom said to Flora. "I guess she hasn't forgiven me yet."

"You are awfully quiet, dear," Flora said to her daughter.

Cedar knew her mother couldn't possibly be so naive as to not know why her daughter wasn't speaking. Tom Evans's presence filled the room like cheer on Christmas morning! And what could Cedar possibly have to say that would be interesting to him?

"Just . . . just thinking, I guess," she offered weakly.

She released the strand of hair she'd been nervously twisting when her mother squeezed her knee with the hand that had been resting there. Still, in the very next moment, she couldn't keep her other hand from reaching up for a strand of hair resting on her other shoulder. Twisting and untwisting the long strand of hair, she forced a smile when she saw Tom's broaden as he looked at her.

"I hear Lucas Pratt has got his eye on you, Miss Cedar," he said.

Instantly, Cedar was irritated. Tom had already heard of Lucas's admiration for her? No doubt he was like everyone else in town and thought she should encourage Lucas's attentions.

However, his next utterance indeed surprised her. "I think ya oughta stay clear of that one."

Cedar's eyes widened. It was quite a bold, opinionated statement to make when he had only become reacquainted with her less than half an hour before.

"That's how we both feel," Flora said in a lowered voice. "I can't quite put my finger on it. All I know is I hope he doesn't come around with courting Cedar in mind."

"He won't, Mama. For pity's sake," Cedar quietly scolded. She was more thoroughly embarrassed than she could ever remember being. What was her mother thinking in discussing such things with Tom Evans?

"What makes ya think he won't come courtin' ya, Miss Cedar?" Tom asked. It was a rather brazen question, and Cedar wasn't quite sure how to answer. She wasn't quite sure whether she should answer. Still, the expression of rather mischievous, daring curiosity on his face tweaked her somehow.

"I-I just don't think he will," she stammered.

Tom's alluring eyes narrowed as he studied her. His grin widened. "Oh, he will," he assured her. "He'd be plumb ignorant if he didn't."

Again Cedar felt herself blush to the very tips of her toes.

"Quit twisting your hair, Cedar," her mother whispered aside to her daughter. "You'll wring it clean off."

Cedar hadn't even been aware she'd still been twisting the long strand of hair. Furthermore, she was mortified at the fact she had been. She hadn't twisted her hair for years! When she'd been a child, she'd twisted her hair anytime she was nervous or extremely delighted. But her mother had helped her break the habit after she'd become engaged to Logan. Now here she sat, mercilessly twisting it and almost entirely unaware of the fact. Even worse, she was suddenly conscious of the fact that her hair hung free, for she had unpinned it upon returning home. Tom Evans must think she was some sort of city-bred tart! She looked to him, certain her musings about him were correct when she heard him chuckle.

"Remember that time when ya was little and I was in town havin' some shoein' done?" he asked. "You was sittin' out in front of the blacksmith's chatterin' away to me like a little chipmunk . . . a-twistin' and a-turnin' yer hair somethin' awful . . . and ya plumb tied it in a knot."

Though she thought it was impossible, Cedar felt her already painful blush deepen. He remembered? He remembered that one little thing? Of course, to Cedar it had been far from a little thing—so it was understandable that the memory should be vivid in her mind. But in his? She was wildly delighted in knowing he would remember such a seemingly trivial incident.

"Yes, I remember," was all she could manage as she dropped the strand of hair she'd been twisting.

"I untangled it for ya. Remember that?" he asked.

"I do," she admitted.

How could she ever forget? She'd been jabbering away to him (just like a little chipmunk) while he waited for his horse to be shod. Jabbering, jabbering, jabbering—and twisting a strand of her hair. Before she knew it, she'd twisted the hair into a tight knot. Knowing her mother would be disappointed in her for having knotted her hair again, she'd burst into tears, spilling out the story to Tom Evans of how her mother was always having to cut knots out of her hair—of how she would certainly be scolded for knotting it again. Tom had taken a handkerchief from his pocket, dried her little tears, and set to work untangling the mess. He'd been so kind, so understanding, so careful—and Cedar had relished the attention from him.

"Took me near to half an hour to get that mess undone," Tom chuckled.

Flora looked from Tom to Cedar and back. "I never knew that! Why didn't you ever tell me that, Cedar?" she asked.

"It was that summer you were always having to cut knots out of my hair, Mama," Cedar explained. "I didn't want you to be mad at me for making another one."

Flora smiled and reached over, lovingly squeezing Cedar's hand. "You were always such a sweet young man, Tom," Flora said.

Tom shook his head. "No, ma'am. I'd just been in trouble enough as a boy . . . had too much understandin' to let her go home with another rat's nest in her hair." Flora giggled, and Cedar smiled too.

To Cedar, the patience Tom Evans had shown that day—the understanding and compassion for a little girl—had proved him to be purely heroic. To a little girl, there could've been nothing more gallant than sitting for half an hour picking a knot out of her hair. No doubt he'd had cattle to wrangle that day—maybe fence to patch or branding to do. Yet he'd taken the time to help a little girl. Cedar felt a long-absent warmth glow in her heart at the memory.

"I'm not too proud to admit that I would be grateful to you, Tom . . . if you really would consider tilling the garden and patching up the roof. But only if you truly have the time," Flora said. "And I'll only let you do those things if you promise to stay for supper in the evenings after you've done them."

"Well, that don't seem quite fair, Mrs. Dale. I'd sure be gettin' the better end of the stick," Tom said.

"Those are my conditions, Tom," Flora said. "Supper or we till our own garden and patch up our own roof."

Tom chuckled. "Well then, I'll take your conditions. I ain't too good a cook, and with Lark runnin' off with Slater . . . I'll be right grateful for a good supper for a change."

"Wonderful!" Flora exclaimed. "Then what day would you like to come on out?"

Tom's eyes narrowed as he studied Cedar Dale for a moment. He still couldn't believe the beautiful young woman sitting across from him had bloomed from the little sprout of a girl he'd known so long ago. What he wouldn't give to untangle her hair for her now! He imagined her chestnut hair was as soft as silk—figured it would feel mighty nice between his rough fingers and against his callused palms. He liked the way her eyebrows arched over her eyes— more defined than the other women he knew. Complemented by the bright blue of her eyes and dark eyelashes, her thin, flawlessly curved brows lent to her striking appearance. He fancied her high-set cheeks were unusually rosy—probably from the walk home from town. Her mouth drew his attention as well. Her berry-colored lips appeared soft and somewhat moist—with the general set of them having an almost flirtatious allure.

Yep. Tom could well see why Lucas Pratt was

so smitten. If Tom himself were a younger man, he'd haul out after the girl like a bee to honey. But he wasn't a younger man. Again, he was inwardly amused by the irony of the fact he'd begun to think like his brother—begun to think he was too old and weathered to pursue a pretty young filly like Cedar Dale. But the fact was he was too old—wasn't he? Still, whether he was too banged up and toughened for the likes of such a young woman, there was nothing wrong with appreciating her sweet beauty—admiring her from afar. At least, he didn't guess there was.

Briefly he let his thoughts linger on how empty and lifeless the ranch house seemed without Slater and Lark, Katherine, and the children. He figured there was more life in Flora Dale's house with just her and her daughter in it—even considering the loss of her good husband—than there was out at his place. He knew he was just missing his relations—adjusting to being a bachelor horse breeder rather than spending his time nagging on his older brother about snatching up Lark, entertaining Kate's children, and worrying over Kate's well-being. He'd spent so much time working out everyone else's lives, he'd pretty much quit living his own. Thus, it made sense that it might take him a while to settle in—that the house being suddenly empty might make his thoughts run off in ridiculous directions—such as thinking on how pretty Cedar Dale might look wearing an apron and waltzing around his own kitchen.

Yep. He just needed to settle in, and he needed to be sure he didn't go from worrying over Slater, Lark, Kate, and the children to worrying over the Widow Dale and her daughter. It wouldn't hurt to help them out here and there, however. The roof did need patching, and he figured the garden might be downright necessary if they hoped to eat in the coming months.

Thus, he answered Flora's question. "I've gotta come into town on Saturday. Would Saturday be all right?"

"Of course, Tom!" Mrs. Dale chirped. "We'll look forward to it."

He could see the spark of hope his simple offer of tilling and patching had caused in her, and it made him glad he'd offered to help—even if the truth of it was he didn't really have a moment to spare.

"I'll get them things taken care of for ya," Tom said. "And if there's anything else I can do, I'd be glad to do it."

He stood then—obviously making ready to leave—and a sudden sense of insecurity washed over Cedar.

As her mother left her seat on the sofa, Cedar rose as well.

"I reckon I better be gettin' on home," Tom

said. Realizing he still held the sack of sugar tucked under one arm, he exclaimed, "Oh!" He offered the sugar sack to Cedar, saying, "Here you go, sugar," and chuckling with amusement when she blushed. Winking, he added, "I mean . . . here's yer sugar, Miss Cedar."

"Thank you, Mr. Evans," she said, accepting the sack of sugar. Running a hand through her hair from her forehead back over the top of her head, she blushed again when he smiled as he watched her perform the simple gesture. Something in the way his eyes narrowed caused a thrill to travel down her spine, and she quickly thought that Logan's simple gaze had never caused such a reaction to rise in her.

Instantly, she felt her brow pucker as she frowned. The thought of Logan—of her father— it dampened the moment for her.

"We'll see you on Saturday then, Tom," Flora said as she preceded the man to the door. Cedar followed behind them, simultaneously relieved and depressed by his leaving.

"I'm lookin' forward to it," Tom said, smiling as he returned his hat to his head. "Maybe Miss Cedar here will find me a little more worth talkin' to by then," he said.

Cedar looked to her mother as she heard her giggle. There was mischief in her eyes, and it caused a great unsettling in Cedar's bosom.

"Oh, she's just bashful 'cause you're so handsome, Tom," Flora teased her daughter. "Isn't that right, sweetheart?"

"Mother!" Cedar scolded—mortified more by the truth of her mother's statement than by the teasing manner of it.

"Do ya think I'm handsome, Miss Cedar?" Tom asked her with a wink.

Again Cedar felt her cheeks turn as red as summer cherries. What could she say? How could she possibly respond?

When she did not answer, he added, "Well, I'm mighty flattered. Maybe wonderin' a bit 'bout yer taste in men . . . but mighty flattered all the same." He chuckled, touched the brim of his hat as he nodded, and said, "Good day to you, ladies. Thank you for lettin' me sit a spell."

"You have a good day, Tom," Flora said. "We'll see you on Saturday."

"Yes, ma'am," Tom Evans said. He winked at Cedar once more and then turned and strode over the threshold and out into the warming spring morning.

Cedar watched her mother close the door. All at once, she felt cold—unhappy—as if there would never be another cheerful moment in her life.

As her mother turned to her, she asked, "What in the world is wrong with you, Cedar?" Flora frowned. "A body would've thought you've had your tongue cut out! I swear you didn't say more than five words to that man. He probably thinks I

69

didn't teach you a breath of good manners! And after he rode all the way out here to bring that sugar."

Instantly, Cedar burst into tears—buried her face in her hands. She'd wanted to burst into tears since the moment she'd been knocked on her seat in town and looked up into the face of an older, more handsome Tom Evans.

"Oh, honey!" Flora exclaimed with instant regret—instant compassion. "What's the matter? Why ever are you going on so? I know your little heart just used to nearly beat itself to death whenever Tom Evans was in town. I would've thought having him sitting right here in the parlor would've been something to delight you . . . not cause so many tears."

"He must think I'm the silliest, most ridiculous thing in the world, Mama!" Cedar exclaimed, returning to the parlor and throwing herself onto the sofa as she continued to sob. "First that preposterous incident in town! Then he arrives at the door to find me here with my hair down and looking like a drowned cat!" She looked up to her mother and added, "And how could you agree to let him till the garden and fix the roof? Isn't it bad enough that the whole town thinks we're pitiful?"

Flora inhaled a deep breath, smiled, and sighed.

"One of the hardest things in the world, Cedar . . . is learning how to let others help you when you're in need. We need Tom's help. Oh, I know we could till the garden ourselves . . . even climb up and fix the roof. But he'll do a better job of it, and we both know that. He knows it. And the only reason folks in town have pity for us is because of who we've lost . . . not what we've lost. Furthermore," Flora continued, "I don't think Mr. Tom Evans would've been going on about how fine you've grown up if he thought you were the silliest, most ridiculous thing in the world." Sighing once more, she said, "That's why I am so surprised at your rude manner toward him. I've never seen you so quiet."

Cedar sat up, wiping the tears from her cheeks. She knew her mother was right, but Cedar had never been able to keep her wits about her where Tom Evans was concerned. Whether it was a decade ago or that very day, he'd rattled her entirely just by being in her presence—and she felt ridiculous.

"Mama," Cedar began, "you remember how I used to follow along after him . . . drive him nearly insane with pestering and chatter. How would you feel?" She paused then, wiping new tears from her cheeks.

"I'd feel very glad that I'd grown up into such a beautiful woman and that he was still unmarried," Flora answered.

"Mother!" Cedar exclaimed. She tried to ignore the fact that the very same thoughts had crossed her mind the moment Mrs. Gunderson had related all the news of the town to Cedar and her mother weeks ago—the moment she'd heard that Tom Evans was still unmarried and not courting anyone.

"Oh, don't pretend to be so astonished, Cedar," Flora scolded. "Mrs. Gunderson says Tom's own brother married a girl some twelve years younger than himself . . . so I know you've thought of it."

Cedar wiped another tear from her cheek. There was no need to argue. Her mother was right.

"And it makes me glad you have," Flora added. "It gives me hope that . . . that what happened with your father and Logan . . . well, it gives me hope you're healing."

Cedar shook her head. "Healing or not, I'm not ignorant enough to think Tom Evans would ever . . . would ever . . ."

"Oh, nonsense!" Flora exclaimed. "I have my suspicions that you're just why he's so anxious to come back."

"Mama, don't try to—" Cedar began.

"Hush, now," Flora interrupted. "Let's get on into the kitchen and get some of those nice potatoes you brought home to baking for lunch. Hmmm?" Cedar sighed and nodded. Putting potatoes on to bake was about the last thing on the face of the earth she felt like doing at that moment, but she and her mother had both learned keeping the body busy helped ease the worries of the mind.

Still, the very essence of Tom Evans seemed to linger, and Cedar found herself wildly distracted. All she could seem to think about was how handsome he was—how kindly he'd treated her and her mother. She couldn't help smiling whenever she thought of his flirtatious manner—his wit in calling her "sugar" when he'd handed the sugar sack to her. Whether it was a pun or not, it had been intentional—and Cedar adored it.

Even so, an odd guilt was plowing around in her mind as well—a feeling of disloyalty and betrayal where Logan's memory was concerned. Logan Davies had died because of her. She'd loved him, and he'd died because of it. How could she be so callous as to have tender thoughts toward another man? How could she allow herself to be so wildly attracted to another man, even one she'd adored since her childhood? It seemed wrong somehow, and the guilt tainted her thoughts of Tom. Besides, Tom Evans was kind to everyone he knew. Cedar knew she was no one special or unique to him. It would be best to tuck her thoughts of him away and concentrate on baking potatoes—best to remember Logan and his ultimate sacrifice for her sake.

Tom settled on one of the kitchen chairs, propping his feet up on another. When he'd left for town that morning to stock his flour, he never would've imagined he'd end up committing himself to an entire day of hard labor outside his own chores that needed doing. The new fence that was the dividing line between what was now part of Reno Garrett's place and Tom's still needed to be finished. The few cattle he'd kept when Slater had taken the rest of the herd were already calving, and the new Clydesdale he'd bought to breed Dolly and Coaly would be arriving on the train in another week. He never would've imagined he'd ride to town and bump into a pretty little filly who'd once been a child he'd known either. He smiled, thinking that if nothing else, the trip to town had been eventful.

He hadn't quit thinking about Miss Cedar Dale—not for one moment the whole way home. The fact was it was a good thing old Fred knew his own way back—for Tom doubted he'd even been paying attention to where the horse was going.

Yep. Little Cedar Dale had grown up into a right beautiful young woman. Tom was a bit uncomfortable with the way his mouth had begun to water as he'd sat studying her in her mama's parlor. She'd make someone a sweet little wife someday—if she ever got over the death of her other lover, that is. Tom wondered if she ever would get over it—or even if she did, could any man ever compete with the memory of one who had died in defending her honor? He thought about the way Cedar had watched him as he sat in her mother's parlor—like a little bunny staring at some ravenous wolf. What a pity it all was. She seemed so timid—frightened and uncertain. He smiled, remembering what a chatty chipmunk she'd been as a child—chuckled in remembering the way she used to beg him to wait for her to grow up so she could marry him. Yep. It was a shame she'd been so beaten up by life already.

Tom glanced around the empty kitchen and sighed. He missed Slater and Lark. He'd have to get himself a dog to keep him company—a dog or a wife. Amelia Perkins was willing enough to take up the job. That he knew. The way she slobbered around after him? He laughed out loud, thinking that Amelia Perkins did follow after him like a dang dog sometimes. Still, he wasn't a hair interested in her—didn't even like her enough to speak to her, unless she spoke to him first and good manners demanded a response. Oh, she was beautiful—that was undeniable—beautiful to look at anyway. And she seemed a kind, caring sort. But Tom's heart didn't seem to give Amelia a second thought; neither did his mind. Nope, his tired old brain would never find Amelia Perkins and the word *love* melting up together. And if Tom Evans knew one thing, he knew a man ought to love the woman he married.

Tom chuckled. He shook his head. The loneliness was getting to him—much worse than he thought it would. The solitude was working on his sanity all right—it had to be. What else could have him thinking on getting a dog—or getting married?

Instantly his thoughts returned to Cedar Dale. She seemed so alone, so frightened, so broken. Even for her mother's company and love, she seemed so vulnerable—and every protective instinct instilled in Tom Evans was wildly alert. He thought of her soft nut-brown hair—the clear blue of her eyes—the rather alluring set to her berry lips—and once again his mouth began to water.

"Time to get to work," he mumbled, pushing himself out of the chair. Yep. He needed a dog. Elvira had a female ready to drop a litter any day. He'd ask her if he could take one of the pups when they were old enough.

Tom left the house, intent on mucking out the stalls in the barn. If he was going to spend Saturday out at Flora Dale's place, he'd better be sure his place was kept up. He shook his head, disgusted at himself for letting his mind wander in the direction of Cedar Dale again. Still he smiled—chuckled. She was such a pretty little thing.

Chapter Four

As the week progressed—as Saturday and Tom Evans's impending visit neared—Cedar's emotions churned. She began to feel nauseated for most of each day, nervous with the anticipation of seeing Tom Evans again. Certainly she knew he thought nothing of her beyond the fact she and her mother were in need of charity. Still, she could think of little else but him, lingering on memories of the past—of how kind and patient he had been with her when she was a child, how little in that regard seemed to have altered in him. Yet guilt became her constant companion as well—guilt over the fact her thoughts so constantly lingered on Tom Evans instead of lingering on the loss of Logan and her father as it seemed to her they should have.

She mused that her father would be pleased to see her thoughts veering from paths of discouragement, loss, heartache, and fear. It was Logan's feelings she worried over. Would he think she was fickle, disloyal, and uncaring? Naturally, her mother attempted to reassure her.

"Logan wouldn't want you to spend your life alone and unhappy," Flora had said that evening after Tom Evans had delivered the sack of sugar. "He'd want you to live a full and wonderful life."

"And what about Daddy?" Cedar had asked. "Wouldn't Daddy want you to live a full and wonderful life too? You make it sound so easy, letting go of Logan . . . letting go of the guilt."

Flora smiled. "I did live a full and wonderful life, Cedar," she said. "I married your daddy when I was fifteen years old, had you a year later . . . and I was as happy as any woman ever could be."

Cedar saw the familiar shadow of grief and longing pass over her mother's countenance. She'd caused her mother's sudden sadness and inwardly scolded herself for being so selfish.

"I've had my love, Cedar," her mother continued. "And though I'm nearly destroyed at having lost it . . . at least I had it. But you're so young, with so much to offer. Don't let the guilt over what happened to Logan keep you from reaching out and snatching up what you deserve. Don't let the fear of having lost Daddy keep you from people the way you've been doing since it happened." Flora smiled, patting her daughter's knee. "Besides . . . I think it's fate that finds us back here and Tom Evans still unattached. Why, you've loved him ever since—"

"Mother, please!" Cedar interrupted, frowning as her heart's tempo increased. "Tom Evans will always see me as the little pest with knots in her hair. Don't tease me about it so. Even if I had a mind to think a man like him would ever . . .

even if I had the courage to . . . well, he's not the type of man who would ever . . . just let's not talk about it anymore."

Cedar had been grateful that her mother had simply smiled and said, "All right, sweetheart. All right."

Still, no matter what she was about over those next few days—whether cooking, washing up supper dishes, mending, or even reading—she found her thoughts always, always, always returned to Tom Evans. The closer the week wore down toward Saturday, the more agitated and anxious Cedar became. Yet her excitement grew as well, and it was her excitement that worried her most.

Two nights before Tom Evans was to arrive to till the garden and patch the roof, as Cedar lay in her bed attempting to fall asleep, she found that each time she closed her eyes, an image of Tom Evans was all she could envision. He was there—tall, handsome, witty, friendly—alluring. Cedar turned her pillow, punched it hard, and rolled onto her side. Gazing out the window into the starry night, she tried to force her thoughts to Logan—to how she had loved him—to how he had loved her enough to lose his life for the sake of her honor. But visions of sweet Logan and his kind, patient smile quickly vanished—vanquished by vivid visions of a man from Cedar's past—a man she'd never forgotten—a man she knew she never would forget.

Cedar sighed as she abandoned the effort to think of Logan. It was a vain struggle, and she knew it. Though she would always love him, Logan was gone, safe in the arms of heaven, at peace and free from worldly fear and strife. Tom Evans was present—gorgeous, alluring, and entirely present!

Cedar felt a slight smile tickle the corners of her mouth as she closed her eyes and let her mind linger on Tom Evans's broad shoulders and delicious smile. Tom Evans had been a man long before Cedar had grown into a woman. She knew he must still see her as he had when she'd been a child chasing him all over creation. No doubt it was why he had smiled at her nearly constantly when he'd delivered the sugar to her home several days before. No doubt he was enjoying a quiet amusement, remembering what a lovesick lamb she'd been for him last time he'd seen her. How would she ever endure sitting at the same supper table with him Saturday evening? How would she keep from staring at his handsome face, blushing crimson under his gaze? She could wring her mother's neck for allowing him to offer to help with the roof and garden space.

Yet Cedar's smile broadened as she surrendered to her visions of him—to her memories. How vividly she still remembered the day he'd found her in town—the day she'd, once again, twisted a long strand of hair into a knot at the back of her head and was sobbing in knowing a scolding was awaiting her at home. She still remembered the way the young, handsome cowboy Tom Evans had promptly sat down on the ground in the alley between the general store and Mr. Gunderson's smokehouse, pulled her into his lap, and begun the arduous task of untangling her hair. She remembered the soothing sound of his voice—the way he kept her talking about lighthearted, insignificant things so that she wouldn't cry in anticipation of a scolding or from the necessary discomfort he was inflicting while unknotting her hair.

Cedar's smile broadened as she thought of how Tom Evans's incredible patience would serve him well as a father. He'd make a wonderful father. He'd make a wonderful husband. He'd make a wonderful anything!

"That's enough of that, Cedar Dale," Cedar growled, forcing her eyes open and punching her pillow to fluff the feathers inside it. "No more nonsense."

Yet as Cedar closed her eyes once more, a quiet giggle escaped her throat as she thought of the way she and Tom Evans had collided in front of the general store earlier in the week. How wonderful to have touched him—even for the uncomfortable circumstances. She thought of the way her hand had tingled when she'd taken his—of how effortlessly he pulled her to her feet—and the thought caused goose bumps to ripple over her arms and legs. Still, it was a delightful way to fall asleep—covered in goose bumps and entertaining visions of Tom Evans.

"I need more flour, Cedar . . . and that's that," Flora explained to her daughter. "There's no way I can stretch what I have with everything I've got planned for supper tomorrow."

"But, Mama, I don't feel up to going into town today. I don't want to face anybody . . . even Mrs. Gunderson," Cedar argued. "As nice as she is—"

"But look who you ran into last time you were in town, sweetheart," Flora reminded Cedar with a smile and a wink. "Wasn't meeting up with Tom Evans worth risking your worry a little?"

"Yes," Cedar admitted. "But I've been sick to my stomach with knots and nerves ever since."

"Well, I don't know why," Flora said as she cracked another egg and emptied its contents into the bowl on the table. "It's obvious he finds you attractive."

"It's obvious he finds me amusing, Mama," Cedar said, taking a strand of her hair between her fingers and twisting mercilessly.

Flora reached out, taking Cedar's free hand in her own. Her smile faded; a frown puckered her brow a moment.

"Tom Evans is a good man, Cedar," Flora said. "Furthermore, he's familiar to you. The fact you already know him . . . it should make it easier to—"

"He is a good man, Mama," Cedar interrupted, pulling her hand from her mother's grasp and turning from her. "And that's why he needs someone . . . someone fresh . . . someone untainted. Someone whose heart won't always belong to someone else."

Though Cedar had fallen asleep to visions of Tom Evans, it had been visions of Logan Davies that had haunted her dreams. All through the night she'd dreamt of Logan—dreamt of his handsome face, his kind nature—his body lying dead and lifeless as his blood soaked the city street beneath him. She'd awakened with the sense that she owed him her very life—that she always would owe it to him. With the morning, all Cedar's happy feelings of excitement and possibility where Tom Evans was concerned had vanished. She felt like a ship being tossed at sea—one minute safe, the next suffering damage.

Flora sighed. "It's all right to move forward, Cedar. It's not unfaithful or disloyal to Logan to find happiness without him . . . to fall in love with someone else. Tom Evans would make a fine—"

"Mother!" Cedar interrupted as her heart began to hammer within her chest at the word *love* being intermingled with her thoughts of Tom

Evans. "How can you even say that? I've seen Tom Evans all of twice since we returned. Twice! How can you imply I would fall in love with him? How could you think I would abandon Logan's memory so quickly?"

"Quickly?" Flora exclaimed. Cedar watched as her mother's pretty brow puckered into a frown—an angry, irritated frown. "It's been two years, Cedar. Two years! And don't try to pull the wool over my eyes either. I haven't seen so much color in your cheeks, such a twinkle in your eyes ever . . . as I saw the day Tom dropped in here. And I do mean I've never seen you light up that way. Never, Cedar. Not even when Logan was—"

"Stop it, Mama . . . please," Cedar begged, covering her ears with her hands. "I loved Logan! I did!"

"I know you did, sweetheart. I know you did," Flora cooed, taking Cedar by the shoulders and turning her to face her once more. "But . . . but I think that, whether it's just the memory of the handsome young man you were so lovesick over as a child . . . or whether some divine intervention has taken place in our lives . . . Logan would want to see you happy, Cedar." Flora paused and brushed a tear from her daughter's face. "If the tables had been turned, Cedar—if you had been killed instead of Logan—you'd want to see him happy . . . married to a nice girl and loved. Wouldn't you?"

Cedar bit her lip and sniffled. She closed her eyes for a moment and nodded.

"But that's just it, Mama," she whispered. "If the tables were turned, I would want to see Logan happily married to someone else, but . . . but . . ."

"But what?" Flora prodded.

"But if it had been Tommy Evans in Logan's place . . . if I had been killed just before I was supposed to marry Tommy Evans . . ." Cedar stammered.

Flora frowned and prodded, "What, darling? What? If you had been engaged to Tom instead of Logan . . . and you had been killed . . ."

"Something in me knows . . . I'd want him to pine away after me forever, Mama," Cedar admitted. "I'd never want to know he . . . that another woman had . . . I'd want him to love me and only me . . . forever."

Flora sighed with contentment as her frown softened—vanished. A comforted smile spread across her face.

"Just because you're afraid you might love someone else more . . . afraid you might find yourself embroiled in passion in a way you never were with Logan . . . doesn't mean you didn't truly love him, Cedar," Flora said.

Cedar shook her head, brushing the tears from her cheeks. "It's wrong to think such things . . . to feel them."

"There are many different kinds of love, darling . . . many different levels of love. Even though Logan died the way he did, it doesn't mean you owe him anything other than your loving gratitude. You don't need to sacrifice your life the way he did. He didn't save you so that you could waste away in guilt and sorrow."

Cedar brushed more tears from her cheeks. She was surprised when she felt a smile at her lips—more surprised when she felt laughter gurgle up from her throat.

Smiling at her mother, she repeated, "*Embroiled in passion,* Mother? Honestly."

Flora smiled too. "But you forget, Cedar," she said. "I watched those Evans boys grow up . . . and even now I'm a bit more experienced than you, my dear. Embroiled in passion is just where you might find yourself . . . if you can find the courage to step out of the shadow of Logan's death and into the light of Tom Evans's rather dazzling smile."

Cedar shook her head and giggled, completely amused by her mother's dramatics.

She giggled as she brushed the remains of her tears from her cheeks. Striding from the kitchen, she took her coat down from the hook by the front door.

"I'll go to town and fetch us some flour, Mama," she called to her mother. "And I'll try not to become *embroiled in passion* while I'm there."

Cedar giggled again as she opened the door to leave.

"You do that, sweetheart," Flora said, wiping her hands on her apron as she walked to the entryway to watch her daughter go. "You do that."

Flora closed the door behind Cedar and leaned back against it for a moment. She smiled—for there was hope. For the first time in two years, Flora was experiencing hope where Cedar's future was concerned. Not only had she seen the way Cedar lit up like a lantern in Tom Evans's presence; she'd seen the way Tom's eyes had smoldered with interest as he'd studied Cedar from across the room. Naturally, Cedar had been far too young to catch his eye when they'd lived on the farm before, but she was a beautiful, kind, loving young woman now—and Tom Evans had been a bachelor long enough. Thank heaven!

Flora returned to mixing the cake she planned to serve as dessert the following day. She smiled when she found herself humming softly—even for the thought that Jim was gone. Oh, how she missed him! How she still wept in the quiet confines of her bedroom late at night—often wept. Still, there was hope for Cedar now, and it gave Flora cause to feel more lighthearted.

She did consider for a moment—consider her own hypocrisy. Flora Dale knew she'd never recover from the death of her beloved husband. They'd had eighteen years together, but it hadn't been nearly enough. Forever wouldn't have been enough. Still, at least they'd had one another, loved one another, and that's what she wanted for her daughter—love.

Thus, she continued to hum as she baked, knowing Jim would be happy that she'd moved herself and Cedar back to the farm. He'd be happy that Flora was encouraging their daughter toward Tom Evans. Hadn't Jim always said he'd wished "that Evans boy" had been younger— young enough to still be around when Cedar was marrying age? Yes, Jim was looking down from heaven, smiling and nodding his approval.

"She'll be happy and cared for, Jimmy," Flora said aloud. "I'll see to it. Don't you worry."

Flora frowned a moment, paused, and turned to look into the parlor. She felt goose bumps prickle the back of her neck—for in that very moment, she could've sworn she'd heard Jim's voice behind her.

And what about your happiness, darling? she thought she'd heard him say.

The sensation of having heard his voice was so powerful that Flora actually found herself whispering, "Jim?" in return.

Yet there came no response. There never did.

In that moment, the bitter ache of loss and loneliness returned. Flora felt tears well in her eyes—wondered how she'd ever feel safe again without Jim near to take her in his arms and protect and comfort her. The fact was she probably wouldn't—but what was she going to do? She couldn't just sit down and quit, now could she? She had Cedar to provide for—to care for. Oh, Flora had certainly had thoughts of defeat—of despair and hopelessness. When Jim had been killed, she thought she'd never be able to pick up and move forward. But having Cedar—loving her more than her own life—Cedar had kept Flora from succumbing to near insanity because of her grief.

Even now, even as a tear trickled down one cheek in missing her Jim, even now the hope of seeing Cedar healed—of seeing her daughter happy and loved—even now it was Cedar that kept Flora Dale from hating life, from hopelessness, from bitter, miserable, cold loneliness.

"You better be the man I remember you to be, Tom Evans," Flora mumbled as she poured the cake batter into the pan she'd prepared. " 'Cause Cedar has a lot of knots that need untangling these days . . . and not just in her hair."

"Hey there, Reno," Tom greeted as he stepped out onto the front porch.

Tom rubbed the sore muscle in his chest as he watched Reno dismount.

"Gettin' a pretty late start, aren't ya, Tom?"

Reno asked as he climbed the porch steps. The man offered Tom a hand in greeting, and Tom chuckled as he accepted Reno Garrett's firm grip.

"Yep," Tom admitted. "I had me a mighty restless night last night. Couldn't seem to catch a wink of sleep. Guess I finally fell to sleep about the time the sun was comin' up."

Reno nodded. "I been there, boy," he said. "That's a man with too much on his mind."

"I guess," Tom agreed. "What finds you out this way so early?"

Reno smiled and chuckled. "That ornery ol' bull of yers. Outlaw, is it?" Tom sighed—nodded with instant understanding. "He's been havin' the time of his life this mornin' with a couple of my cows. I thought maybe you could help me get him headed home. He's meaner'n hell."

"I'm sorry, Reno," Tom began. "That's my fault. I meant to have the boys check the fencin' 'round his pasture. Ol' Outlaw has been wound up tighter than a wasp since Slater rode off with most of the herd. Let me get saddled up, and I'll come fetch him."

"I'd sure appreciate it, Tom," Reno said. "But . . . ya might wanna hold off on saddling up for a minute or two. I saw that little filly Amelia Perkins headin' this way in her daddy's buggy."

"Oh, help me now," Tom grumbled.

Reno chuckled. "What's the matter, Tom? You don't like purty girls droppin' in of a mornin'?

Seems a might nice way to start the day, if'n you ask me."

Tom laughed. "Well, it might be . . . if it weren't for the fact that it's Amelia Perkins comin' up the road," he said. He smiled at Reno and winked. "Now, if ya like . . . I can send her on over to yer place for a spell . . . bein' as you think purty girls is a nice way of startin' off the mornin'."

"Hell no!" Reno laughed. "I'm old enough to be that girl's daddy," he said, smiling. "That just wouldn't do for me."

"Now, Reno . . . we both know you ain't old enough to be Amelia's daddy," Tom said.

"Forty years to my name, Tom . . . and clickin' another one off at Christmas," Reno said, shaking his head. "Besides . . . I ain't got time for it. I never have had."

"Well, I sure wish you had time for it now," Tom said as he looked to the horizon to see Carl Perkins's horse and buggy headed straight for the house, Amelia at the lines.

Reno chuckled. "I hear she's a real little she-devil," he said.

Tom nodded. "Yep. I best head her off 'fore she gets too close to the house."

Reno chuckled again. It was obvious he was amused by the situation.

"Well, I'll see ya in a bit," he said. "We gotta get that ol' bull of yours corralled 'fore he does any more damage."

"Yes, we do," Tom said as Amelia tossed a wave to him from her seat in the buggy.

Reno mounted his horse, chuckling all the while.

"Good luck there, Tom," he said. "Ain't much a man can do once a woman decides she's gonna wrangle him."

Tom smiled—even chuckled. "Well . . . we'll see about that," he said.

"Get," Reno mumbled, spurring his horse.

Tom laughed, noting that Reno Garrett rode off in the opposite direction from which Amelia Perkins was approaching, even though it would be out of his way.

Tom stepped off the porch and headed out a ways from the house. He didn't want Amelia anywhere near the ranch house—didn't want to give anybody a reason for gossiping, even the stock.

"Mornin', Tom!" Amelia greeted in her familiar, all-too-syrupy manner.

"Mornin', Miss Amelia," Tom said. He wasn't one to be ill-mannered too often, after all—even when he wanted to. "What brings you out this way?"

Naturally he already knew what brought Amelia to the ranch, but he feigned ignorance all the same.

"You," she answered simply, although very flirtatiously. "I just can't imagine you've really been eatin' proper since Lark and Slater left you out here all alone, so I thought I just might drop some fixin's by today."

Tom gritted his teeth and forced a friendly grin. He didn't care for Amelia Perkins. Furthermore, he liked to do the pursuing when it came to things between a man and a woman. He didn't like being preyed upon—and certainly not by Amelia Perkins. It was the second time in a week she'd ridden out to his place. Two days ago she'd pretended she was just out wandering in need of a little fresh air. No town-living woman in her right mind wandered miles outside of town just for a breath of fresh air. Oh, she was pretty enough—green-eyed and hair as black as pitch. Nice figure too. But she didn't inspire a lick of heartfelt interest in Tom Evans.

"Well, that's mighty thoughtful of ya, Amelia. Mighty thoughtful," he said as he watched her alight from the buggy. He should've helped her down—he knew he should've. It was downright rude not to. Still, Tom had learned to be very wary of Amelia—learned not to offer any sort of encouragement.

He watched as she lifted a large pot from the floor of the buggy, and he accepted it as she held it out to him.

"Now, Amelia," he began, "you know you and your mama don't need to worry none about me."

The girl ignored him, however—ignored his attempt to draw her mother into it.

"I've got two pies too," she told him. "I didn't know which kind you'd like best, so I just made both . . . apple and rhubarb."

She was past him and up on the porch before Tom had a chance to stay her. Quickly, he hurried into the house after her, setting the pot down on the floor just inside the door.

Amelia Perkins rather pushed her way into everything. Tom figured there probably wasn't a lick of anything he could've done to keep her outside. She glanced around the inside of the house as she removed her gloves.

An odd sort of panic rose in Tom. *How long is she plannin' on stayin'?* he thought to himself.

"Well, ya certainly need some straightenin' up in here, Tom," Amelia sighed. "A woman's way . . . that's what it's needin'." She turned and smiled at him. "And ya must get awful lonesome out here all by yerself."

"Not really," Tom lied. " 'Sides, I'm thinkin' on gettin' me a dog soon as Elvira Gunderson's litter is weaned."

Amelia playfully tossed her head as she laughed. "A puppy? Tom Evans . . . don't you know that a puppy will tear this house down right around your ears?"

Tom frowned a bit. "Do yer mama and daddy know you're all the way out here, Miss Amelia?"

he asked. For sure and for certain it wasn't proper for her to keep dropping in on him alone like this. The gossip in town fed faster than a prairie grass fire, and Tom didn't want to find himself at the wrong end of a shotgun wedding.

"Of course, silly goose," she assured him. "I always tell my mama when I'm headed out yer way, Tom."

"I'm sure you do," Tom mumbled. It was just what he feared. Rather paternally, he took Amelia by the shoulders and turned her around. As he urged her back over the threshold and out of the house, he said, "Thank ya for stoppin' by, Miss Amelia . . . and for the supper. I'll get yer pot back to ya Saturday when I come into town."

"But . . . but I'd thought I'd stay and do some mendin' for ya or somethin'," Amelia stammered.

"Oh, that's a mighty nice offer," Tom said, nearly shoving her out onto the porch. "But I gotta get out to Reno Garrett's place to help him round up my old bull and see to some fencin'."

Instantly Amelia turned to him. Her eyes narrowed, and her smile faded. Scowling, she said, "Well, at least do me the courtesy of bringin' in the pies I made for ya, Tom Evans."

Tom forced another smile and said, "Sure thing, Amelia. And I do thank ya for comin' out to check up on me."

As he hurried out to the buggy, he felt bad for being so rude. Still, what else could he do? He couldn't have Amelia Perkins dropping by any time she wanted. He quickly retrieved the pies and sauntered back toward the house.

"I do thank ya, Miss Amelia," he said, more out of guilt than true appreciation. "It's mighty kind of you and your mama to look out for us poor ol' cowboys." He set the pies on the porch railing and then took hold of Amelia's elbow and guided her down the steps and toward her buggy.

"You'll tell your mama I said thanks, won't ya?" he asked.

"I suppose," Amelia pouted as she climbed into the buggy.

Tom nodded and forced one last smile. He almost burst into laughter as Amelia Perkins angrily slapped the lines at the horse's back, sending the buggy hauling off like a cat with a firebrand tied to its tail.

As he watched her go, he felt bad for the horse. Releasing a heavy sigh of relief, he turned back to the house. He needed his hat, after all. Probably oughta saddle up Fred and get over to Reno Garrett's place before Outlaw caused too much more damage.

Still, sometime later—as he rode toward Reno Garrett's place—Tom caught himself wishing he were settled down with a woman of his own. Instantly, the companion to his thoughts became pretty little Cedar Dale. He thought of the frightened doe expression he'd seen in her mesmerizing blue eyes when she'd realized who he was after knocking her to her seat outside the general store days before. He chuckled to himself when he remembered the way she'd sat twisting a strand of hair when he'd lingered in her mother's parlor after he'd ridden out to deliver the sack of sugar. He thought it was sweet— entirely adorable—the way she still twisted her hair just the way she'd done as a child. He could remember her so many years before, running around town in her bare feet, several knots of hair at the back of her head. The memory warmed him inside like he couldn't remember being warmed in a long time.

"She's awful young though," he said aloud to himself. He chuckled in the next breath, however. "And I'm beginnin' to sound more and more like Slater every day."

Tom frowned a moment. He was figuring ages—his and Cedar's—Slater's and Lark's. The way he figured, Cedar was a bit older than Lark had been when she'd married Slater—and Slater was two years older than Tom.

What's nine or ten years difference in age anyhow? he mused. After all, his grandmother had been all of fifteen when she'd married his grandfather—who was thirty-three when they wed. In the scheme of things, nine or ten years wasn't so much. Maybe he would let himself think on that little Cedar Dale for a while.

"I see you managed to escape with your life," Reno teased as Tom reined in next to him.

"Just barely," Tom chuckled.

Reno smiled and then sighed. He rested his arms on his saddle horn and nodded toward the place where Outlaw stood watching them with heightened suspicion.

"He ain't gonna take too kindly to you drivin' him away from these lady cows," Reno said.

Tom chuckled, thinking for a moment that he wished Slater would've taken Outlaw up north with him.

Tom dismounted, and Outlaw pawed the ground with one front hoof, lowered his horns, and snorted.

"Yep," Tom said. "He's gonna be ornerier than all get out now."

"I tried to get close to him and get a handle on the ring in his nose," Reno explained, "but he wouldn't have none of it."

"I'm sure he wouldn't," Tom chuckled.

It was going to be a chore, getting Outlaw back. Tom would probably have to drag him by the nose ring all the way home.

Handing Reno Fred's reins, he said, "Me and that old bull . . . we've been goin' around this way for years."

"I had me a girl like that once," Reno laughed.

"Any time I turned my back on her, it seemed she was tryin' to do me harm."

Tom chuckled. "Some women is like that, I guess."

"Women and cattle," Reno teased. "We could rope him maybe."

"Yeah," Tom said. "But it'd just make him madder. I'll just have to get him by the ring and walk him home."

"All right then," Reno said.

Tom looked up to Reno. Smiling, he said, "Actually . . . why don't you tie both them horses up? Now that I think of it, it always took both me and Slater to get that ol' bull to mind."

Reno smiled. "You bet."

Tom stared down Outlaw as Reno tied the reins of Fred and his own horse to a nearby fence-post.

"Yeah, I see you . . . you sorry ol' piece of leather," he mumbled. "But yer comin' on home . . . whether you want to or not."

Reno stepped up beside him then, and Tom looked to him.

"You ready for some hard cowboyin'?" Tom asked.

Reno chuckled. "You bet. Ain't been a bovine I met yet that can get the better of me," he said. "And I got the scars to prove it."

Tom chuckled—nodded. "Let's go then."

As Tom and Reno carefully approached Outlaw,

Reno said, "I hear that new widow in town is a mighty purty woman."

Tom watched as Outlaw snorted and stomped the ground with one powerful hoof.

"Yep. And her daughter's one to start yer mouth to waterin' somethin' awful," he said.

"Well, I'd like to get a peek at both of 'em," Reno mumbled, pausing as Outlaw took a step forward.

"I thought you were an ol' bachelor rancher for life," Tom chuckled. He was a little unsettled suddenly, however—for he didn't like the idea that Reno Garrett might take to letting his thoughts linger on Cedar Dale.

"Oh, I am," Reno assured him. "But I figure . . . there ain't no harm in lookin'. Right?"

Tom glanced to Reno and nodded as an understanding smile spread across the man's face.

"That's right," he agreed.

The earth began to shake then—the ground rumbling as Outlaw charged.

"Oh, he's mad now!" Reno shouted as he readied to help round up the bull.

"Wouldn't you be?" Tom laughed. But even for the danger of a charging bull, Tom found himself distracted by thoughts of Cedar Dale—thoughts that maybe he wasn't the only man who might have his eye on her.

Chapter Five

"Well, good mornin', Cedar!" Mrs. Gunderson cheerily greeted as Cedar stepped into the general store. "Back already? Why, you were just in here Monday!"

Cedar smiled and nodded to the jolly woman. She was beginning to feel comfortable with the elderly lady—and she was glad.

"Yes," Cedar replied. "Mama and I are in need of some flour. I guess she hadn't noticed it until this morning."

"Sugar on Monday and flour today, is it?" Mrs. Gunderson asked, still smiling. Mrs. Gunderson held such a kind and happy countenance. Cedar wondered how anyone could ever keep from catching her merry mood.

"Yep." Cedar sighed, shaking her head a little. "I wish Mama would've noticed she needed flour before I came in here on Monday. It would've saved me the trip today."

But Mrs. Gunderson chuckled, her eyes fairly twinkling with mischief. "Oh, why save a trip into town . . . especially when ya live so close, honey?" she asked. "And besides, ya never know what might happen . . . or who ya might run into. Ain't that right?"

Cedar blushed, certain the woman knew exactly

whom Cedar had "run into" the last time she'd ventured into town. The fact was the closer Cedar had gotten to the general store, the faster her heart had beat at the anticipation of perhaps seeing Tom Evans again. The sense of conflict raging inside her was nearly overwhelming, however. One moment the thought of seeing Tom again caused her very soul to soar, her heart to wildly hammer, her insides to quiver. Still, in the very next breath, a severe anxiety would wash over her, sending nausea to churn her stomach, perspiration to bead at her temples and forehead.

As if the older woman had read her thoughts, Mrs. Gunderson said, "In fact, Tom Evans was in yesterday. He said he's comin' out to yer place to patch up yer mama's roof tomorrow." The old woman's eyes twinkled again as she added, "He said he's stayin' for supper."

Cedar's blush intensified, this time burning to the very tips of her toes.

"Yes," she admitted. "He's been kind enough to offer to help Mama and me with a few chores . . . the roof . . . tilling the garden space."

"Mmm," Mrs. Gunderson hummed, winking at Cedar. "I'll bet his kindness won't stop there, sweet thing."

"Well, I can't think of anything else that needs doing or fixing out at our house," Cedar began, "so I'm sure he won't have need to—"

"Cedar Dale!" Mrs. Gunderson scolded. "What

are you thinkin'? Honey, a women can always think of things that need doin' 'round the house or farm . . . especially if there's a handsome cowboy nearby to do 'em."

"Well . . . well, Mama and I wouldn't want to take advantage of Mr. Evans's kindness and charity," Cedar said.

Mrs. Gunderson chuckled. "I think yer missin' my meanin' entirely, Cedar," she said. Cedar felt a puzzled expression wrinkle her brow. "First of all, whether there's things needin' doin' or not . . . a clever woman can always find some task to keep a man around. And second of all . . . you go right ahead and take advantage of that man! It'll keep life more interestin'."

"Do you mean we should make up things for him to do for us?" Cedar asked, entirely astonished as she realized exactly what the woman was implying.

"Of course!" Mrs. Gunderson exclaimed. "How do you think I finally caught my Theodore? Mr. Gunderson worked for my daddy when we were young, and whenever he had nothin' to do . . . I'd always find somethin' for him." Mrs. Gunderson lowered her voice, leaned over the counter, and said, "Men like to feel needed, ya see. They want to feel like a woman needs a hero . . . and that they happened along and turned out to be just that."

Cedar giggled. "Why, Mrs. Gunderson!" she

exclaimed in a whisper. "I think you're an imp wearin' angel's wings. Who'd you steal that halo from?"

Mrs. Gunderson laughed. "Oh, I didn't steal my halo, honey. I earned it by way of experience."

"Hey there, Miss Dale," Lucas Pratt greeted as he entered the general store. "It's always nice to see you in town."

Instantly, Cedar's lighthearted mood vanished.

"Good morning, Mr. Pratt," Cedar greeted— nervously.

She should be flattered by the way the young man's gaze lingered on her face—traveled over her as he studied her from head to toe—but she wasn't. Certainly Lucas was tall and quite handsome with his dust-colored hair and green eyes. His smile was inviting, he was well-mannered, and most folks in town took to him easily enough. But Lucas didn't cause Cedar's heart to leap—not in the least. She didn't feel excessive joy at seeing him—didn't own some delicious desire to linger in his company. She didn't sense any malice or ill-intent in him. He just didn't interest her. It was as simple as that.

"Do you and yer mama need any help out there at yer place, Cedar?" Lucas rather unexpectedly asked.

Mrs. Gunderson arched one eyebrow and went about pretending to be busy writing something on a piece of paper.

"Um . . . um . . . not just now. We're . . . we're doing fine," Cedar stammered. "For the time being," she added as an odd sort of guilt washed over her. Why didn't she just tell him Tom Evans had already offered to help and that her mother had accepted his offer?

"Well, you be sure and let me know if there's anythin' I can do," Lucas said, smiling at Cedar.

"Thank you, Lucas. You're very kind," Cedar said.

The way he stood gazing at her—the bright light glowing in his eyes—gave Cedar great discomfort. She felt sorry for him, knowing she could never return his interest in her. She began to slightly tremble, unnerved by the way her mind had to struggle to remember she had loved Logan Davies—and the way her hands began to shake as her heart leapt at the thought of Tom Evans.

Cedar gasped and startled as Amelia Perkins stormed into the general store like a thundercloud ready to burst.

"What on earth is wrong with that man?" Amelia exclaimed. She stood with her hands on her hips, shaking her head, her bosom rising and falling with the labored breath of anger and frustration. "Supper and two pies, Mrs. Gunderson! Two! I worked all yesterday on them fixin's, and all he can do is hurry me out the door with a, 'Thank ya, Amelia,' and not even a smile!"

Cedar frowned, perplexed by the outburst.

Amelia Perkins owned the look of a woman scorned. Her ebony hair was pulled back but windblown, and her bright green eyes smoldered with the same fierceness of a summer tornado.

Mrs. Gunderson sighed. Cedar fancied the old woman's smile indicated she held some secret delight.

"Tom Evans is set in his ways, Amelia," Lucas said. "I told ya, yer plumb wastin' yer time a-tryin' to reel him in like yer doin'."

Instantly Cedar's cheeks began to burn with jealousy. She studied Amelia Perkins. She'd never liked Amelia—even as a child. She always felt Amelia was a bit too full of self-importance and pride. And now—now she'd taken supper to Tom Evans? In that moment, Cedar consciously, yet silently, determined to think of Amelia as the enemy. It was obvious by Amelia's perturbed appearance, as well as by her verbal explanation, that she hadn't received the attention from Tom Evans she had hoped to receive. Cedar was more than merely glad at hearing it—she was elated! She quietly scolded herself for owning such joy in Amelia's disappointment, however.

Amelia straightened her posture. She smoothed her ebony hair, inhaling a calming breath. Her moment of vexation was passing, to be replaced by an obvious return of determination. Amelia's lips tightly pinched together, and Cedar knew her resolve was complete.

"He'll come around," Amelia announced, nodding with emphatic assurance. "He'll get lonely without his brother and their kin out there with him . . . and he'll come around."

Amelia paused—nodded to Lucas and then Mrs. Gunderson. "You all have a good day, now . . . you hear?" she chirped. Then she looked to Cedar—studied her from head to toe a moment before adding, "And give your mother my kindest regards, Cedar Dale."

Spinning on her heels and flouncing as she exited the general store, Amelia Perkins was gone—nearly as quickly as she'd arrived.

Cedar was surprised when Mrs. Gunderson and Lucas simultaneously burst into laughter.

"Ya think she'll ever give up, Mrs. Gunderson?" Lucas asked between chuckles.

Mrs. Gunderson shook her head, wiping the tears of mirth from her eyes. "Not as long as there's a breath left in him and no weddin' ring on his finger," she answered.

"Amelia Perkins has been sweet on Tom Evans for years," Lucas explained to Cedar. "She's tried everythin' short of tyin' him up and beatin' him into marryin' her . . . but he just don't seem to wanna come around."

Cedar forced a smile—though in truth, she felt like crying. It infuriated her that Amelia was so determined where Tom Evans was concerned. She had no right to be vexed—no reason to own such sudden and thorough animosity toward Amelia—but she was—and she did.

"You know, children," Mrs. Gunderson began, "a body can learn just about anything they wanna know concernin' the goin's-on in this town . . . just by lingerin' a minute or two at our little general store."

"Amen to that," Lucas chuckled.

"Why do you suppose that is?" Cedar wondered aloud. She turned to Mrs. Gunderson and continued, "I mean . . . what you just said is so entirely true. Anything I've learned about anybody or any of the goings-on here . . . I've learned either from you or while I was in the general store. Why is that?"

Mrs. Gunderson smiled, her eyes twinkling with amusement. "Every town has a place where folks feel comfortable, cared for . . . where they feel at home," she answered. She shrugged. "Church is friendly enough . . . but it seems to me that folks feel they need to keep church as where they put on their Sabbath faces, all serious, like they ain't done nothin' wrong . . . even though the Lord knows they have and probably just wishes they'd be a little more sincere. Now, though the Lord don't hold to gossip, I know he does hold to folks carin' about one another, helpin' out when they can. And my Theodore's general store seems to be the place folks feel they can come to for just that . . . for someone to care about 'em."

Cedar felt her own smile broaden. She looked closely, just to make sure Mrs. Gunderson wasn't actually wearing a halo.

"There's always someone passin' through the store that can help another person," she continued. "Oh, I know there's plenty of gossip and chitchat that goes on here too," she added with a gesture of waving away something insignificant. "But I like to think the good that bumps into everyone meetin' up in here outweighs anything bad that might breeze through. What do you think, honey?"

She winked at Cedar, and Cedar knew Mrs. Gunderson was implying that the delight of bumping into Tom Evans earlier in the week far outshone any irritation Amelia's grumbling might have caused.

"I think you're right," Cedar giggled.

"I know you are!" Lucas exclaimed.

Cedar blushed as she glanced to Lucas to see a rather dreamy-eyed expression lingering on his face.

Once again her discomfort made itself known, and she said, "I guess I better be getting back to the house. Mama's going to need that flour." She accepted the small sack of flour Mrs. Gunderson produced from behind the counter.

"Five pounds won't last you too long, honey," Mrs. Gunderson said. "So you tell your mama I'll see to it that a nice big sack of flour gets out your way soon enough. After all . . . I seen that the sugar got there, now didn't I?"

"Yes, ma'am," Cedar giggled. "And I meant to thank you for that."

"Oh, you're welcome, sweet thing," Mrs. Gunderson said. "You certainly are welcome."

Cedar giggled with understanding and turned to Lucas.

"It was so nice to see you again, Lucas," she said. The sudden remembered realization that she would see Tom Evans again the next day added to the rather unfamiliar lighthearted mood—and she realized her compliment to Lucas had actually been sincere.

"You too, Miss Cedar," Lucas said, removing his hat and nodding to her.

"And thank you ever so much, Mrs. Gunderson," she said. She paused a moment and then added, "For everything."

"Oh, honey . . . you come in as often as you can," Mrs. Gunderson told her. "I do so enjoy your visits. Now, you and yer mama . . . you two have a nice supper tomorrow evenin', ya hear?"

"We will," Cedar was certain her mother's cooking could outdo anything Amelia Perkins could concoct in attempting to please Tom Evans.

"Let me know if you all need anythin', Miss Cedar," Lucas called after her. "Anythin' at all."

Cedar nodded, delighted in the knowledge Tom

Evans would be near her soon—delighted in the knowledge that he'd vexed Amelia Perkins so thoroughly.

As she left town and headed back toward the house, Cedar was surprised to find she was humming to herself—surprised to find that a smile had been lingering on her face. Even when she returned to the house to find a note from her mother waiting on the kitchen table, explaining she'd gone down to the creek for a "sniff of spring," her humming didn't cease. The house smelled welcoming, like warm bread and sweet cake. For the first time in almost two years, Cedar had something wonderful to anticipate. Tom Evans would be there the following day, and not just for a short visit—but more likely for most of the day and then supper.

She wondered what he was doing at that moment. She knew he wasn't with Amelia Perkins, and the memory of Amelia's frustration made Cedar giggle aloud—though she did scold herself a moment later for such impish thoughts.

Reno followed the coyote tracks leading away from the Evans place. When he and Tom had arrived back at Tom's ranch to find Tom's hired hands putting down a new calf, they'd known something was wrong. Getting that damn bull of Evans's back behind an Evans fence had been hard enough. Reno knew his bones would be aching for a week from wrestling Outlaw by the ring in his nose for such a long distance. They were lucky they'd got the better of him. Reno figured Tom was right: if that old bull had been any younger, he would've about sent them both to pushing up the daisies.

Still, he hoped Tom was able to whipstitch the gash Outlaw's horn had left in his ribs quick enough. They couldn't let the coyote get too far or have the opportunity to attack any other animals. Knowing horses as he did, he knew Tom Evans was relieved the rabid coyote still had enough sense in him to go after Tom's new calves and not the new stallion he had in the corral near the barn. Still, to lose two calves—it was a shame.

"Come on, boy," he urged his horse as he saw the coyote tracks veer off toward the creek. Yep, the sick coyote was sticking close to the creek bed—stopping far too often to drink.

Reno wondered how many other animals may have been infected. One of Tom's cowboys said he heard baby coyotes yipping out near an old barn on the Evans place. Tom meant to find them and put them out of their misery after he'd quit bleeding and sewn his flesh shut. Reno had decided to take out after the sick animal right away. Sure, he was near to worn out from wrestling with that old bull, but if the rabies spread, it would mean disaster for everybody's stock. It was dangerous for folks too, of course. It had to be hunted, killed, and its infected carcass burned as soon as possible.

"Ah! There you are," Reno whispered to himself, reining in his horse and watching the animal for a moment. Yep, there was saliva foam at its mouth, and it was pacing back and forth, seeming disoriented.

"Now you stay right there, old girl," Reno whispered as he drew his rifle from its saddle sheath and took aim. "Right there. That's it . . ."

Before he could fire, however, the coyote bolted, sprinting ahead through the trees lining the creek bank.

"Dammit!" Reno growled, spurring his horse. "Take it easy, boy," he told his horse. "We don't want to . . ."

Reno's heart nearly leapt into his throat then as he saw a woman walking along the creek bank some ways in front of the rabid coyote—a ways in front but directly in the sick animal's path. Reno Garrett was good with a rifle, but was he good enough to take the coyote down with one shot before it reached the woman? And what if he missed? What if the bullet missed the coyote but hit the woman? He was so astonished at his pause of thought and sudden doubt in his own rifle skills that he decided not to risk it.

"Come on, Ace! Ride!" he shouted, spurring his horse to a gallop.

· · ·

Flora paused, thinking for a moment that she'd heard something other than the quiet, soothing babble of the creek. She loved to escape to the creek, even if the water was still too cold to wade in. Her conversation with Cedar before she'd left for town, and the lingering sensation that she'd heard Jim's voice, had found her in need of a walk. Thus, she'd ambled down to the creek to toss in a few rocks, listen to the calming burble of the water, and let her mind breathe. She worried now that she'd lingered too long—that Cedar might have returned from town already and need her there.

Flora stopped—stood still—listened. She did hear it then—the drumming of horse hooves. She shrieked and covered her ears as she heard the report of a rifle—a sound that always caused fear and pain to return to her heart.

Turning, she first saw the man approaching on horseback at a dead gallop. He was headed straight for her, raised his rifle, and fired into the air.

"Run, woman! Run!" he shouted.

Flora was momentarily astonished into immobility—frozen with fear as she watched the rider and horse bearing down on her.

"Run!" the man shouted again. And then she saw it—ahead of the rider—a coyote racing directly for her.

Some instinct she didn't know she had told her the coyote was the true danger—though she'd never known one coyote to pose a danger to an adult human before.

Hitching up her skirt, Flora ran—to where she didn't know. She simply ran. She heard the rifle again and understood the first two shots fired by the rider were meant either to get her attention or to distract the coyote. This one, however, she heard whir past behind her. The man was shooting at the animal now.

She glanced back to see the coyote was undaunted, however.

"Rabid!" she breathed as full understanding overtook her. Again the man on horseback fired, the shot hitting the ground near the coyote. The animal stopped—turned—snarled and growled as the rider neared.

Caught in a living nightmare, Flora heard the man shout, "Lady!"

As the rider popped back over his saddle to sit on his horse's haunches, he extended one arm, and Flora understood. Screaming as the coyote advanced toward her once more, she reached out as the man neared, gasping as his arm caught her at her waist, pulling her up to flop stomach-down over the saddle. The brutal gesture knocked the air from her lungs, but the cowboy simply spurred the horse a ways on before reining it to a jolting halt.

The horse turned back toward the way they'd come, and the rider said, "Whoa, Ace. Hold steady."

The coyote was close—growling and barking—its jowls dripping with foamed saliva.

Flora didn't have to hold her breath as the man leveled his rifle. She had no breath in her.

The coyote bolted toward them, and the man fired, dropping the beast not fifteen feet from where the horse stood.

Instantly the man dismounted and none too gently pulled Flora from the saddle. She found she could hardly stand and was still gasping to catch a good breath.

"You all right, ma'am?" the man asked.

Flora couldn't speak. She still hadn't caught her breath. For the sake of the fear gripping her and the astonishment of the appearance of the man standing before her, she wondered if she'd ever be able to speak again.

"My apologies, ma'am," the man began, "but the coyote was rabid . . . and I didn't see no other way of keepin' it off ya."

Flora nodded—swayed to one side as blessed air finally filled her lungs. The man's hands were instantly at her shoulders to steady her. An over-whelming sense of safety washed over Flora then, and she gazed up and up into the deep blue eyes of the man before her. He was tall—unusually tall—and handsome—unusually handsome—

with the most piercing blue eyes, shaded by thick, dark lashes. At the corners of his mesmerizing eyes he owned the creased evidence of many years spent squinting into the sun (or perhaps smiling), and Flora felt herself smile, delighted by it. He grinned in return—seemed relieved, as if her smile was proof she had not been harmed. His smile, in itself, was captivating, as was the way he removed his hat, raking a strong, bronzed, and callused hand through black hair that was peppered with the silver salt of experience.

"I think you just burnt ten years off my life, ma'am," he chuckled, obviously relieved.

"Oh, I hope not," Flora heard herself say.

He chuckled again and offered a hand to her.

"Reno Garrett, ma'am," he introduced himself.

Flora was slightly embarrassed when she heard herself giggle the way Cedar had as a child. Accepting his handshake, she said, "Flora Dale. And I thank you for saving my life, Mr. Garrett. If the coyote hadn't mauled me to death . . . well, enduring death from that horrible disease would've been . . ."

"I'm sorry if I frightened ya, Mrs. Dale," he said, still holding her hand in his. "But I didn't know what else to do. I didn't want to risk shootin' at the ol' prairie wolf, missin', and hittin' you."

Flora's hand began to tingle where he held it—first her fingers, then her palm, until her whole hand was as warm as a new calf's belly. As the sensation began to travel up her arm to her shoulder, she was disappointed when he released their shared handshake.

"Still, I'm sure I roughed ya up a bit too much there," he added.

"Oh, it's fine, Mr. Garrett," she said, giggling again—much to her own astonishment. "After all, it's been quite some time since a handsome cowboy whisked me away on the back of his horse."

She watched as his smile broadened—inwardly scolded herself for such scandalous flirting. What was wrong with her? She sounded like some saloon hussy!

"Well, now I find that a might hard to believe, ma'am," he flirted in return. "Seems to me a purty little thing like you would have all the cowboys in the county out pretendin' to chase rabid coyotes . . . just in case you needed rescuin'."

Though she would've thought it impossible, Flora's smile widened. She felt her cheeks pink up in a manner they hadn't in years. Since Jim's death, she hadn't been affected by another man— not the way Reno Garrett was affecting her now anyway. It truth, her heart was beating so wildly she had a notion time had been reversed and that she was a girl of fifteen again—instead of a widowed mother of a grown-up daughter.

"Mama!" she heard Cedar cry out. "Mama!"

Instantly, Flora's lightheartedness at nearly

being devoured by a rabid coyote only to be rescued by a handsome cowboy was squelched. When she turned to see her daughter racing toward her—an expression of pure terror on her face—she knew the gunshots had caused Cedar's worst nightmares to begin again.

"Mama!" Cedar said, brushing tears from her cheeks as she slowed her pace to a walk and approached. Flora watched as Cedar studied Reno Garrett for a moment. "I heard the gunfire, and I-I thought . . ."

"It was just a rabid coyote, ma'am," Reno said. "Nothin' too much to worry over."

"Exactly," Flora added. "Mr. Garrett shot the animal long before it could've posed any danger to me."

"Oh, thank heaven," Cedar breathed, placing a hand to her bosom over her heart. "I was so afraid that . . ."

"Oh, there's nothing to be afraid of," Flora lied. She smiled at Reno Garrett and added, "Especially with such kind neighbors to look out for us."

Reno nodded and said, "That's right."

He studied Flora Dale's daughter for a long moment. She was very beautiful—the image of her mother. He felt an odd twitching pain in his heart for a moment. One of his cowhands, Hadley Jacobson, had told him about the Widow Dale and her daughter—told him the story of their loss, of their terrible tragedy. It was how he'd instantly understood the necessity of keeping the entire tale of her mother's danger from the coyote to himself. He could see on the girl's face the absolute terror lingering in her, mingled with the fear concerning her mother's safety. He wanted to reach out and gather the pretty girl in his arms—but for different reasons than he wanted to reach out and gather her mother into his arms. Still, he wished he could reassure them both somehow.

"You bought part of the Evans ranch. Isn't that right?" Cedar asked, extending a hand in greeting to the tall, handsome man.

"Yes, ma'am," Reno Garrett said, accepting her hand and firmly shaking it.

"Well, thank you for shooting that coyote, Mr. Garrett. I can't imagine what might have happened if you hadn't come along," Cedar said. She suspected the man had saved her mother's life and was just trying to protect her from worry. She liked him for the fact.

"Yes. Thank you so very much, Mr. Garrett," Flora said, offering her hand to the man again. Even for the residual fear causing her to tremble, Cedar did not miss the color that rose to her mother's cheeks when the man shook her hand. "If there's anything we can offer as our thanks . . ."

"No, ma'am," Reno Garrett said. "Your well-bein' is more'n plenty."

Cedar smiled and felt her eyebrows arch as she heard her mother giggle.

"Well, I'll just drag this poor varmint back to the Evans place to burn it. Tom will need to burn the pups if he finds the den anyhow . . . so we might as well not smoke up your sweet air." Reno said, returning his hat to his head.

Taking an old piece of a blanket from his saddlebag, Reno Garrett wrapped the coyote's carcass up in it, flung it over his horse behind the saddle, and mounted. "You ladies have a nice day."

"Thank you," Cedar responded when her mother only continued to stare rather adoringly up at Reno Garrett.

"Anything you ladies need . . . you just give me a holler," Reno said. "Bye now."

He touched the brim of his hat, offered one more broad, dazzling smile to her mother, and rode away. Cedar watched him go—watched her mother watch him go.

"He's handsome, isn't he?" she said.

"Oh my, yes," Flora said, exhaling a heavy sigh.

Cedar's thoughts immediately went to her father. Her mother had loved her father. She knew how deeply she'd loved him—as deeply as a woman could love a man. Yet as she studied the bright pink in her mother's cheeks—the twinkling sparkle in her eyes—Cedar understood that Reno Garrett had touched a place in her mother's heart in exactly the same way Tom Evans had touched a place in her own.

It was the look of fascination—of anticipation and breathlessness in her mother's
countenance—that caused Cedar's heart to soar,
to swell to an even greater delight in eagerness
of Tom Evans's arrival the next morning.

Reno Garrett frowned. The rabid prairie wolf had
nearly got the pretty Dale widow! Fact was, his
heart was still hammering from the fear of it—
either that or from the sight of the pretty Dale
widow herself. Maybe it hammered for both
reasons. Either way, it was still hammering.

His frown deepened, furrowing his handsome
brow even further. He'd been awful rough with
her. He knew dang well he'd knocked the breath
out of her nice little figure when he'd hefted her
up onto Ace's back. Still, what else could he
have done? The coyote was right at her heels! It
might have buried its teeth in her otherwise. The
thought caused an uncomfortable shiver to travel
up his spine. Rabies was a terrible way for anything to die—especially humans. He couldn't
even think of that pretty little widow dying of
anything, especially rabies contracted from a sick
coyote.

He thought how much Flora Dale looked like
her daughter—hair the color of chestnuts, eyes as
blue as the bluest lake he'd ever seen up north
when he was cowboying way back. Yep, a man
could go swimming in eyes the likes of Flora

Dale's. But what was the girl's name? He'd been so distracted by her mother and the goings-on with the coyote that he'd clean forgotten to pay attention to whether the girl even introduced herself to him. He figured she hadn't—because he couldn't think that she had. After all, in all the excitement, introductions didn't seem too important.

"Go on, Ace," he said, spurring Ace into a gallop. Too much dawdling never did anybody any good. He needed to get back to the Evans place and burn the dead coyotes and calves.

He shivered once more at the thought of what could've happened to the pretty Dale widow. He wondered how far the rabies had spread—figured he'd lose the rest of the day to warning the neighbors and folks in town.

A moment later, he smiled however. She knew how to flatter a man—that was for sure. Reno thought about his apologizing to her for being so rough—chuckled when he remembered her response. *After all, it's been quite some time since a handsome cowboy whisked me away on the back of his horse,* she'd said.

"Oh, I hope you keep an eye wide in my direction, Flora Dale," Reno muttered to himself. " 'Cause I might just whisk you away some other day . . . to somethin' a might more to yer likin' than rabid coyotes."

Chapter Six

"How many were there?" Cedar asked as she tossed another rock into the pile to one side of the house. "I mean, counting the one Mr. Garrett killed?"

Tom Evans paused, leaning on the tip of the shovel handle.

"Let's see . . . on my place, we burned seven pups, the one Reno shot, the male we found nearby, and the two calves that got bit and chewed on. We found a skunk wanderin' around in circles in the middle of the day over at Reno's place and shot that ol' boy . . . and Eldon Pickering says he shot three coyotes this mornin'."

Cedar frowned. "That's too many rabid animals for me to be able to sleep well tonight," she said.

"Oh, don't you worry, Miss Cedar," Tom said as he drove the shovel into the freshly weeded soil. "We most likely got 'em all. And if we didn't, everyone's keepin' watch . . . and we will get 'em. I been through rabies outbreaks before. We'll get a handle on it soon enough."

Still, Cedar was unsettled. A rabid coyote had nearly attacked her mother! If it hadn't been for Reno Garrett happening by—but Cedar had determined not to linger on what might have happened. Reno Garrett *had* happened by, and her mother was fine.

"You know, I didn't offer to till up yer mama's garden so as you would have to work harder than me," Tom said.

"I'm not working harder than you," Cedar said, smiling up at him. She shook her head as she glanced down to see another rock in the soil. "I just can't figure out how all these rocks got here." She laughed. "I mean, Daddy paid me three shiny pennies to pick them all out when I was seven years old."

She heard Tom chuckle, and the sound warmed her. She looked up to him once more. She was still astonished that he was there—that she was there with him. When her mother had opened the door that morning to reveal Tom Evans standing on their front porch, Cedar had thought for a moment that her heart might beat itself to death with pounding so hard. And now—now he was right there next to her, working the soil while she pulled weeds and removed rocks.

He was so handsome! So unfairly handsome! Cedar quickly studied him for a moment. She adored the dazzling smile he blessed her with every time he glanced down at her—the way the deep brown of his eyes seemed as dark and inviting as sweet molasses. She loved his hands—their callused palms—the way the veins on the backs of them rather bulged out the same way the veins on his powerful forearms did each time he lifted the shovel. She was glad he'd rolled up his shirtsleeves, for she liked watching the muscles in his forearms move as he worked.

Everything about Tom Evans was attractive—drew Cedar to him like ants to honey. She studied his boots a moment, worn with hard work and rugged living—studied his blue jeans, letting her gaze linger on the worn tear at the back of one thigh as he turned to pick up a large stone he'd felt with his boot while tilling. She liked the way his shirt hung loose and untucked—the way he paused to remove his hat and rake a strong hand through his nut-brown hair. Yep, everything about Tom Evans was attractive—absolutely everything.

"What's that?" Cedar asked as her gaze fell to a place on Tom's shirt at his side. Just where his ribs would be beneath his shirt, something was beginning to stain the fabric.

Instantly, Cedar gasped as realization struck her.

"You're bleeding!" she exclaimed.

"What?" Tom asked, pausing in shoveling.

"Right there at your side," Cedar said, pointing to the place—the place where a bright red stain was spreading.

"Oh, that," Tom said. He shoved the spoon of the shovel into the dirt and pressed one hand to the place at his side. "That's just a scratch from yesterday."

"Yesterday? The same yesterday when you were chasing down rabid coyotes?" Cedar gasped.

When Tom removed his hand, the bloodstain on his shirt was larger.

"Well, yeah . . . but I didn't get bit or nothin'," he said, pressing his hand to the place again. "Me and Reno had to haul ol' Outlaw back to my ranch and—"

"An outlaw?" Cedar exclaimed. She'd heard the stories of the outlaw that had come gunning for Tom's brother, Slater. Mrs. Gunderson had told her the whole story when she and her mother had first moved back. But she could've sworn Mrs. Gunderson said the outlaw had been killed. "I thought your brother killed that outlaw," she breathed.

"Oh, he did," Tom chuckled. "I meant my bull, ol' Outlaw. That's his name. He broke through the fence again and was . . . consortin' with some of Reno's cows. We had a hell of a time . . . a hard time gettin' him back to my place. He got a horn to me, but it's just a scratch. I thought I sewed it up better than this though."

This time when Tom removed his hand from the place, however, the fabric of his shirt was saturated.

"You thought you sewed it up better?" Cedar asked. She was trembling—fearful over his well-being. "Didn't you go into town and have Doctor Prichard have a look at it?"

127

"Well, of course not," Tom said. "I just did what I usually do . . . took me a needle and thread and . . ."

As Cedar's concern increased, she reached up, taking hold of the shovel handle and pulling herself to her feet. However, as her attention was held by the blood soaking Tom's shirt, she released the shovel handle once she was standing—not realizing that she'd been pulling so hard on it. Thus, when she released the shovel—its spoon being so firmly sunk into the soil—the handle sprang forward, knocking Tom Evans solidly across one cheek.

"Whoa!" Tom exclaimed as his hand went from pressing the bloody shirt at his ribs to pressing the red welt now evident along his left cheek.

"Oh! I'm so sorry!" Cedar exclaimed. Tears were already welling in her eyes. She was so clumsy! She'd always been clumsy, but she'd hurt someone else this time. Usually her clumsiness only had ramifications for her own well-being, or lack thereof. But this time—this time she'd hurt someone else. And not just anyone else—she'd hurt Tom Evans.

"Oh my!" she breathed as he removed his hand from his face, studying it for a moment. "I'm so sorry, Mr. Evans!"

Tom frowned a moment as he studied at his hand. Then he smiled—even chuckled.

"For a minute there, I thought my face was

bleeding too," he told her, his smile never lessening. "But it's just the blood from my shirt."

"Mama!" Cedar called then. "Mama, Mr. Evans is bleeding!"

"Oh, it ain't nothin' to worry about, Miss Cedar," Tom said. Cedar watched then as Tom Evans put a hand to the back of his shirt, took hold of the fabric there in one fist, and stripped it from his body in one smooth motion.

Cedar watched, mouth agape, as he then wadded up the article of clothing, pressing it to the wound at his side. The sight of Tom Evans standing before her bare from the waist up was entirely astonishing! His shoulders and chest were broad—broader even than they looked when his shirt was on him. He was bronzed too, revealing that he more often than not worked outside in such a condition as he now stood. The muscles in his shoulders, arms, and torso were perfectly formed, giving him the appearance of having been chiseled out of some sort of copper-colored stone.

Tom noted the way the pink had completely drained from Cedar Dale's pretty face. Apparently she didn't handle the sight of blood well—though he could've sworn she'd always been pretty banged-up as a child. The way he remembered it, both her knees and sometimes both elbows were constantly in the process of healing from bumps, scrapes, and bruises. The sight of blood hadn't seemed to bother her then.

He wondered if perhaps it had something to do with the deaths of her father and lover. She had witnessed it, after all—no doubt seen both men bleeding out on the street.

"It'll simmer back down in a minute or two," he said, offering a reassuring smile. His wadded-up shirt should soak up the blood well enough now. Maybe she'd recover her color a little bit.

Flora Dale exited the house by way of the back door then.

Tom frowned, puzzled as she looked at him, gasped, and covered her mouth with both hands, exclaiming, "Oh my!" Apparently both women had been so traumatized over the violence that had taken their loved ones that the sight of blood unsettled them.

"Oh, it ain't but a scratch, Mrs. Dale," Tom assured her. "It'll quit oozin' out here in a jiffy."

"What happened to your face, Tom?" Flora asked as she hurried toward him.

He glanced to Cedar. She was still staring at him in awed astonishment.

"Oh, uh . . . I just . . ." he stammered.

"I hit him in the face with the shovel handle, Mama," Cedar confessed. He could've sworn there were tears welling in her eyes.

"You hit him with the shovel handle?" Flora exclaimed. "What on earth for?"

130

He watched as Flora Dale studied him from head to toe a moment—as she suspiciously quirked one eyebrow.

Tom figured what she was thinking at once. There he stood—shirtless—while her daughter looked terrified and had obviously hit him with the shovel handle. She was thinking he'd been inappropriate toward Cedar.

Quickly, he began explaining, "Oh, it weren't intentional, Mrs. Dale. It was an accident. You see . . . she saw my scratch here bleedin' through my shirt and was just—"

"He's bleeding something terrible, Mama," Cedar interrupted. "Look there."

Tom frowned as Cedar stumbled back a few steps as she pointed to the place at his ribs where he still pressed his shirt to his wound. Was she really that disturbed by even the thought of the sight of blood?

"What have you done here, Tom Evans?" Flora asked then. She tugged at Tom's hand until he pulled the wadded-up shirt away from the wound. Flora gasped. "Tom Evans! Don't you know better than to keep a wound uncovered like this?" she scolded.

"Well, they heal faster if ya let 'em breathe," he told her. He smiled, realizing he felt as if his own mother were scolding him.

"What on earth?" Flora exclaimed as she studied the wound more closely. "Four stitches,

Tom?" she asked him. "In a wound that size, you only put four stitches?"

Tom raised his arm and looked at the wound at his side oozing blood.

"Well, yes, ma'am," he answered. "It seemed plenty enough at the time."

Flora sighed, clicked her tongue, and shook her head in gestures of disapproval. "Cedar," she began, "get the bandaging out please, and pour that water in the tea kettle into a bowl. Let's clean this boy up a bit."

"Yes, ma'am," Cedar said.

Tom watched as Cedar fairly fled into the house. He wondered how she was ever going to handle the sight of blood in a washbasin—for he had no doubt Mrs. Dale meant to mother-hen him and take care of the wound properly.

As Cedar hurried into the house, Tom leaned forward and whispered to Flora, "She ain't too good with blood, huh?"

Flora smiled—giggled a little. Reaching up, she pinched Tom's cheek as if he were a little boy instead of a grown man approaching thirty.

"Oh, blood doesn't bother Cedar much," she whispered. "It's a half-naked man she isn't too comfortable with . . . especially one the likes of you, Tom Evans," she added with a wink.

Tom understood then—smiled and nodded.

Flora laughed. "Oh, how I remember the fits you two boys used to give your poor mother over running around only half-dressed most of the time."

Tom nodded once more. "Yep," he said. "Mama never could keep us dressed proper." He glanced toward the house, lowered his voice, and said, "Sorry if I rattled Miss Cedar there, Mrs. Dale."

Flora Dale smiled, however. "Oh, you go on and rattle her all you want, Tom. It reminds her she's alive." Tom nodded, amused at the woman's insight and honesty. "Now," she said, taking hold of his arm, "let's get you cleaned up. It's almost time for supper."

Tom smiled as he followed Flora into the house. So Cedar Dale's sudden pallid complexion was due to the fact she'd become bashful when he'd stripped his shirt off, was it? Tom liked the notion—liked the little brown-haired, blue-eyed gal more for it. Furthermore, Tom Evans wasn't one to forget such a thing. He figured the knowledge might come in handy one day—one way or the other.

Cedar gulped as Tom Evans stepped into the house behind her mother. He smiled at her, and she knew she blushed—scolded herself for being such a ninny. Why was she so affected by his appearance? He was already unlawfully handsome and attractive. Didn't it make sense that the rest of him would be as unsettling as his visible persona?

She was grateful her mother had sent her into the house to prepare the bandages and water. It had given her a moment to regain control of her senses. Oh, certainly the sight of Tom Evans so bronzed and perfectly formed was as unsettling and as wildly thrilling as it had been only moments before, but Cedar had owned a moment to recover her decorum—and she was thankful.

"Come here, Tom . . . and we'll dress that wound right," Flora said, leading Tom Evans into the kitchen. Shaking her head, she said, "You Evans boys must've kept your mother in fits over laundry." Taking the wadded-up shirt from him, she handed it to Cedar. "Cedar, toss that bloody thing in the sink. We can wash it out later."

"It sure smells invitin' in here, Mrs. Dale," Tom said, drawing a deep breath.

"Well, you let us dress this *scratch* of yours, and then we'll sit down to supper," Flora said.

"Yes, ma'am," Tom mumbled.

He looked to Cedar, winked, and said, "Sorry for concernin' ya over the blood, Miss Cedar."

"I wasn't concerned over the blood, Mr. Evans . . . just you," Cedar heard herself respond. She couldn't believe she'd confessed to being concerned for him! She felt the heat increase in her cheeks and wished she didn't feel so entirely flustered.

He smiled and said, "Well, thank you."

Ever since her trip to the general store the day

before and Mrs. Gunderson's encouragements—ever since having seen the excitement Reno Garrett had unearthed in her mother during the coyote incident—Cedar had begun to simmer on the idea that perhaps wonderful things could happen—that perhaps Tom Evans taking notice of her wasn't so entirely unfathomable.

Still, as she studied the red welt on his face, she said, "And I'm so sorry about . . . about the shovel handle."

Tom chuckled as Flora dipped a cloth in the bowl of water Cedar had placed on the table. "Oh, it's all right. A man needs a shovel handle to the face now and then . . . for one reason or the other."

"Dry this off while I take the chicken out of the oven . . . will you, sweetheart?" Flora said to Cedar, handing her a small towel. "Bind it up good with the bandages. You'll need a few of the longest ones. Then hop on into my wardrobe and dig out one of your daddy's old shirts for Mr. Evans to wear for supper. All right?"

"Yes, ma'am," Cedar said.

With slightly trembling hands, Cedar accepted the towel from her mother and went about dabbing at the tender flesh around Tom Evans's wound.

"I suppose you're lucky you weren't skewered by that bull, Mr. Evans," Cedar mumbled as she studied the rather brutal-looking wound. She estimated the laceration was at least four inches in length—and deeper than she liked to think on.

"I guess so," Tom Evans said.

As Cedar continued to gently dab at the battered flesh in preparation of bandaging it, she was nearly overcome with some provocative sort of stupor caused by the heat she could feel radiating from his body. The scent of his skin was nearly intoxicating—the scent of sun, heat, and perspiration that smelled like some sweet, moist sort of grass instead of being unpleasant in any way.

Once she'd dried the wound as best she could, she began bandaging it.

"Hold this please," she told him, placing one end of a long length of cotton at the ribs of his other side.

Tom Evans did as she asked, holding the end of the bandage firm as Cedar worked to wrap the strip of cloth around his torso in covering the wound.

"Make it tight enough to keep it from bleeding too much . . . but loose enough he can breathe, Cedar," Flora instructed.

"Mm-hm," Cedar managed to reply. Tom Evans's nearness, however, was beginning to have a rather dizzying effect. She kept wishing he would lower his arms at just the right moment and capture her in an accidental embrace. She wanted to press her cheek to his chest—feel the warmth of his skin against hers.

Risking a glance at him, she found that he was unwaveringly watching her—an almost knowing grin on his attractive face.

She blushed once more and pulled another long bandage from the basket filled with strips of cloth.

"Sweetie," her mother began as she removed the large roasting pan from oven, "try that red shirt of your father's for Tom. I think it'll be the closest to fitting well."

"Yes, ma'am," Cedar said as she wound another bandage around Tom Evans's broad torso.

"I best wash up first, Mrs. Dale," Tom said.

Cedar looked up to see him still staring at her—still smiling. She felt her own smile broaden a moment—until her attention was drawn to the long welt running vertically over his left cheek.

"I'm so sorry about the shovel, Mr. Evans," she said.

"Tom," he said, his gaze never leaving her eyes. "You can call me Tom, Miss Cedar." He chuckled and added, "Or Tommy . . . the way you used to . . . if you'd like."

Cedar giggled and felt an odd, almost forgotten delight flitter through her limbs.

"All right," she whispered. She returned her attention to the bandaging, adding, "Then you can call *me* Cedar."

"Yes, ma'am," Tom Evans said.

Cedar breathed a sigh. "There. That should keep it from seeping too awful much again," she told him. "That and the fact that you won't be on the roof or tilling up soil anymore today."

"Thank you kindly," Tom said. "I noticed you ladies have a rain barrel out back, Mrs. Dale," he began. "Is that for washin' up cowboys before supper?"

Flora smiled. "I think it might be for just that purpose, Tom," she said.

"Then I'll hurry on out and try to make myself presentable."

"That's fine . . . and Cedar will bring a shirt and towel out for you," she assured him.

"Thank you, Mrs. Dale," Tom said with a nod.

He turned and strode from the house by way of the back door.

"Fetch him a towel while you're getting the shirt, Cedar, honey. All right?"

"Yep," Cedar said as she hurried to her mother's room.

Quickly she snatched a small towel from the linen cupboard and then went to her mother's wardrobe to find her father's red shirt. She smiled as she removed the shirt from its place, knowing her mother had quite often slept in her father's old shirts during the first year following his death. She buried her face in the cloth, wishing his scent still lingered there—but it didn't. She held the shirt up, wondering if Tom Evans's broad shoulders would indeed fit inside the width of the shirt. She surmised the color of the shirt would complement Tom Evans's eyes—then immediately scolded herself for such ridiculous and feminine musings.

"Now don't you get those bandages too wet, Tom Evans," Flora called from the kitchen.

"Yes, ma'am," he called in return, chuckling to himself afterward.

Tom smiled, thinking all mothers must be alike in many, many regards—for he could almost hear his own mother's voice echoing Flora's instructions.

"Here you go, Mr. Evans," Cedar said as she stepped out of the house, offering a towel to him.

"Tom," he corrected her, amused by the bashful blush that pinked up her pretty cheeks.

"Tom," she managed—though he could see she was uncomfortable in being so familiar.

"Thank you," he said, taking the towel. He proceeded to dry his face, arms, and shoulders. He rubbed the towel over his chest, smiling when he saw Cedar shyly glance away.

"I hope my father's shirt fits," she said. "I wouldn't want you to be uncomfortable all through supper."

Tom smiled as he felt the mischievous imp that lingered in the Evans men rise to his consciousness.

"Well, I hope it fits too," he began. "I wouldn't want *you* to be uncomfortable all through supper either."

He winked at her, and her blush deepened. "Oh, I'm not uncomfortable . . . about seeing you . . . seeing you without your shirt," she lied.

"You're not?" he teased.

"No. Of course not," she said. "I've see lots of men without their clothes on."

"You have?" he chuckled.

"Of course!" she assured him. Then, realizing exactly what she'd said, she stammered, "I-I mean . . . not without any clothes at all . . ."

"Mm-hmm," he said, taking a step toward her.

He smiled when she took a step backward, shaking her head and adding, "I just meant that . . . well . . . I remember when we lived here before and Daddy had men working for him . . . cowboys and such. They were forever running around without half their clothes on. I mean, even you . . . I remember you. You just weren't quite so . . . so . . ." He almost laughed out loud as she gestured toward his chest. She was entirely rattled—and he was enjoying it entirely too much.

"I mean . . . you were just a boy then," she continued, "and not quite so . . . I mean, I think my daddy's shirt would've fit you fine then, but now I'm not so sure it will . . . you know . . . because you're so much more . . . so much more . . ."

"I'm so much more older," he finished for her, coming to her rescue.

"Yes!" she breathed, so relieved he could almost reach out and touch her reprieve. "Exactly!" Her smile of relief was short-lived, however, and she began to wade around in a new venue of humiliation. "I mean . . . not that you're old. I certainly don't think that . . . not for a moment. You're just . . . you understand you're just . . ."

"Older than I was then," he finished for her again.

"Yes! Exactly!" she breathed, again relieved.

As Tom Evans moved closer to her, for a moment he considered reaching out and taking hold of Cedar Dale instead of taking hold of the red shirt she now offered him. There was a radiance in her eyes—a brightness he remembered from her childhood—a twinkle that had been absent the day he'd bumped into her in front of the general store. Still, he saw it now—the brilliant sparkle of delight—and it drew him to her even more strongly than he'd been drawn to her the day he'd bumped into her, the same day he'd hauled the sugar out to her and her mother. It drew him to her even more powerfully than it had that morning when he'd arrived and begun to patch the roof.

Tom accepted the shirt she held toward him, smiling as she instantly clasped her hands at her back, as if she were resisting the urge to touch him.

Again the imp in him leapt to the lead, and he asked, "Can you help me on with it, do you think?" When she paused—eyes wide as supper plates with astonishment—he added, "All that fiddling with this scratch has made it kind of sore, so if you wouldn't mind helpin' me . . . I'd sure appreciate it."

"Of course," she said, though her renewed blush told him she was wildly unsettled. "Put your left arm in first," she instructed. Once Tom had slipped his left arm into the left sleeve of the shirt (wincing with an expression of feigned discomfort for the wound at his side), Cedar assisted him in drawing his right arm through the right sleeve.

Tom was pleased when he did not have to coax her any further, for she immediately pulled the two sides of the front of the shirt together and began fastening the buttons.

"This was my daddy's favorite shirt," she told him, smiling as she fastened one button at the middle of his chest. "Red was his favorite color." She fastened another button—and another. Tom smiled as she fastened a button at his stomach and then one at his waist before realizing that perhaps it wasn't proper to continue.

"There," she said, leaving the last two buttons unfastened. "How does it fit?" She reached up, smoothing the taut fabric at one shoulder, and then seemed to think the gesture was too familiar and again clasped her hands behind her back.

"It'll do fine. Thank you," he said, swallowing the excess moisture borne of desire gathering in his mouth.

She smiled at him. Yet almost immediately her pretty smile was lost as a frown puckered her delicate brow.

"I am sorry about the shovel handle," she whispered, studying the welt on his face.

Tom wished she would reach up and touch the mark the shovel handle had made. In that moment, he wanted nothing more than to feel her touch—no matter how lightly applied or how brief. Still, he knew she was fragile—not physically perhaps. But he knew her loss and the great harm it had reaped on her. He would have to be careful—careful, but reassuring.

Therefore, as he said, "It ain't nothin'," he moved toward the door leading into the house, lightly placing his hand at the small of her back for a moment to urge her to precede him in entering. Tom didn't miss the goose bumps that erupted on Cedar's forearms, and he was encouraged. He affected her—he knew he did. He also knew Cedar Dale had no idea how wildly she affected him. This gave him a firm advantage, and he smiled.

"Like I said, a man needs a shovel handle to the face now and then . . . just to make him behave if nothin' else," he said.

Cedar smiled, and as she stepped into the house, Tom's gaze traveled from the top of her head to the heel of her boots. He resisted the urge to slap her on her cute little petticoat-padded, pink-calico-skirted fanny—chuckling to himself in the next moment for even considering on it.

"Yep," he mumbled in a whisper, "sometimes a man deserves to be downright slapped."

Chapter Seven

Flora smiled as she watched Cedar—watched Cedar trying *not* to watch Tom Evans. The fact was Tom's brawny build was nearly busting Jim's old shirt out at the seams! She almost laughed out loud as she remembered the look on Cedar's face—the pale expression of over-whelmed astonishment borne of Tom Evans standing in the garden without a stitch on but his trousers. Yep, Tom Evans was the man Flora wanted for her daughter—and for a million different reasons. Not only was he a hard-working man with a profitable business, he was handsome, charming, witty, and, she suspected, very patient and understanding. Flora knew that Tom Evans was the type of man to value a woman and be thoroughly aware of every vulnerability she owned. Tom was a protector as well as owning a nurturing nature. Flora well remem-bered how highly Jim spoke of Tom years before when he'd hired out to the Dales' one summer. She remembered her own good opinion of him too, and he hadn't changed much. Oh, he was larger—much larger—even more handsome with the look of a man instead of a boy. But his presence, his personality, and character were exactly as Flora remembered.

Suddenly, Flora was determined to see Cedar settled with Tom. In her heart she truly knew there could be nothing on earth—no one on earth—who would care for Cedar the way Tom would. She smiled when she glanced to Tom to catch him studying Cedar as she placed the basket of bread in the center of the table. He grinned, and Flora didn't miss the rather predatory expression of desire on the man's face.

Her own smile broadened. Tom Evans was interested in her daughter—greatly interested. The fact gave Flora a deep sense of hope she hadn't known in a long time. She'd worried so long and so hard over Cedar—her pain—wondering if anyone would ever pierce the shield of guilt and anguish the circumstances of the loss of Logan had forged. Yet now, as she watched Tom's gaze linger on Cedar as she sat down at the table, she finally owned hope that her daughter would know true happiness once more.

"Thank you for fixing the roof, Tom," Flora began, ladling gravy over the mound of mashed potatoes she'd heaped on Tom's plate, "and for tilling up the garden spot. I'll sleep better tonight knowing the rain won't get in and that we can start planting as soon as the frosts are past."

"I'm more'n glad to do it, Mrs. Dale," Tom said, tucking his napkin in the collar of the otherwise overly tight-fitting shirt. "And I'd do it every day if a supper like this was waiting at the end every time. I ain't lyin' when I say this is the best meal I've had since Slater carried Lark off to matrimony."

Cedar smiled, pleased that Tom would be enjoying a good meal.

"Well, I certainly hope so," Flora said, smiling. She ladled gravy over her own plate and winked at Cedar. "Still," Flora continued, "Mrs. Gunderson was telling me last week that Amelia Perkins has been seeing to your suppers now and again."

Instantly, Cedar's pleasant mood dampened. Why had her mother seen the need to bring up the subject of Amelia Perkins? Cedar looked to Tom to see him sigh with obvious exasperation, however.

"Well, yeah," he admitted. "Amelia does wander out my way once in a while with a pot of stew or a couple of pies in her pocket. I don't know how to keep her from it . . . 'cause I think her mama has somethin' to do with it."

"I'm sure she does," Flora said.

Cedar frowned, thinking an expression something like guilt flittered across her mother's face.

"Have you ever given any thought to courting Amelia, Tom?" Flora asked then.

"Mother!" Cedar exclaimed. She was aghast— not only because her mother had posed such a personal question but because she didn't want anyone planting any ideas in Tom Evans's mind where Amelia Perkins was concerned.

"What, honey?" Flora asked, shrugging in feigning innocence.

"You can't ask Mr. Evans things like that!" she scolded in a whisper, even for the fact that Tom Evans sat directly across the table from her. His chuckle told her that scolding her mother in a whisper had been in vain.

"Why not?" Flora asked, smiling. "We're just having conversation, Cedar." Flora then turned to Tom and repeated, "*Have* you ever given any thought to courting Amelia?"

Cedar felt as if her cheeks were on fire! She was horrified—humiliated—thoroughly embarrassed. Furthermore, she realized that she was sitting in dread anticipation of Tom's answer. What if he *had* given thought to courting Amelia Perkins? In that moment, Cedar was certain her heart would break if his answer proved to be that he was.

"No, ma'am," Tom answered, however. "Not for one breath of a moment."

"Whew!" Cedar felt herself sigh. She glanced up, relieved to find Tom's attention on his plate. He hadn't heard her breath of solace.

"Amelia Perkins ain't my type of woman," he added.

"What is your type of woman?" Flora asked.

"Mother!" Cedar scolded, again in a whisper.

Tom chuckled, obviously amused by Cedar's discomfort.

"Oh, I like 'em short, brown-haired, and easy to embarrass," he said, winking at Cedar.

And Cedar was embarrassed—nearly to bursting apart. Still, she couldn't keep from smiling— couldn't begin to hide her delight at his flirting.

Flora giggled. "Well, I'm glad to hear you aren't interested in Amelia, Tom," she said. "You deserve better."

"Well, thank you, Mrs. Dale," he said.

"Flora, if you please, Tom," Flora said. "You make me feel like the preacher's wife with all that Mrs. Dale nonsense."

"Yes, ma'am," he chuckled.

"Mrs. Gunderson says that Hadley Jacobson says that your new neighbor is a real fine man," Cedar began. "We met him yesterday, and he seems to be just that."

"Reno?" Tom asked. "Yep. Slater and me were lucky he come along when he did. It wasn't so hard sellin' off half the place when we knew someone deservin' was takin' it."

Cedar smiled. She felt an impish delight rising in her bosom. Glancing to her mother, she said, "He's very handsome . . . isn't he, Mama?"

Touché! she thought as a crimson blush rose to her mother's cheeks.

"Yes, he is," Flora answered without pause. "I

guess you know, Tom . . . that he honestly saved my life yesterday."

But Tom frowned, looking to Cedar for explanation. "What?"

"He didn't tell you that he met us?" Cedar asked.

"No," Tom mumbled.

Cedar shrugged. "Well, Mama was down by the creek . . . when all of a sudden she hears something."

Tom couldn't help but grin, charmed by the sudden expression of excitement on Cedar's lovely face.

"So she paused," she continued, "and listened for a moment . . . and that's when she heard a rider. She turned to see a horse and rider approaching, and the man was shouting at her to run. Then she saw the coyote . . . so she started running."

Tom chuckled as Cedar—rapt in the excitement of the story—leaned toward him, reaching across the table to place a soft hand on his forearm. Her eyes fairly sparkled with the thrill of the tale, and Tom fancied that a man could be happy in drowning in such an alluring blue.

"Then, before she quite knew what was happening, Reno Garrett rides up, whisks Mama up onto his saddle, and saves her from the certain and ghastly fate of writhing to death with rabies!" she finished.

"Did he now?" Tom asked, still too distracted by the intensity of her expression and the feel of her touch to say much else.

"Yep," she assured him. She seemed to realize then that she was touching him and quickly drew her hand away. Still smiling, however—blue eyes still dazzling him with their radiant excitement—she said, "Oh, and he shot the rabid coyote too. You know . . . one of the ones you burned yesterday."

"Hm," Tom said, still gazing into Cedar's mesmerizing eyes. "He didn't say a word about it. Just said he'd killed the coyote down by the creek."

"Do you think he forgot that he met us?" Flora asked.

Tom looked to Cedar's mother to see an expression of almost panicked pain on her face. He felt his eyebrows arch as understanding swept over him all at once. For a moment, he'd been uncomfortable, thinking Cedar had been dazzled by Reno Garrett's good looks and heroics—for even Tom could admit to Reno being a handsome man. But now—now he understood. He recognized it then—the other expression on Cedar's face, the one lingering just beneath the excitement—hope for her mother.

"I mean, you'd think a man would remember rescuing a woman from certain death," Flora mumbled. The woman's lips were slightly pursed, almost as if she were pouting, and a worried frown furrowed her lovely brow.

"Oh, I think he remembers, all right," Tom began. "Reno's a very private man . . . keeps to himself." He smiled at Flora. "He probably just don't want people thinkin' he's boastin' about his heroic good deeds." He lowered his voice, adding, "Or it could be he just don't want to draw too much attention . . . too much competition . . . if you understand my meanin', Flora."

Flora smiled, appearing somewhat reassured.

Tom smiled and winked to Cedar. Warm delight drizzled over him when she smiled and winked in return.

"Well, anyway . . . I'm very grateful that Mr. Garrett came along when he did," Flora said.

It seemed like a dream! As Cedar sat at the supper table, studying the way her father's shirt futilely attempted to fit Tom Evans's muscular form, she could not keep feelings of elation from welling up within her.

There had been something very reassuring—a sense of safety lingered in having Tom Evans near that day. As he'd worked on the roof, he'd whistled, offering a smile each time Cedar had come and gone from the house on some errand and glanced up at him. And then when he'd started working the garden space and her mother had suggested it might not be right to expect him

152

to do all the labor in preparing the garden—that perhaps Cedar should help with the weeding and clearing the stones—it was then that Cedar found herself wrapped in sensations of bliss, security, and hope the like she had never known—never.

She allowed herself to gaze at Tom Evans a moment as he conversed with her mother. Oh, how she'd adored him when she'd been a little girl! How she'd dreamt of growing up and belonging to him! A sense of trepidation began to trickle through her mind—a fear that she might just begin dreaming of belonging to him again. But she was a grown woman now, and such dreams were for little girls. Weren't they?

Cedar's attention snapped back to the discussion in flow between her mother and Tom.

"Well, the way Elvira tells it . . . you're going to have a pretty tough time squirming out of this one," Flora was saying.

Tom nodded. "I suppose so," he sighed.

"I'm sorry," Cedar ventured. "But squirming out of what?"

Flora rolled her eyes with exaggerated exasperation. "Out of Amelia Perkins's plans to rope Tom, Cedar. For goodness sake! Where does your mind wander to sometimes?"

"Oh," Cedar mumbled. Somehow, while Cedar had been daydreaming, the conversation had doubled back to Amelia. The fact of it irritated her.

"Well, I guess all I can do is hope that some

purty little thing will come along and snatch me up 'fore Amelia sneaks in one night and hogties me."

"Oh, I'm sure some pretty little thing will," Flora laughed. "In fact, I know just the—"

"Mama," Cedar interrupted, fairly leaping from her seat, "you've left the pie in too long." She knew exactly what her mother was implying, and she hoped it wasn't as obvious to Tom Evans as it had been to her. What on earth had gotten into her mother? Although her heart hammered madly at the thought of snatching Tom away long before Amelia Perkins could lay a finger on him, she had to be sensible—realistic.

Hurrying to the oven, Cedar pulled the door open, fanning the heat that puffed into her face as she looked for something to use to remove the pie with. Snatching a cloth from the counter, she removed the pastry, setting it next to the cake her mother had made the day before.

"Oh dear, you're right, Cedar," Flora said as she watched Cedar close the oven door. "Thank you for remembering before it got too crisp and was spoiled altogether."

Inhaling deeply in trying to dispel the embarrassment her mother had nearly heaped upon her, Cedar smoothed her skirt and returned to the supper table.

"Thank you, Cedar," Flora said as Cedar took her seat.

"Jim was wise to keep hold of this place, Flora," Tom noted.

"Yes. I'm so very glad he did. I don't know what we would've done had we been forced to stay in that horrible city," Flora agreed.

"This place is so close to town . . . you ladies shouldn't have too much trouble in winter. Just be sure yer prepared. It's more'n once we've had whiteouts this late," he explained.

"Oh, Tom, surely not this late," Flora said. "I mean, we're prepared, of course . . . but truly . . . this late?"

"Yep. Just last April a young mother and her little baby froze to death just fifty or so feet from the schoolhouse," he explained.

"How awful!" Cedar exclaimed, her heart aching with empathy for the loss. "It's not more than a few hundred feet from the schoolhouse to the boardinghouse on the corner."

"If ya even think a storm is brewin' this time of year, it's best to just stay in," Tom said.

Cedar looked to her mother, sensing her mother's concern was as deep as her own.

Tom must've noted their changed demeanors, for he quickly added, "Now, here I've gone and rattled you two lovely ladies. I sure didn't mean to scare ya. Yer two right smart fillies, and I'm sure you'll be just fine. Probably won't be another snowstorm 'til November now." Tom smiled and ate another bite of mashed potatoes and gravy. Attempting to lighten the mood once more, he said, "This is the best roast chicken I've ever had, Flora," he said.

Cedar watched as her mother's frown of worry slowly curved upward into a smile.

"Why, thank you, Tom. I'm glad you're enjoying it," she said.

"Cedar," Tom began, "I was wonderin' if you'd—"

He was interrupted, however, by a loud knock on the front door.

Cedar's heart landed with a thud of disappointment in the pit of her stomach. What was he wondering? She may never know.

"Now whoever could that be?" Flora asked, folding her napkin and setting it on the table beside her plate as she rose from her chair. "At supper time?"

Cedar was more curious about what Tom Evans had begun to say. However, his attention had obviously turned to the knock on the door, and he rose from his seat as well. Cedar stood, exhaling a frustrated sort of sigh. Their isolation with Tom Evans was thwarted. It didn't matter who was at the door; the moment was ruined. If President Benjamin Harrison himself were at the door, Cedar Dale could not have cared less.

Tom nodded and gestured that she should precede him to the front of the house.

"Thank you," Cedar said, smiling as she passed him.

As Flora Dale opened the door, Cedar winced—her heart tumbling to another thud in her stomach—when she saw Lucas Pratt standing just beyond the threshold.

Removing his hat, Lucas greeted, "How do ya do, Mrs. Dale?" as he stepped into the house. He glanced to Cedar and smiled. His smile tapered, however, when his gaze moved beyond Cedar to where Tom Evans stood.

"I'm sorry, Mrs. Dale," Lucas began, "and I didn't know you all had company."

"O-oh, it's fine, Lucas. Just fine," Flora stammered, closing the door at his back. "What brings you all the way out here this evening?"

Lucas glanced from Cedar to Tom—then back to Flora. Something in his expression hinted at the reason for his visit, and Cedar began to tremble—stepped backward—closer to Tom. Somehow the closer she was to Tom Evans, the safer she felt. As she took another step in retreat, she felt his hand press the small of her back. His touch was comforting—protective in a manner. It sent warming reassurance streaming through her. She resisted the urge to take another step back—to step back into Tom Evans's arms—and the thought of being in his arms caused goose bumps to race over hers.

Cedar hoped that perhaps Lucas already

realized his imposition on their supper and guest and would not linger.

"Well, I-I . . . I just wanted to . . ." Lucas stammered.

Yes, that's it, Cedar thought. She'd guessed the reason for his visit and wished he would simply take his leave.

"What is it, Lucas?" Flora prodded.

"Well, ma'am," Lucas continued, "truth be told . . . I stopped in to ask yer permission to court yer daughter, Mrs. Dale."

Cedar felt her knees weaken and begin to give way beneath her. Only Tom's hand at her elbow kept her from crumpling to the floor. She'd seen it in Lucas's eyes—known it was coming— somehow known he'd come to ask her mother's permission to come courting.

Desperate panic began to rise in Cedar. She had no desire to be courted by Lucas Pratt. None— ever! He was a kind young man, considerate, generally well thought of—but Cedar held no attraction to him. There was only one man she was attracted to—near violently attracted to—and he stood just behind her, one hand at her elbow and wearing a red shirt that had once belonged to her father. Why couldn't it be Tom Evans asking permission to court her? Yet Tom—older, wiser, and more experienced—hardly seemed the type to ask permission, or to court. Cedar guessed that Tom Evans, kind and good-natured as he was,

was probably beyond the timid tradition of courting a girl.

As unsteady as Cedar felt, however, her mother seemed to remain calm, completely unflustered for all outward appearances. Yet when her mother responded—when the astounding utterance left Flora's lips to linger in the air like a tangible thing of awe—Cedar knew her mother's outward demeanor mirrored none of her inward turmoil.

"Oh, Lucas . . . I'm so sorry," her mother said, donning an expression of great sympathy. "You are such a sweet young man, but I do feel very strongly that a young woman should only be courted by one man at a time . . . and it's just this very evening that I've already granted Mr. Evans permission to court Cedar."

As a quiet gasp of amazement mingled with relief escaped her lips, Cedar's eyes widened as she felt Tom's grasp at her elbow tighten.

"Mother!" she exclaimed in an astonished whisper.

Turning to her daughter, Flora said, "Well . . . I must keep firm on this, Cedar. One beau at a time is plenty . . . and proper." Cedar saw then the distress brewing in her mother's eyes. "Don't you agree, Tom?" she said, looking to Tom for sheer deliverance.

Cedar heard Tom clear his throat. She dared not chance a glance back at him. He must think her mother was a madwoman!

Again Tom cleared his throat, saying, "Yes . . . yes, I most certainly do agree, Mrs. Dale."

Cedar looked to Lucas. The disappointment visible in his expression was pitiful. Cedar's knees were shaking—her hands were shaking—every thread of her being shaking. She could see the annoyance and resentment in his eyes, and for a moment, she feared he might not leave without some argument.

Lucas straightened. His jaw visibly set in an angry grit, he said, "I see. Well . . . I guess I'll just have to wait my turn then, won't I?"

"Oh, you are *such* an understanding young man, Lucas Pratt," Flora sighed. She reached out, offering a hand to him. Lucas accepted her hand, and she patted the back of his. "Now, don't be a stranger. You drop by anytime, you hear?" She opened the door once more—an unspoken suggestion that he should leave.

"Yes, ma'am," he said, touching the brim of his hat as he looked from Cedar to Tom and back. "I'll do just that."

"Bye-bye now," Flora called as he stepped into the evening. "Have a nice evening, Lucas."

Closing the door, Flora Dale sighed and turned to face Cedar and Tom.

"For pity's sake, Mother!" Cedar breathlessly exclaimed. "What on earth were you thinking?" She felt her body sway a little—felt her knees buckle. In the next moment, she found herself being supported by one of Tom Evans's powerful arms.

"Hey, hey, hey," Tom said, taking her chin in one hand. "Hold on there, little filly. Take a deep breath. Look me in the eye now."

Cedar tried to focus on his handsome face, his handsome face now owning a puckered brow of concern. "Mother! H-how could you?" Cedar breathed, trying to keep her mind alert—to keep it from sinking into stunned and humiliated unconsciousness.

Flora began wringing her hands, tears filling her eyes as she whimpered, "I-I don't know! I just didn't know what to say! He's not for you, Cedar. You know that . . . and . . . and I couldn't think of any good reason. And Tom was here . . . and standing just there and . . ."

"Excuse me a moment," Cedar breathed as she managed to find her strength again and hurry out of the room.

"Oh my . . . oh my," she gasped as she made her way through the kitchen to the back door. Quickly she stepped into the cool evening— forced herself to draw slow, even breaths. What had her mother done? What would Tom Evans think of her now? He'd think Flora Dale was trying to trap him into courting her daughter in much the same way Amelia Perkins's mother was encouraging her. Much the same way? Cedar felt nauseous—for it was nothing the same. At least

Amelia's mother played at being charitable, sending her daughter out to take supper to the lonely old bachelor on the Evans place. Cedar's mother had simply ambushed Tom—ensnared him before he'd even suspected the trap had been set.

Cedar covered her mouth to keep the contents of her stomach from escaping. Turning to the rain barrel just outside the kitchen door, she patted cool water to her burning cheeks. Oh, what he must think of her—of them both!

"I don't know what came over me, Tom," Cedar heard her mother say. She held her breath a moment, listening. The evening air clearly conducted the sound of her mother's voice to the kitchen—and she listened. "I-I just didn't know what to say. He's a nice young man. I have no reason to doubt him, but . . . but . . ."

"It's all right, Flora," Tom said then. "I understand. You were backed in a corner and protectin' yer young."

"Well, yes . . . I suppose when you say it that way . . . it doesn't seem quite so bad," Flora said.

"What?" Cedar gasped from her place on the back porch. Of course it seemed bad—just as bad!

"Oh, but whatever will I do, Tom?" Flora asked. "I can't let people know I'm a filthy liar!"

Cedar held her breath when she heard Tom's

laughter echo from the house. "You ain't a filthy liar," he said. "You just told a fib. It ain't like we all haven't done it."

"Oh! My reputation will be ruined!" Flora wailed, however. "I'll be known as Widow Dale, the liar! 'Oh, there goes that poor Widow Dale,' folks will say. 'You know she's a liar, don't you?' That's what they'll say, Tom, and no one will trust me again and—Cedar! Oh, my poor baby! She'll be drug down to hell with me for this!"

Again Tom chuckled. "Now it ain't like that at all," he said. "I'll just . . . I'll just court Cedar for a while. That'll fix it all up, won't it? I'll just make out like it all happened just the way you said it did. That'll save your reputation, you fibbin' widow . . . and it'll keep Lucas at a distance for a time too."

He meant to actually do it? Tom Evans meant to pretend to court her? For a moment, Cedar's joy knew its zenith! Courted by Tom Evans— heavenly! However, in the very next moment, she reminded herself that he'd only be pretending— pretending to court her in order to salvage the Widow Dale's reputation.

"Oh, Tom, I couldn't ask you to do that," Flora said. "I mean . . . it's a little different than patching up the roof or tilling the garden space."

"Yes, ma'am, it is," Tom said.

Cedar still felt as if she might vomit, but she couldn't let the ridiculous situation continue.

Storming back into the house, she'd meant to let her temper fly at her mother.

Instead, when her mother and Tom both turned to look at her—her mother's face so pleading, Tom's so benignly amused—she simply stammered, "I-I . . . I can't believe you've fallen into this quicksand pool, Mother. I can't believe you've dragged Mr. Evans in with us!"

"I know, Cedar! I know!" Flora cried, brushing tears from her cheeks.

"Mr. Evans," Cedar began, summoning every shred of courage her wild humiliation would allow. "I—"

"Tom," he interrupted, smiling at her.

Cedar almost smiled for the obvious patience he'd been blessed with. She did not miss the amused expression on his face, yet she persevered.

"I am so sorry for all of this," she said. "It's obvious Mother has completely lost her senses." Cedar glanced to her mother, still astonished at what she'd told Lucas. "I don't know. Maybe that coyote did nip her yesterday. Nothing else can explain such mad behavior from a woman I know to be as proper and as honest as a preacher's wife!"

"Cedar, I'm not rabid. I was just . . . just befuddled," Flora explained.

Tom's sudden laughter was like music. Shaking his head, he wiped a mirthful tear from his eye.

"Oh, don't go frettin' on it, Cedar," he said.

"We all find ourselves in the briar patch at one time or the other. Fact is . . . I think it's a might entertainin'." The lingering amusement evident in his molasses-brown eyes was evidence enough that he was, if nothing else, entirely entertained. "And besides," he continued, "maybe it'll keep Amelia Perkins off my trail for a while."

Reaching out, he patted the top of Cedar's head as if she were a favorite puppy—in the exact manner he had sometimes patted the top of her head when she'd been a child. Oddly enough, she wasn't offended by the gesture—but rather delighted.

"Anyhow, we can't let folks think yer mama is a liar. Now can we?" he asked.

"Well, it wouldn't be anything she didn't deserve," Cedar told him, glaring at her mother. Reaching up, she loosened a strand of hair and began twisting it this way and that with one index finger.

"Besides," Tom added, "I might be an old plow horse . . . but when the colts are all corralled, maybe you'll decide to keep me. Why set yer aim at a fawn when ya can drop yerself a full-grown buck?"

Cedar blushed—tried to ignore the wild pounding of her heart. She knew he was only teasing, of course, yet the fact he was willing to play at courting her was beginning to sink in. Tom Evans, the man of Cedar's lifelong dreams, was going to court her—for all assumed appearances anyway.

"Oh, Tom," Flora exclaimed with a sigh. "However can I thank you? Truly . . . I can't express how horrified I am with myself. I know I shouldn't ask you to do this."

"Ya didn't," he told her.

"Even so, how do I ever thank you?"

Tom smiled at Cedar, reached out, and tweaked her nose.

"How 'bout roast chicken next Sunday?" he asked.

Cedar smile as he winked at her.

"Of course! Sunday supper!" Flora exclaimed. "After all, if a man's going to have a girl, he should be in every Sunday for supper. Isn't that right, Cedar?"

"Mother!" Cedar gasped. "You cannot ask him to—"

"Oh, preen yer purty feathers back, cluckie," Tom chuckled. "If there's one thing me and Slater loved as kids . . . it was gettin' the best of folks by way of a good prank."

But suddenly Cedar didn't want to be a prank. She certainly didn't want to be courted by Lucas Pratt, but she didn't want to be ridiculous in Tom Evans's mind either.

"Come on, Cedar," her mother begged. "It might be fun!"

"But it's . . . it's not . . ." Cedar stammered.

"Oh, come on, girl," Tom said. Daringly arching one eyebrow, he added, "How 'bout I take ya waltzin' in the moonlight next Friday night? Then we'll see if you still think it ain't worth a little fib to have some fun."

"What?" Cedar breathed, simultaneously puzzled and elated.

"You just leave it to me, Cedar Dale," Tom said. "I'll keep my secret 'til Friday." He strode to the wall hooks near the front door and retrieved his hat.

"Thank ya, Flora," he said. "Thank ya for the best supper and the most interestin' evenin' I've had since I can't remember when."

"You're welcome, Tom," Flora said, humbly smiling as he placed his hat on his head.

"And thank you, Cedar Dale," Tom chuckled.

"Whatever for?" Cedar asked. "A shovel handle to the face and more trouble than you could've ever imagined up on your own?"

He shook his head, obviously still amused by it all.

"I ain't been nobody's beau for a long time," he said. "Hope I ain't forgot how to go sparkin' proper."

"What?" Cedar exclaimed. The impish twinkle in his eyes and accompanying deep chuckle told her he was only teasing her, however.

"Now, Flora," he began, "you know this is gonna spread faster than a windswept flame on the prairie." He sauntered toward the door, ready to take his leave. "You two best be prepared with straighter faces than you were wearin' here tonight."

He opened the door to leave, but Cedar's mind was empty. She could not think of one word to speak to him.

"We'll see you on Friday then?" Flora asked.

Cedar looked to her mother, her mouth agape. Was her mother truly going to let the thing play itself out?

"Oh, I'm sure our paths will cross long before Friday," Tom said, touching the brim of his hat and winking at Cedar. Cedar blushed—wished her heart didn't hammer so hard every time he looked at her. "Good night, ladies," he said.

"Good night, Tom," Flora sighed, closing the door behind him.

"Mother!" Cedar exclaimed, bursting into tears. "How could you . . . how could you cause such a mess?"

"Somebody else made a mess once," Flora said, smiling. "It turned out they called it pumpkin pie. And we both know how sweet that is."

"But, Mama . . . he must think I'm—"

"If he thinks you're anything but something to catch . . . he wouldn't have agreed to it, Cedar," Flora interrupted.

Cedar closed her eyes, trying to sort the conflicting emotions leaping about in her stomach.

168

In truth, she was elated at the prospect of having Tom Evans's attention—sickened by her mother's ridiculous lie, of course—horrified at what Tom must think of her—but near euphoric at knowing she would see him again, and soon. She thought of the way he'd patted her head and tweaked her nose—again remembering he'd offered the same gestures to her as a child.

"I feel ill," Cedar mumbled.

"Well, no wonder," Flora told her. "Running off like a silly ninny the way you did."

"I was horrified into it, Mama . . . by your antics," Cedar reminded her.

"I was horrid, Cedar," her mother admitted. "I don't know what came over me! I've just felt like some silly little girl all the day long . . . ever since yesterday when . . ." Flora paused, burying her face in her hands for a moment. "I just lost all sense of thinking. I couldn't fathom how to tell the boy no. Then I looked to Tom, and . . . well . . . it seemed a good thing at the moment."

"I'm going to bed, Mama," Cedar mumbled. "Rabid coyotes, seeping wounds, and bare skin . . . and now lies and ramifications. I'm wrung out from it all." She paused and turned, wagging a scolding index finger at her mother. "And as penance for your sinful lies . . . you can do the supper dishes yourself tonight."

"That's fine, dear," Flora said, smiling. She kissed Cedar affectionately on one cheek. "You

169

need your rest anyway. We don't want you looking tired when Tom comes around, now do we?"

Cedar shook her head, irritated with her mother's lightheartedness concerning the situation. For pity's sake! A body would've thought she was sixteen instead of a grown, widowed woman with a grown-up daughter.

Still, as Cedar tied the ribbon of her night-dress at her throat some time later, she was oddly happy—happy in her mother's sudden silliness—the silliness she suddenly realized had been missing since her father's death. Likewise she was happy in her own ridiculous considerations. What fun it would be to see Amelia Perkins's face when she heard Tom Evans was courting Cedar Dale. Cedar wondered how far Tom would carry the game. How long would he be willing to play it? Long enough for Cedar to truly capture his attention?

As she lay in bed that night, twisting and untwisting a long strand of her hair, she lingered in a vision of Tom's face as he grinned at her—wondered at the bright amusement in his eyes. Once when she was a child, she'd fallen down in the road in front of the livery stable and scraped her hand. Tom Evans had picked her up, kissed the little skinned-up palm, and dabbed at her tears with his dusty handkerchief. Cedar had never forgotten that kiss. She wondered now what it would feel like to kiss Tom Evans again—really kiss him—square on the lips kiss him. Perhaps—thanks to her mother's ridiculous lie—perhaps she would find out before the theatrics were over.

Cedar shook her head and giggled. The entire situation sounded just like something those eccentric actors Lucas Pratt's father employed might play out in his drama house.

As the clock struck midnight, Tom Evans tossed and turned in his bed—fought off two quilts and a sheet. What in tarnation had he gotten himself into? Cedar was right. Flora Dale had lost her mind when Lucas Pratt had shown up on the doorstep of the Dale house. Still, he was astonished at his own reaction—at how willing he was to save Flora Dale's reputation—at how desperate he'd felt—desperate to keep Cedar from being courted by Lucas Pratt.

Even now he could still sense the sweet scent of her hair—still see the bright flash of her sapphire eyes as the firelight danced in them. Oh, these musings were dangerous indications indeed—indications that Tom was near to being—well—near to being entirely smitten.

Tom Evans hadn't had a girl on his mind the way he now had Cedar Dale on his mind ever! He flittered through his thoughts—his emotions. Perhaps he simply felt sorry for the girl, compassion for the loss of her father and her lover. At the thought of the murdered man who

171

was to have married Cedar, Tom was instantly and unexpectedly jealous—ferociously so. Naturally, guilt was the next emotion to whisper to him—guilt for owning calloused feelings toward the murdered man. Tom then began to wonder if he were merely small-minded—simply attracted by Cedar's youth and beauty.

He gave up identifying any reasons for anything for the time being, but he could not chase the images of Cedar Dale from his mind.

"Waltzin' in the moonlight?" he grumbled aloud. Whatever had possessed him to say something so dramatic?

Exhaling a heavy sigh—for he had worked hard all the day long and was painfully tired—he shook his head. He knew dang well what had possessed him to say something the like—that pretty little Cedar Dale. Tom had wanted to reassure her that all would be well. He'd wanted to protect her from gossip, humiliation—anything he could protect her from. So he'd said what he had to imply that he really did want to court her. Yet as Tom exhaled another heavy sigh, he admitted the truth to himself. The fact of the matter was he did want to court pretty little Cedar Dale.

Chapter Eight

"I knew it! I knew it, I knew it!" Mrs. Gunderson exclaimed, slapping one knee with glee. Lowering her voice, she continued, "I knew them two was meant for each other. The minute I saw how right pretty Cedar had grown up to be . . . I knew there was no other girl for Tom Evans."

"Well . . . they're just courting, Elvira," Flora stammered. "It might not stick."

"Oh, it'll stick just fine, Flora," Mrs. Gunderson said. "That girl's been purrin' for Tom since she was a kitten . . . and it don't take bein' beat on the noggin to see she's caught Tom's eye."

Cedar frowned and continued to feign interest in several bolts of fabric Mrs. Gunderson had strewn on a nearby table. She had tried not to eavesdrop on the conversation between her mother and Mrs. Gunderson. Still, the moment she heard Mrs. Gunderson mention Tom Evans, her good manners were forgotten.

It was sorely obvious that Tom had been correct in his prediction that news of his "courting" Cedar would spread like a windswept flame on the prairie. From what she'd heard of her mother's conversation with Mrs. Gunderson so far, Lucas Pratt had sulked and pouted for three

173

whole days before Mrs. Gunderson had managed to weasel the information out of him just that very morning. Thus, the moment Cedar and her mother had stepped into the general store later that afternoon, Mrs. Gunderson had whisked her mother aside to collect further details.

Cedar had remained almost perpetually nauseated since the Saturday supper with Tom—since her mother had momentarily lost her wits and told Lucas Pratt she'd agreed to allow Tom to court her daughter. She hadn't seen Tom since—not that there should've been any reason that she should have seen him, of course—but the hope constantly lingered in her that she would see him. Now, however, at seeing Mrs. Gunderson's reaction to the utter (albeit secret) falsehood that Tom Evans was courting Cedar Dale—in knowing that the entire town had heard it, no doubt—she wondered if Tom was simply irritated by all the ridiculous gossip. Perhaps he'd changed his mind about playing at the farce. Still, she hoped he had just been kept too busy with his horses and such to make an appearance in town. The truth was it was entirely irrational for Cedar to have even expected to see Tom Evans for any reason. He was a busy man. All men were, but especially ones like Tom Evans who ran horse or cattle ranches.

Cedar sighed—discouraged, embarrassed, and agitated. Mrs. Gunderson's excitement was beginning to take its toll on her, and she felt desperate to escape.

Turning to where her mother and Mrs. Gunderson stood steeped in conversation—her mother owning the countenance of discomfort borne of deception and guilt, Mrs. Gunderson owning the countenance of exuberant enthusiasm—Cedar said, "Pardon me, Mrs. Gunderson." When Mrs. Gunderson nodded, Cedar looked to her mother. "Is it all right if I just start home, Mama? You don't have too much to carry, do you?"

"Not at all, sweetheart," Flora said. She smiled an understanding smile—an apologetic smile. "I'll see you in a little while, all right?"

"Yes, ma'am," Cedar said, exhaling a sigh of relief. She looked to Mrs. Gunderson and smiled. "It was so nice to see you, Mrs. Gunderson . . . as always."

"And it was sure nice to see you too, Cedar," Mrs. Gunderson gushed. The old woman winked. "Didn't I tell you bumpin' into good things outweighs trippin' over the bad?"

"Yes, ma'am," Cedar said, forcing her smile to broaden. "Have a nice afternoon, Mrs. Gunderson."

"You too, honey," Mrs. Gunderson called as Cedar turned to leave.

As she strode toward the door leading out onto the boardwalk, however, she heard Mrs. Gunderson say, "She's probably just rushin' off to some secret rendezvous with Tom."

"Probably," she heard her mother respond.

If only it were true, Cedar thought. But it wasn't. She wished Mrs. Gunderson would cool her enthusiasm over the whole thing. After all, it was a lie—a terrible, shameful lie!

Stepping out onto the boardwalk, Cedar glanced across the street. It seemed more folks were milling about than usual. She blushed, hoping it wasn't the sinful lie about her and Tom Evans that had people standing in groups here and there, seemingly steeped in quiet conversation. Still, she figured, with Mrs. Gunderson so wound up, that it was very likely the reason.

Cedar had no wish to be questioned about whether or not it was true. She could just imagine folks firing questions at her as if the salvation of the world depended on it. Therefore, slipping into the alley to the right of the general store, she hurried along the back of the buildings, heading for the creek instead of the house. She'd have to be careful, of course. Mrs. Gunderson had told her and her mother that no one had reported any other rabid animals in the area since Tom Evans, Reno Garrett, and Eldon Pickering had killed the ones they had. Still, she'd be watchful. She knew rabid animals were drawn to water, so she wouldn't linger long at the creek—just for a while—just long enough to settle her stomach and try to get hold of her tumultuous emotions.

Soon Cedar found herself lingering on the creek

bank near the house—very near to where Reno Garrett had saved her mother from certain, agonizing death. For a moment, a wave of terror broke over her as she thought of how close she'd come to losing her mother. Tears welled in her eyes, and she began to tremble. Yet she hadn't lost her mother; Reno Garrett had saved her. All was well. She silently reminded herself that her mother was fine—that all was indeed well—as she tried to concentrate on the fresh, invigorating atmosphere of early spring.

The daffodils were blooming in bunches along the creek bank—sunny yellow and bright with cheer. Cedar smiled, thinking they looked exactly like vivid bouquets of captured sunshine. She loved daffodils—simply adored them! Oh, how she had missed them when she'd lived in the city. Not that they didn't grow there too, but in the city they grew in hothouses and flower boxes—in manipulated patterns in the parks. But some-how—somehow daffodils were more beautiful thriving in pastures and along the creek bank. Oh, she knew her father had planted the bulbs there when she was a little girl. She'd helped him—helped him place the fragile daffodil bulbs into the ground one early autumn, delighting when they bloomed the next spring, the same spring she'd turned six years old. Perhaps that was why these daffodils seemed more beautiful to Cedar—because she and her father had planted them—because they stood as a lovely reminder of him—because every spring they would bloom and announce to the world that James Dale had once walked the path they now adorned.

Once again, Cedar tried to conjure a vivid image of Logan Davies. She even closed her eyes—as she'd done so very many times since having spent an entire day and most of one evening in Tom Evans's overwhelming company. Since Saturday, she tried to pull forth a clear image of Logan in her mind, but she just couldn't seem to remember every detail of his face the way she'd been able to before. Eventually, she'd gone to the trunk at the foot of her bed and found the photographs she'd placed there—the photographs of Logan Davies, the man she'd been engaged to marry. It was only then that his features were clear in her mind. She'd tried to feel sick to her stomach over his loss—frightened and sad the way she had for two years. But she found that the uncomfortable feeling in her stomach was borne of worry over, and desire for, Tom Evans—not for the misery of losing Logan. Oh, she felt sad—felt the loss of love and a friend—but it wasn't the same sadness and loss she'd known for so long. Even her guilt at not being overwhelmed with misery seemed less present, and she wondered if perhaps she really had begun to heal.

She thought of her mother—the expression of

pure admiration, delight, and excitement that had been on her face the day Reno Garrett had rescued her. Could it be her mother was healing as well? Cedar smiled, thinking her mother had looked exactly the way Cedar felt inside whenever she was in Tom Evans's presence.

"Tommy," she whispered aloud. She smiled. She loved the word and repeated it. "Tommy." The very feel of the name on her tongue—the way pronouncing it caused her lips to press together—the way it curved the corners of her mouth upward. It was what she'd always called him as a child—Tommy. Furthermore, it was still what she called him to herself—in her thoughts —and in her dreams.

"It's awful chilly to be without a coat or somethin'."

Startled by the sound of his voice, Cedar gasped and whirled around to see Tom Evans standing just behind her. She'd been so lost in her own thoughts, she hadn't heard him approach. She was thankful it wasn't a rabid coyote that had caught her so unaware.

"Oh! Hello," she managed.

He grinned—a rather impish, roguish grin— and hunkered down, snapping off a bloomed daffodil and stem and offering it to her.

Cedar smiled as she accepted the bloom, delighted by the simple, yet rather romantic, gesture.

"What brings you out this way?" she asked.

Tom removed his hat long enough to rake one strong hand through his nut-brown hair.

"I was plannin' on stoppin' in on you and yer mama, and I saw ya out here by the crick," he answered. "Since I *am* yer beau . . . I thought it might be all right if I imposed on yer privacy a bit."

Cedar blushed, feeling elated yet embarrassed. Glancing to the pretty flower she held in her hand, she began, "I do understand that it's your kind heart that finds you in this mess—"

"Maybe me fixin' yer roof was kind, Cedar," he interrupted, his smile broadening as he winked at her, "but this I'm doin' for the pure fun of it."

"What fun could you possibly find in all this?" she asked, uncertain she wanted to hear his answer.

"Are you pullin' my leg?" he chuckled. "Puttin' on the whole town? Keepin' Amelia Perkins from showin' up on my front porch?" He nodded, adding, "Not to mention gettin' to call a purty little thing like you my girl. Seems I'm comin' out smellin' better and better all the time."

Cedar giggled, more than merely pleased by his exuberant response.

"Still, I would think that if you have to do things like this to have fun . . . then you're working far too hard, Mr. Evans," she said.

"I thought we worked this all out the other day, Cedar. My name's Tom . . . unless you think somethin' the like of 'honey' or 'sugarplum' might better suit," he teased with a wink. "Now," he began, sitting down on the grass at her feet. She felt her smile broaden as he leaned back on one elbow, stretching his long legs out in front of him. "Tell me about this Cedar Dale filly I'm courtin'."

"What?" Cedar asked, wrinkling her nose with bewilderment. "What do you mean?"

"We're courtin', ain't we?" he explained. "Ain't that what courtin' is . . . gettin' on with knowin' each other?"

Cedar was enchanted by his easy manner. She'd almost forgotten how effortlessly he could make anyone feel comfortable. He had a way of appearing sincerely interested—of soothing anxieties.

"Well . . . what do you want to know?" Cedar asked.

As his eyes narrowed, his smile unexpectedly fading, her heart began to beat even more quickly than it already had been beating since she'd turned to see him standing behind her.

"Can I ask ya anythin'?" he asked.

Instantly, Cedar felt her body stiffen. Still, she couldn't possibly refuse him—not after all he'd done for her and her mother—after all he was doing. The simple fact he was Tom Evans would've kept her from refusing to answer him, even if all the other considerations had not existed.

"Yes . . . I suppose so," she stammered.

"Then tell me about the boy who was killed with yer daddy," he said.

Cedar was disturbed at the dulled heartache in her bosom. Instead of pain—near to unbearable pain the like she'd experienced for so long each time she thought of Logan—a rather soft sort of peaceful calm bathed her. The sort of melancholy a person felt when thinking of an old friend who'd moved away was there in her bosom—but not overwhelming pain.

"His name was Logan," she began, studying the daffodil she still held. She fancied for a moment that the blossom smiled at her—nodded—encouraging her to let go of her remaining fears. She sighed. "His father owned the bank, and Logan worked with him. He was a kind and caring young man."

"Handsome?" Tom asked.

Cedar grinned, thinking the inquisitive, curious expression on his face was very much like that of a young boy when asking a question he wasn't certain he truly wanted to know the answer to.

"Yes. Very handsome."

"Wealthy?" he asked next.

Cedar felt an amused giggle tickle her throat. "Yes. I suppose so."

Tom nodded—appeared thoughtful—glanced away for a moment.

Looking back to her, he forthrightly asked, "Was he a good lover?"

"I beg your pardon?" Cedar breathed. The forthrightness of the question—coupled with the content of it—caused her to blush.

"Was he a good lover?" Tom repeated. "Did he know how to kiss you and do a good job of it?"

Cedar kept her mouth from gaping open in astonishment by lightly biting her lower lip. She was surprised to a complete loss for words for a moment. Logan had kissed her—often—but she'd never considered whether or not he had done a good job of it. She enjoyed his kisses, yes. But were she to be truthful—in the deepest core of her feelings, she'd always been a bit disappointed in kissing. Somehow the exchange of affection never quite measured up to what she'd always dreamed it should be. And until that moment, with Tom Evans sitting at her feet, asking her if Logan had done a good job of kissing her, she'd never really considered that in reality a kiss could be more affecting.

"I-I . . ." Cedar stammered.

One of Tom's masculine brows arched inquisitively. He picked up a nearby twig, snapping it in two between his thumb and index finger.

"I'll take that as a no," he said, adding, "no disrespect to your young man, ya understand. I'm bettin' he was as good as they come, and ya should remember him fondly. Still . . . and again I'm meanin' no disrespect of yer young hero . . . still, it's plain as day he never put yer knees to knockin'."

"Didn't put my knees to knocking?" Cedar exclaimed in a dismayed whisper as a heated scarlet rose to her cheeks.

"Yep," Tom said. She watched as he sighed, tossed the remnants of the twigs into the stream, and rose to his feet. "Ya know what I mean, don't ya?" His brow puckered when she did not immediately respond. "Ya know . . . he didn't put your knees to knockin'. He didn't stir up yer blood."

Cedar swallowed the lump of embarrassment gathered in her throat. She tried to steady her heart's erratic hammering—tried to understand why she couldn't seem to draw a regular breath.

"I'm quite sure I don't know what you mean, Mr. Evans," she admitted.

"Tom," he corrected with a smile. He winked at her, bent toward her, and whispered, "That's why I'm sure . . . good a boy as he was . . . that he didn't do neither knee-knockin' or blood-stirrin'." He moved closer to her—closer—until he stood so close she could feel the warmth of his breath on her forehead. "But don't you worry none, Miss Cedar Dale," he said, taking one of her hands in his. "Come Friday . . . when we're waltzin' in the moonlight . . . I'll show ya just what I mean."

Her hand burned in being held by his. She could feel the calluses in his palms, the strength of his fingers, the capable power barely masked by his gentle grip. It was only then Cedar realized her free hand had dropped the tender daffodil bloom and was busily twisting and untwisting a long strand of her hair with one index finger.

Releasing her hand, Tom Evans bent then, placing a soft, briefly lingering kiss on the bridge of her nose. In that instant—for the sake of such a trifling, seemingly small gesture—Cedar knew that as much as she'd loved Logan, he had never put her "knees to knocking" the way Tom Evans could.

"Tell yer mama I said hello, will ya?" he mumbled. He smiled, winked, touched the brim of his hat as he nodded, turned, and sauntered away.

Cedar's hand he'd been holding went to her throat in a useless effort to steady her breathing. Tom Evans would be the death of her! He'd suffocate her with wanting to belong to him—drown her with the unquenched desire to be in his arms! All at once, she felt free from pain, fear, and unwarranted guilt. All at once she was breathless with titillation—felt that if she stretched her arms out to her sides she might actually take flight.

She lingered for a time—lingered in the tranquility of healing—bathed in the bliss of delicious anticipation. At last, she turned and made her way back toward the house, wondering—if a chance meeting by the creek had sent her senses crashing into such waves of delight, what would the effects to her body, mind, and soul be if Tom Evans did intend to keep up the pretense of courting her? What if he really did intend to waltz with her in the moonlight on Friday?

There was only one road before her—waiting.

"Hey there, Elvira."

"Afternoon, Reno," Mrs. Gunderson cheerily greeted. "And what brings you to town today?"

Flora Dale gulped as she turned to see Reno Garrett striding into the general store. She inwardly scolded herself for the way her heart leapt in her bosom—for the butterflies taking flight in her stomach. After all, she was no longer a tender-aged young girl. She was a full-grown woman, widowed, weathered by life, with a daughter old enough to capture the attention of just such a man as Reno Garret. Still, Flora could not keep her senses from reacting to the tall, intimidating, and wildly alluring man as he smiled at her—gazed at her—did not take his attention from her face for even one moment as he crossed his muscular forearms, resting them on the counter as he leaned toward her.

Speaking to Elvira Gunderson but still looking at Flora, he answered, "Well, seems I got me a bit of a sweet tooth today." Flora blushed as Reno quickly studied her from head to toe. "Thought I might come in and see what you had in the general store that might satisfy my cravin'."

As Flora's blush intensified, she lightly bit her lower lip, trying to mask her delight with his unrestrainedly inappropriate flirtation.

"Well, I-I . . ." Elvira stammered.

Flora glanced to Elvira to see her mouth agape in disbelief. The older woman stood perplexed, frowning as if she weren't quite sure whether Reno Garrett really was looking for some confectionary treat or whether he was uttering some metaphorical implication.

At last Reno Garrett pulled his gaze from Flora and looked to Elvira Gunderson.

"I was in last week, and Theodore give me a little sack of lemon drops," he explained. "But I was wonderin' if ya had somethin' a little different today . . . maybe along the lines of some of them candy corns . . . or even chocolates."

"Oh!" Elvira sighed at being assured that Reno hadn't been in any way improper. Flora, however, was as disappointed as Elvira was relieved. "Why, I'm sure we've got somethin' for that sweet tooth of yours, Reno," Elvira chirped. Turning around, she studied the collection of jars housed on the shelves behind the counter containing a variety of sweets.

Again Reno looked to Flora—a smile of pure enticement spreading across his handsome face. "Oh, I've no doubt of that, Elvira," he said with a wink. "No doubt at all."

A soft giggle escaped Flora's throat—for he *was* flirting with her. She began to squirm under the intensity of his gaze but didn't make one move to avoid it. She was too drawn to him—too mesmerized by his mere presence.

"Hey there, Mrs. Dale," he greeted at last.

"Hello, Mr. Garrett," Flora said, wishing her smile wasn't quite so accepting of his attention.

He was so handsome! Quickly, Flora studied the two or three days' whisker growth on his square, rugged jaw—the way trails of silver whiskers cascaded over his chin from the corners of his mouth, emphasizing the ebony black of the others. His thick, dark eyelashes were a stark contrast to the bright blue of his eyes, and his gaze seemed to pierce every defense against his charms she might have managed to muster.

"Flora and I were just discussin' yer neighbor Tom Evans. He's courtin' her daughter, you see," Elvira said as she took down a jar filled with candy corn and placed it on the counter in front of Reno.

"Is he now?" Reno asked, still staring at Flora.

"Yes," Elvira said as she removed the jar's lid. "Has Tom said anything to you about it yet?"

"Nope," Reno said. "Can't say that he has."

"Well, it *has* only been a few days since he asked Flora's permission," Elvira sighed, dropping several pieces of candy into Reno's hand when he offered his palm to her. "I guess word travels slower out to the ranches and such. After all, I just found out about it this mornin' myself."

Flora smiled as she watched Reno Garrett toss the pieces of orange and yellow candy into his mouth one at a time.

"So Tom Evans has got his eye on yer daughter, is that it, Mrs. Dale?" he asked.

"It would seem that way, wouldn't it?" Flora answered. She felt a little ill, hoping the way she'd worded her answer would keep her from having the weight of owning another lie on her conscience.

"What do you think of the candy corns, Reno?" Elvira asked.

Reno looked to Elvira, smiled, and nodded. "Give me a couple a fistfuls of 'em . . . if ya wouldn't mind."

"Not at all," Elvira chirped. "I got a little bitty sack here I've been savin'."

Returning his attention to Flora, he said, "Tom Evans is a good man."

"Yes, he is," Flora agreed. "A very good man."

"I'm a bit surprised he didn't come courtin' after you, Mrs. Dale," Reno flirted.

"Reno Garrett!" Elvira exclaimed. "What a thing to say! Why, Flora don't know you like the rest of us. She's gonna think yer some sort of—"

"Oh, I think Mrs. Dale knows how purty she is, Elvira," Reno interrupted. "I'm sure she's left quite a long string of broken cowboy hearts behind her," Reno chuckled.

"I very seriously doubt that, Mr. Garrett," Flora said.

His smile hadn't faded since the moment he'd sauntered into the general store. Even now it remained stretched across his handsome face, and Flora was purely captivated by it.

"So is yer daughter as happy to be in Tom Evans's company as he no doubt is about bein' in hers?" he asked.

"I'm sure she is!" Elvira answered before Flora could begin to open her mouth to respond. "Cedar Dale has been sweet on Tom Evans nearly since the day she was born!"

"Is that right?" Reno asked.

"Yep!" Elvira answered. It didn't seem to bother Elvira that Reno's gaze had hardly left Flora's face since he'd arrived. She prattled on like it was the most natural thing in the world. "And if you've seen Cedar . . . have you ever met Flora's daughter, Reno?"

"Yes, ma'am, I have," he answered. "She's the spittin' image of her mother."

"Then you understand why it is she caught Tom's eye," Elvira said. Smiling and releasing an understanding giggle, she added, "Obviously."

"Yep," Reno said.

"Anyhow, I was just tellin' Flora here that them two was made for each other . . . just made for each other. Flora's worried that it might not stick, this courtin' between the two of them, but I told her not to worry. It'll stick permanent. Mark my words, Reno Garrett."

"I always do, Elvira," Reno said. "I always do."

He looked to Elvira then as she handed him the small sack of candy. "Thank ya kindly," he said, reaching into his pocket and producing two pennies. Placing them on the counter, he winked at Elvira Gunderson.

Flora giggled as Elvira blushed, batted flattered eyelashes at the handsome cattle rancher, and said, "Oh, go on with you, Reno Garrett . . . you bad, bad man."

Reno chuckled, straightening to his full height.

"Might I offer you a ride home, Mrs. Dale?" he said. "I brung the wagon today. It would save ya the walk."

"Well, I-I don't know if . . ." Flora stammered. Propriety was battling with rebellion inside her. If she accepted Reno's offer, she risked sparking a thread of gossip. However, if she didn't, she

191

somehow knew she'd regret it for the rest of her life.

"Oh, go on, Flora," Elvira impishly encouraged. "After all, you don't want to have to carry this whole sack of flour home by yourself." Elvira reached beneath the counter and struggled to lift a twenty-five pound sack of flour.

"But, Elvira, I just came in for the needles and—" Flora began.

"I forgot to send it home with Cedar last week," Elvira interrupted, still fighting to heft the sack of flour. She smiled at Flora, winked, and added, "I wouldn't want you to walk out of here without it and regret not havin' taken it today."

Instantly, Flora understood. Elvira was providing an excuse for Flora to accept Reno's invitation. No one in town would've expected the Widow Dale to carry a twenty-five pound sack of flour all the way home.

"That's right," Reno said, reaching over the counter to haul the sack of flour up onto one broad shoulder. "And I'm headed out yer way . . . so it just makes good sense for you to allow me to haul this flour on home for ya."

"I suppose it does," Flora said. She looked to Elvira and smiled. "Thank you, Elvira. I swear, you do think of everything."

Elvira's smile broadened with pride. "Well, I do try to. Now you have nice afternoon, Flora. And you too, Reno Garrett."

"Thank you, ma'am," Reno said. "I plan to."

Opening the general store door, Reno stepped aside, allowing Flora to precede him.

"Thank you," she said as she stepped past him.

"My pleasure, Mrs. Dale," he mumbled. "The wagon is just here . . . yonder," he explained, nodding to the team hitched to a wagon across the street.

"Thank you," Flora said. She felt ridiculous—ridiculous, elated, and giddy as a puppy as Reno escorted her across the street. She silently told herself to settle down—that he was just a neighbor offering his assistance to the new widow in town. Yet each time she looked at him, her heart would race, and her stomach would turn somersaults.

Reno put the large (although surplus) sack of flour into the wagon bed. He then climbed up onto the seat, offering her a hand to assist her.

Flora giggled as she accepted his hand. His touch caused goose bumps to spring over her arms. She was so affected by the sensation that she nearly lost her footing while climbing up onto the wagon.

"There now," he said once he'd seated himself beside her. "Now, do you wanna get home as fast as I can haul ya there? Or would ya rather maybe meander the long way a spell?"

For a moment, Flora was anxious, thinking she'd made mistake in accepting a ride from a man she'd only met once before—a man she knew nothing about.

Trust him. You'll be safe.

Quickly, Flora glanced over her shoulder— half expecting to see Jim seated in the wagon bed, for it had been his voice that whispered reassurance in her ear. She felt moisture in her eyes as a calm assurance of being just where she belonged warmed her heart.

"Oh, it's been quite some time since I was offered a wagon ride by a charming man," she said, smiling at Reno. "I think I might prefer the long way . . . if that's all right with you, Mr. Garrett."

"Yes, ma'am," Reno Garrett chuckled, smiling as he slapped the lines at the backs of the horses. "That's more fine with me than you'll ever know."

The wagon lurched forward, and Flora felt an odd breathlessness rise in her. She fancied the sense of freedom and wonderful anticipation suddenly washing over her was some sort of message—an assurance from Jim or from heaven (or perhaps both) that all would at last be well— that she might begin to find true joy in life once more.

As the wagon rumbled out of town, Flora sighed. The afternoon breeze was a little too cool to be entirely pleasant, but it refreshed her. Furthermore, she adored the fact that it was Reno

194

Garrett holding the lines. She glanced to him, noting how handsome he was—adoring the crow's feet wrinkles at the corners of his mesmerizing eyes.

"So," he began, jostling her from her easy thoughts, "tell me about yerself, Mrs. Flora Dale."

"Flora," she instantly corrected him. She didn't want him to address her as Mrs. Dale. There was something uncomfortable about it—even though that's who she was. He nodded, a slight grin of satisfaction curving the corners of his mouth.

"Tell me about yerself, Flora," he said.

Flora smiled. She sighed and propped her feet up on the front of the wagon. She owned the sudden urge to unpin her hair—to shake it out and let the breeze play through it. Still, she again reminded herself that she wasn't a girl of fifteen and that she hardly knew the man she was with. It would be best to maintain her matured widow persona—at least for the time being.

"Well, I lost my husband two years ago," she began. It wasn't a happy beginning, but many times she had a difficult time remembering anything else. "I brought Cedar back to the old place here in Lamar to get away from the noise and chaos of the city."

"What about before you lost yer man?" Reno asked. "Where were you born? Are you a city girl by birth? Do ya have other family?"

Flora smiled. He seemed sincerely interested in her.

"I was born in Boston," she told him.

He chuckled. "Ah . . . that explains it."

"Explains what?" Flora giggled.

"Why you talk so proper," he answered. "I figured you were from somewhere up east. Local folks don't talk so straight and proper as you do."

"What about you?" Flora asked. "Were you born near here?"

His smile broadened. "We were talkin' about you, remember?"

"Yes . . . but where are you from . . . originally?"

"A little place called Charleston," he told her.

"Charleston, South Carolina?" she asked.

"Yep."

"How in the world did you end up raising cattle way out here?"

"Now that's a long story . . . best kept until a warmer day when we have us a couple hours alone."

Flora giggled, bit her lip with delight, and blushed.

"Anyhow, we were talkin' about you, not me," he reminded her. "So you were born in Boston. How'd you meet yer husband and end up out here?"

Flora studied him for a moment. Did he truly want to know how she'd met Jim—about her life with him?

"I met Jim when I was fourteen," she began. A familiar pain pinched her heart, but she fancied it was not quite so miserable to endure as it had been a few months before—fancied that the memory now brought more joy than pain. "My mother and I had traveled to Missouri to help my grandparents . . . her parents. They were both very ill. Jim was working for my grandfather. My grandfather loved Jim . . . admired him and felt greatly indebted to the fact that Jim continued to work so hard when . . . but I'm beginning to babble. You don't really want to know all of this, do you?"

Reno Garrett smiled, however, nodding his assurance.

"I want to know everything about you, Flora Dale," he said. "You've caught my eye somethin' fierce, ya know . . . and there ain't many women who can say they've done that."

Again Flora felt such a thrill of pleasure rise within her that she couldn't begin to stifle the delighted giggle bubbling in her throat.

"Furthermore, I ain't a man to waste a whole lotta time," he continued. "When I want somethin', I don't skip after it. I run. So, Flora Dale . . . tell me everything."

He smiled and slowed the team a little,

indicating he would make their journey back to the house as lingering as possible.

"Everything?" she teased.

"Yep," he answered. "Tell me about Jim. I ain't afraid of hearin' it."

Flora smiled as her heart melted. He was a confident man—there was no doubt about that. Furthermore, she sensed he owned compassion for her loss—that Reno Garrett would be the kind of man to respect a woman's lost love— to understand a pain that would never fully heal.

"Very well, Reno Garrett," she began. "I'll tell you my tale if you promise to tell me yours one day . . . one day soon."

"I promise," he said. She watched as he transferred the lines from his right hand to his left, offering her a handshake.

When she took his offered hand, however, he not only grasped it but drew it to his lips, placing a firm kiss to the back of it.

"Now," he said, "tell me everything ya can fit in before we reach yer place."

Flora sighed—entirely titillated by his gesture— entirely attracted to him—entirely lost in more joy than she'd known in a very long time.

Cedar peered through the lace curtains at the small window by the front door. When she'd heard the rumble of wagon wheels, her heart had leapt so hard that it was nearly painful. Instantly, she'd thought of Tom—hoped that by some miracle it was Tom Evans's wagon she heard. However, disappointment twisted in her stomach as she saw it was not Tom Evans arriving but rather Reno Garrett.

Cedar frowned, quickly sweeping the curtains aside.

"Mama?" she whispered. For a moment she thought she was imagining the vision as she watched Reno Garrett hop down from the wagon seat and then reach up, taking her mother's waist between his large hands in helping her down.

The color on her mother's pretty cheeks was no less than sunset pink, and Flora Dale's gaze followed the handsome rancher as he lifted a sack of flour out of the wagon bed.

Cedar dropped the lace curtains, for both her mother and Reno were walking toward the front door. She turned and hurried into the parlor as she heard footsteps on the porch. A moment later, the front door opened, and her mother stepped into the house.

"Would you mind just setting the flour on the kitchen table, Reno?" she heard her mother inquire. She heard the heavy steps of a man's boots striding across the floor as her mother called, "Cedar? Are you here, sweetheart?"

"Yes," she answered. She stepped out of the parlor and into the kitchen in time to see Reno

Garrett deposit a large sack of flour onto the kitchen table.

"Afternoon, Miss Dale," Reno greeted, removing his hat and nodding at her.

"Hello," Cedar said. She noted how large a man he was—how small the kitchen looked with him standing at its center.

"Mr. Garrett was kind enough to offer me a ride home from town," Flora explained.

"Oh, how kind, Mr. Garrett," Cedar said, smiling at the man. Her mother's eyes were bright with pure felicity, and the sight made Cedar's own joy swell.

"It was my pleasure, miss," Reno said.

From the blush on my mama's face, I'm sure it was hers as well, Cedar thought.

"Well, ma'am . . . I oughta be gettin' on home," he said. "I hope to be seein' ya soon, Flora."

"Yes," Flora said. "And thank you, again, Reno."

Reno nodded, and Cedar smiled as she watched his gaze linger on her mother's face for an excessive amount of time.

"You ladies have a good evenin' now, ya hear?" he said, placing his hat back on his head and striding toward the front door.

Flora followed him, but Cedar lagged behind. In another moment, he was gone. Flora watched through the small front window until Reno Garrett was no longer visible.

Cedar smiled as her mother sighed.

Flora turned to face her daughter, leaning back against the front door and whispering, "Isn't he just the handsomest man?"

Cedar giggled, absolutely elated by her mother's dreamy expression. "Almost, Mama," Cedar said, envisioning Tom. "Almost."

Chapter Nine

Even her mother's obvious euphoria where Reno Garrett's attentions were concerned could not outshine Cedar's own wild anticipation of seeing Tom Evans again. All week Cedar could think of nothing else. The hope that Tom really would arrive to collect her Friday evening to whisk her away to waltzing in the moonlight—whatever that implied—kept her almost dangerously distracted. She couldn't concentrate on mending or embroidery and ended up picking out entire sections of stitching. She ruined a batch of bread, for she'd lost track of properly measuring the flour. She'd cut herself with a knife, almost set too large a fire in the parlor hearth, and accidentally let the chickens loose when she left the coop door open.

Even when Logan Davies had been courting her, Cedar hadn't been so distracted and nervous. Delighted and excited with anticipation, yes—but not a bumbling, clumsy goose the way she was where Tom Evans was concerned. She thought it was perhaps his age—the fact that Logan had been more near Cedar's own age, whereas Tom was much older, more experienced, more confident. Perhaps Cedar's giddy agitation was simply for the fact that Tom Evans was only playing at courting, whereas Logan had been sincere.

Still, whatever the reason, Cedar was entirely out of harmony with anything resembling composure or serenity. And as the sun sank lower in the western sky—as Friday began to wane—Cedar sat at the kitchen table with her mother—trembling, anxious, and uncertain.

"Settle yourself, darling. You'll make yourself ill," Flora said, reaching across the table to take one of Cedar's hands in her own. "Tom will be here all in good time. No doubt he's had a busy day. Elvira told me Tom's having quite a time with that new Clydesdale he acquired. I guess when the train arrived and the stud was led into town, it near trampled anything in its path."

Cedar knew her mother was just trying to reassure her. The sun was low; supper had been over for nearly an hour. She was beginning to worry that Tom wasn't coming for her—that he truly had changed his mind about pretending to court her. Oh, it wasn't the anticipation of the gossip in town that would spring up over the fact Tom Evans had changed his mind about the Dale girl that bothered her. It was the fact that she'd so looked forward to seeing him—to pretending he found her interesting.

"It seems to me that horses would be harder to breed and maintain than cattle," Flora mused. "I wonder why Tom didn't just keep the ranch going with his own herd when Slater left."

"Tom has always preferred horses, Mama," Cedar answered. "Don't you remember? He was always breaking horses for every rancher and family around when we lived here before. I remember him breaking a horse for old Mr. Owens . . . then refusing to let Mr. Owens pay him. He knew Mr. Owens didn't have much money and needed to be able to sell the horse. He knew Mr. Owens couldn't sell it if it wasn't broken. So Tommy Evans broke it for him . . . for nothing in return. Do you remember that?"

"I do," Flora admitted. The light in Cedar's eyes when she spoke about Tom Evans both delighted and frightened Flora. Tom was a good man, and she was glad Cedar's heart was finally allowing her to let go of the pain caused by Logan's death. However, she worried that Cedar could not endure another heartbreak—and she knew Tom Evans had the power to break Cedar's heart in a far different manner than Logan's death had broken it. Still, she would not let fear overpower the hope she owned that her daughter's greatest chance at true happiness was embodied in Tom Evans.

"So it makes sense that Tom would want to run horses instead of cattle," Cedar continued, "at least to me."

Cedar was silent for a moment then, and Flora knew her thoughts.

"Do you think he'll really come for me, Mama?" Cedar asked. The worry, the hurt, and the fear on her daughter's face nearly brought tears to Flora's eyes.

However, having faith in hope, Flora smiled her most reassuring smile and said, "Of course, sweetheart! While I'm sure he's just—"

The loud knock on the front door caused both Cedar and her mother to startle. Cedar put a hand to her bosom to slow the hammering of her heart.

Flora smiled. "You see, Cedar? How could you ever doubt the word of Tom Evans?"

"It might be someone else," Cedar suggested as her mother rose from her chair. Rising from her own and following her mother toward the front door, she added, "It might be Reno Garrett."

"Oh, don't be ridiculous, Cedar," her mother said—her face pinking up like a rose, however. "What reason would Reno Garrett have for coming out this way on a Friday night?"

Cedar held her breath as her mother peered out through the small window by the front door.

She turned to Cedar, smiling, and whispered, "It's Tom!"

A wave of nervous trepidation washed over Cedar in that moment. All week she'd looked forward to seeing him; all week Tom Evans was all she'd thought about. Now, however, with only a thin wooden door between them, a strange sense of panic rose in her.

"Oh, I can't, Mama!" she breathed. "He's only here to cover for your lie. I can't . . . I can't . . ."

"Of course you can, darling," Flora interrupted. "Now hush."

Before Cedar could draw another breath, her mother opened the door and greeted, "Good evening, Tom. It's so good to see you again. Do come in, won't you?"

"Yes, ma'am," Tom Evans said as he stepped over the threshold and into the house. He was dressed in a freshly, if not badly, pressed white shirt and new blue jeans. As he removed his hat, Cedar noted that his hair was neatly combed. She fancied she almost preferred his hair tousled— the way it looked when he'd just finished raking his hand through it. She wished in that moment that she could bury her own hands in the soft brown of his hair. He replaced his hat as he glanced to her, smiling. He was so thoroughly attractive! His very presence was so affecting that Cedar found herself overwhelmed by his proximity, and she stepped back from him.

"Would you like to take a little ride with me, Miss Dale?" he asked. "I promise yer mama I'll behave myself." He winked at her, adding, "As best I can, anyway."

Cedar watched as her mother placed a tender hand on Tom's forearm.

"Tom . . . you don't have to continue with this charade, you know," she said. "I don't know what got into me. I've never in my life told such a fib, and I can't expect you to—"

"Why, Flora Dale," he interrupted, "are you havin' second thoughts about allowin' me to court yer daughter?"

Flora smiled. "Of course not."

Cedar gasped as Tom took hold of her arm then, pulling her from behind her mother to stand next to him. Even after he'd maneuvered her body to be closer to his, he didn't release her arm—as if he were afraid she'd run away if he did. His firm but gentle grip caused Cedar to relax somewhat. An odd sense of security and comfort enveloped her.

"I'll have her back in before too late, Flora," Tom said as he guided Cedar out through the front door. "I'm just gonna wet her whistle a little."

"You mean *whet* her whistle, I think," Flora corrected teasingly.

But Tom smiled, winked at Cedar, and said, "No, ma'am. I mean wet it . . . as in water her kisser . . . moisten her mouth."

As Cedar's jaw dropped in astonishment, Flora laughed.

"Now, Tom," she playfully scolded. "Cedar's going to think you're serious about sparking with her."

He was teasing—of course he was teasing. Cedar was simultaneously relieved and disappointed.

But Tom Evans chuckled. Stepping out of the house, still gripping Cedar's arm in one strong hand, he took hold of the door latch, smiled at Flora, and said, "But I am serious, Mrs. Dale. Good night."

Closing the door behind them, Tom smiled as he guided Cedar toward his wagon and team waiting nearby.

He chuckled as they walked, and when Cedar inquisitively looked up to him, he said, "Now she's standin' in there wonderin' just what I'm plannin' to do with you tonight."

Cedar swallowed the nervous excitement that had gathered in her throat. "Wh-what are you planning on doing with me?"

"Oh, nothin' too improper," he answered.

Placing his hands at her waist, Tom lifted Cedar up into the wagon and then climbed up after her.

"Uh-oh," he said, frowning as he studied her a moment. "I probably shoulda paused long enough to have you fetch a shawl or a coat or somethin'. It's warm now . . . but it might cool down later."

"I'll be warm enough," Cedar assured him. She wasn't sure she would be, of course, but she didn't want to leave him—not for a moment—not even long enough to run back to the house for a shawl.

"Yes, you will," he said, winking at her. "I'll make sure of that."

Cedar couldn't keep the smile of delight from curving her lips. He was far too flirtatious, of course—too insinuative to be proper—and she adored it!

Settling himself on the wagon seat next to her, Tom took hold of the lines and urged the team forward.

It was all a lie—a terrible, sinful lie! Still, in those first moments Cedar didn't care. She felt as if some lifelong, insatiable desire were being fed—as if she were lost in the pages of some book and had forgotten who she really was. Tom Evans was there, sitting next to her—so close that his arm brushed against hers. His presence was consuming. Even for the soft breeze carrying perfumes of evening to her, she could smell him. Over the fragrance of new spring flowers and rich soil, she breathed the scent of oats and sweet new grass—of leather and smoked ham.

"It's a beautiful evenin', ain't it?" he asked.

Cedar followed his gaze to the west—to where the sun was just beginning to set. The sky was pink and orange and alive with brilliance.

"Yes," she mumbled. "I'm so glad winter is over."

She felt Tom's arm brush hers again and quickly looked to see him shrug his broad shoulders.

"Well, it ain't over yet," he said. "We'll probably have a couple a mighty ornery storms yet before spring sweeps him out this year." He looked to her, frowning. "Maybe I oughta go back so you can fetch a coat."

"I'm fine," Cedar assured him. She didn't want to go back to the house—afraid something would keep her from leaving with him again if she did.

"Well, I got mine in the wagon bed. I guess we could just wrap you up in that if we need to." He looked to her, grinned, and winked. "And I have other methods of keepin' you warm too."

"You're a terrible flirt, Tom Evans," she giggled.

"I ain't flirtin'. I'm serious," he chuckled.

But Cedar shook her head. "I remember how you'd set the girls to blushing with your charming smile and sugar-words." She giggled. "Why, Agnes Hollar nearly fainted that time you kissed her under the mistletoe at the town Christmas social. And you didn't even kiss her on the lips!" Cedar giggled again at the memory. "I'll never forget that . . . the look on Agnes's face when you kissed her cheek. A body would've thought the clouds had parted and heaven had revealed all its secrets. Then she swooned so hard that if her brother hadn't been standing just behind her, she would've hit the floor." She heard Tom chuckle at the memory as well and continued, "I knew you weren't sweet on Agnes Hollar. You had your eye on Olive Allan then, and everybody knew it . . . so I couldn't believe you even kissed Agnes."

Tom shrugged. "Well, we were standin' under the mistletoe together . . . and I didn't want to hurt her pride in front of everybody."

Cedar sighed, giggled once more, and gazed out to the pink horizon.

"Wasn't that the same year your brother was asked to leave the social? Yes! It was the same year somebody did something to the punch and your brother became inebriated and was asked to leave the social." Cedar would never forget that Christmas social of long ago, for she'd watched the Evans brothers kissing the girls under the mistletoe—all the while wishing she were old enough to lure Tom Evans to standing with her under the miraculous plant.

"Actually, Slater wasn't asked to leave. They threw him out," Tom said. "And, yep . . . I believe that was the same year." He looked to her, smiling and frowning at the same time as if he were astounded with her memory. "I can't hardly believe you remember that."

"Oh, I remember it all right," she said.

"But why?" he asked.

"Because I was jealous," she blurted before she could stop herself.

"You were?" he asked, grinning at her.

Cedar shrugged. Blushing, she admitted, "Of course I was. Remember I had calf eyes for you back then." For what else could she have done?

"So you don't have calf eyes for me now?" he teased.

"Where are you driving us anyway?" she asked, desperate to change the venue of their conversation.

Kindly he allowed the subject to change. "Oh, just a little place I like to go when I need to let my mind wander a bit," he answered. "I thought we might just sit and talk awhile before the waltzin' begins."

Cedar smiled. "So there's a place where your mind can wander *and* you can waltz?"

"*Our* minds can wander, and *we* can waltz," he answered. "After all, ain't that what courtin' is? Talkin' and gettin' to know one another and such?"

"Yes," Cedar admitted. "But you're not really courting me."

Tom Evans smiled. "Ain't I?"

Cedar frowned, looking away from Tom and toward the setting sun once more. She wished he wouldn't tease so mercilessly. But then, he had no way of knowing how much her heart longed for his sincere intentions.

Soon Tom pulled the team to a halt in the middle of a small meadow surrounded by a gathering of young trees. Cedar watched with curious interest as Tom climbed over the wagon seat into the back of the wagon.

"Now then," he began as she watched him

spread a worn quilt in the bed of the wagon, "this is how the good Lord meant for folks to watch the day end and the night begin."

"What?" Cedar asked.

Tom held out both arms, gesturing to her that he would help her climb over the wagon seat into the bed of the wagon.

"Come on now," he said when she paused. "Don't go bashful on me yet."

Drawing in a deep breath of courage, Cedar stood and let Tom take her by the waist and lift her into the bed of the wagon.

"There you go," he said. Cedar watched as he then proceeded to lay himself out on the quilt he'd spread. "Ahhh!" he sighed as he stretched out on his back, crossed his ankles, and tucked his hands behind his head. "Now hurry up and get on down here or you'll miss it."

"Miss what?" Cedar asked.

"What we come out here to watch," he answered.

Swallowing the clump of nerves that had lumped in her throat over the impropriety of it all, Cedar did as Tom instructed and lay down next to him in the wagon bed.

"It helps if you breathe out a long sigh," he told her. "Somethin' like this . . . ahhhhh!"

Cedar giggled, delighted by his boyish manner.

"Ahh," she breathed—and she fancied it did make her feel more relaxed.

"Now, the sun's goin' down. It's almost gone, in fact. Then, one by one, the stars will start appearin'," he explained.

Cedar gazed up into the purple of an evening sky. It was a lovely hue—cool and soothing to her senses. Slowly the purple darkened into blue, the blue fading to black as the moon became more visible overhead.

"So you like to watch the stars come out?" she asked.

"Yep," Tom admitted. "I like to study the constellations as they start to show up . . . think about the fact that since the beginning folks have stared up at the same stars . . . that I'm seein' the same stars my daddy saw . . . and his daddy . . . and his."

Cedar looked over to him smiling, for it was a very sweet and sentimental notion.

"Of course, we won't get to watch 'em too long tonight," he added.

"Why not?" she asked, disappointed that she couldn't lie in the wagon bed with Tom Evans forever—gazing up at the stars—feeling the warmth of him so close to her.

He smiled and answered, "You'll see. But we still got a little while to watch 'em before . . ."

"Before what?" Cedar asked, impatient to know what Tom Evans was planning.

But he simply chuckled and said, "I got me a couple of new horses you oughta come out to my place and see sometime. The thoroughbred ain't been too much trouble, but that Clydesdale . . . dang! He about—oh, wait a minute. I almost forgot."

Cedar watched as Tom reached up to the space beneath the wagon seat and withdrew a bunch of daffodils tied together with a pink ribbon.

"I forgot to bring 'em in to you before," he said, handing the bouquet to her. "Now they'll most likely wilt."

"Then I'll press them," she said, rendered nearly breathless by his thoughtful gesture. She realized only then that if Tom Evans was going to pretend to court a girl, then he was going to pretend to the greatest lengths possible. "I love daffodils," she whispered.

"I know," he said. "The autumn before you all moved to the city, yer mama gave my mama a bunch of the bulbs you all planted out there by the creek. They still bloom every spring right out on the east side of our house. Though I guess it's just my house now. Yer mama said she didn't want Cedar's daffodils to be lost. That's why she brought some of 'em out to us. So I figured if you liked 'em then . . . you probably still do."

She almost rolled over and hugged him—nearly kissed him—nearly burst into tears! Whether or not he was pretending to court her, his considerations of her were astounding.

"Thank you," she said, drawing the bouquet of

yellow beauty to her face and inhaling their sweet perfume.

"Yer welcome," he said. She looked to him in time to see his eyes narrow as he gazed up into the sky. "Tell me some more about what yer life was like after yer family moved."

"Sometimes . . . sometimes I don't think I can remember much past . . . well . . . two years ago," she admitted.

"Darlin', if you can remember me kissin' ol' Agnes Hollar at that dang Christmas social . . . surely you can remember other things," he chuckled.

Cedar smiled, giggling, "I suppose you're right."

And he was. For near to an hour, Cedar lay in the wagon bed next to Tom Evans, sharing memories and gazing up into the night sky as, one by one, the stars appeared. She told him of her schooling in St. Louis, of her father's business ventures, and of how she'd missed living on the farm. He shared things with her too—the story of the outlaw that had come gunning for his brother months before and killed one of the Evans's cowboys, his reasons for giving up cattle to concentrate on horses. All the while the stars blinked and flickered overhead like a million tiny candle flames—bright, warm, and comforting.

At last, Tom sat up. "We picked a perfect night for moonlight waltzin'," he said, smiling at her.

"What is this moonlight waltzing you keep going on about?" Cedar asked as she watched Tom stand and then jump down from the wagon. She stood as well, disappointed somehow that their stargazing was at an end.

"Come down here, and I'll show ya," he said, holding his arms out toward her.

Cedar giggled and placed her hands on his broad shoulders, entirely delighted when he took her waist between his own powerful hands. He lifted her down, taking her hand in his and leading her toward a small hill on the west side of the meadow.

Tom chuckled, pleased with Cedar's obvious delight. He'd figured she'd warm up to him—and she had. Still, he knew he must tread carefully. She still believed he was only courting her to save her mother's good name. A part of him worried that maybe she was only allowing him to court her for the same reason. Yet he knew better. He knew he wasn't imagining the way her smile broadened and her eyes lit up when he flirted with her—at least he hoped he wasn't imagining it.

He thought then about how thoroughly she rattled him. Usually he was pretty sure of himself—of his ability to read folks—but Cedar Dale was different. She seemed to be scared to death of him one moment, ready to reach out and hug him the next. He figured it was just her wounded little heart making her so uncertain—

that or his being almost ten years her senior. He wasn't always sure which.

Truth was, the past week had been pretty rough on him. Tom had inwardly struggled with whether he was doing the right thing in pretending to court Cedar Dale. The moment her mother had stepped into the fibber's trap the week before, Tom had seen an opportunity. Somewhere between bumping into Cedar at the general store and the moment she'd smacked him in the face with a shovel, he'd realized he wanted to know her—truly wanted to possess her attention and affection. Flora's deception with Lucas Pratt had simply offered up an easier way to go about getting what he wanted. Part of him—the part he had begun to realize was a twin to his brother— didn't believe he could really win her—thought that she'd be happier with a younger man, some-one who could grow old with her instead of growing old ahead of her. Still, the part of him that was himself—the eternal optimist part— thought there couldn't be any harm in trying.

Cedar Dale was kind, tenderhearted, amusing, and beautiful. Furthermore, she mesmerized him. Oh, she'd pestered him when she was a little girl—pestered him something fierce—but even then he'd found her very entertaining, interesting, and too adorable for her own good. But now— now she sent something racing through him— something that caused his mouth to water every time he thought of her, something that piqued his protective nature, something that set an almost permanent smile to his face.

Therefore, as he'd waited the week out—waited for Friday to arrive and the pretense of courting to begin—Tom Evans had decided to go fishing—to go fishing with himself as bait and see if he could catch Cedar Dale.

Still, as he held her hand, as the anticipation at what was about to happen rose in him, he wondered. If he did manage to hook her, even for a moment, could he keep his desire to possess her—to hold her, kiss her, and have her—could he keep it all measured and cautious? She'd been wounded, terribly and deeply wounded. She wasn't like Amelia Perkins—bossy, confident, batting her eyelashes, and wanting to be in his arms. Cedar's lips had known another man's kiss; her heart wore the scars another man had left there. Tom had to be patient—careful.

But temptation was pressing him. And as Johnny Thornquist's fiddle playing began to float out across the meadow, Tom gave in to it.

Chapter Ten

As Tom stopped, placing one hand at her waist and raising her other in his in waltz position, Cedar frowned—for, incredibly, she could hear music—fiddle music.

"What are doing?" she asked. "And where's the music coming from?"

"Didn't I tell ya we were gonna go waltzin' in the moonlight?" Tom asked. His voice was low, provocative—somehow hypnotically alluring—and the very tone of it caused Cedar's heart to flutter in her bosom.

"Well, y-yes . . . but . . . I truly hear music," she stammered—awed by the fact that the soft, sweet song of a fiddle floated on the night air.

"That's my cousin Johnny. His stepdaddy owns the ranch yonder, and his mama makes him practice his fiddle for an hour every night startin' about now," he explained. "If I promised to take ya waltzin' in the moonlight . . . didn't ya think I'd have music to waltz to?"

Cedar smiled, suddenly overcome with admiration, appreciation—and wild attraction. She fancied he held her more closely than was proper but relished being so near to him. He smelled like smoked ham and potatoes slathered in sweet cream butter. It made her mouth water.

"Well, I didn't really think you meant we were literally going to be waltzing in the moonlight. And for the brief moment when I did think you meant . . . I thought maybe you were just planning on singing or something," she said, feeling breathless and weak as he began to lead her in a waltz.

"Sing?" he chuckled. "I don't know if I can do *that* . . . but I can whistle pretty good."

"I remember," Cedar breathed, remembering how he'd often whistled when riding through town when she was a child—how he'd whistled while fixing the roof the Saturday before.

He continued to smile at her as they waltzed for a moment.

"I do know a few of the words to this song though," he mumbled.

Cedar knew the words too, but she only smiled and asked, "You do?"

"Yep," Tom said.

She held her breath a moment as Tom Evans began to quietly sing along with the wafting fiddle music. *"Oh, I'm floatin' down the Pecos on a moonbeam, dreamin' dreams of comin' back to you . . . where I know that you'll be waitin' at the millstream . . . and I'll drift into your pretty eyes so blue."*

Cedar smiled as he winked at her and continued, *"Oh, a cowboy, he knows where each lonely river flows, and the Pecos roams the desert* to you. *Oh, I'm floatin' down the Pecos on a moonbeam, dreamin' dreams of comin' back to you.*"

"You do know how to sing," she exclaimed in a whisper, delighted by the low, smooth tone of his voice.

"Maybe," he chuckled.

She trembled as he pulled her body flush with his. She could feel his breath in her hair as he continued to sing, *"Oh, I'm floatin' down the Pecos on a moonbeam . . . dreamin' dreams of you, held in my arms . . . when we'll linger, and you'll kiss me by the millstream . . . and corral me with the fencin' of your charms."* He tipped his head to one side as it descended just enough that his mouth hovered over her ear. *"Oh, the old Pecos knows . . . how I miss my Spanish rose . . . so it's floatin' me on moonbeams to you. Oh, I'm floatin' down the Pecos on a moonbeam . . . dreamin' dreams of comin' back to you."*

He chuckled as the fiddle music abruptly stopped—and then began again.

"I guess Johnny's mama figured he could do better," he said.

Cedar giggled—breathed a sigh of delight as Tom continued to dance with her. His arms were so strong, and the feel of his hand at her waist sent a rapturous shiver racing through her. She could feel the muscles of his torso beneath his shirt, for her body was still flush with his.

Tom was grinning at her when she glanced up to him.

"Tell me somethin' else, Cedar Dale," he said.

"About what?" she giggled.

"About you," he urged.

"There isn't much more to tell," Cedar said, wondering if she were imagining Tom Evans was caressing the top of her head with his chin. Yet she could feel his rough whiskers pulling at her hair. Goose bumps rippled over her arms, and her trembling increased.

"Are ya too cold?" he asked.

"Oh, no . . . not at all," she breathed.

"So ya don't have nothin' left to tell me?" he teased. "Come on now. There has to be somethin' else. Maybe instead of tellin' me about yer past, you could tell me what yer hopin' the future brings. You got any dreams yer willin' to share?" he prodded.

Dreams? Of course she had dreams—the same dreams she'd had for nearly her entire life—dreams of Tom Evans! Cedar was utterly baffled by the fact that, in that moment, she couldn't remember having ever dreamt of anything other than him—though she also knew she probably had. Still, she couldn't possibly confess such a thing.

When her silence continued, he said, "Come on, Cedar. Everybody has dreams. For instance . . . I dream of someday havin' the best horses in the state."

Cedar smiled, delighted by the sparkle leaping in his eyes as he talked about his plans.

"Now . . . watch this," he said, slightly changing the steps of their waltz. "This here's called the hesitatin' step. Learned it from my brother's wife."

Cedar giggled, enchanted by his mastery of the dip-step waltz. He was quite the accomplished dancer, and she was surprised, as well as pleased.

"You're very good!" Cedar exclaimed.

"I'm good at a lot of things," he said, winking at her. The brilliance of his smile flashed like starlight.

"I like your teeth," Cedar stated. Instantly, she felt ridiculous for letting such a thought slip from her lips.

"You do?" Tom chuckled. "Well, I don't think anybody's ever told me they like my teeth before."

Cedar blushed, glancing away—nearly overcome with humiliation.

"Though I did once pass by a saloon girl in the street who told me she liked my hind end," he said. "Elvira Gunderson always says she likes my smile . . . but nobody ever said nothin' 'bout my teeth."

"I say the most ridiculous things sometimes," she said. "I always have. I'm glad you don't remember that about me . . . or, at least, didn't. I haven't changed a whit in that regard. I'm taller than I was when we were here before . . . but sometimes I don't think I have any more poise or manners at all."

"It wasn't ridiculous. I liked it," Tom mumbled. "In fact . . . if the truth be told . . . I been spendin' an awful lot of time thinkin' about how much I like the look of yer lips."

Cedar felt her eyes widen as she looked up to him.

"I'm just bein' honest," he assured her. "Why, just the other day I was wonderin' what it might be like if my mouth—the one with the teeth you like—well, I was wonderin', that if my mouth and yer mouth—the one with the purty lips—if my mouth and yer mouth were to up and meet one evenin' out in the moonlight while Johnny Thornquist's fiddle practice was singin' out over the meadow . . ." He slowed their waltz to a smooth halt. "What do ya think that might feel like, Cedar Dale?"

The violent beating of her heart was next to painful! She was certain he could feel its frantic pace against his chest. Her breathing was short and labored, and when she did draw a long gasp, it filled her senses with the comforting scent of his shirt and hair—his skin.

Gazing up into the warm molasses of his eyes, she whispered, "I-I don't know."

He chuckled. He lightly kissed the tip of her nose, whispering, "Well, I think it might put *my* knees to knockin'."

Cedar's realized her own knees had been knocking since the moment Tom had arrived to collect her earlier in the evening. She feared if he kissed her now, her knees would dissolve altogether and send her crumpling to the ground.

"You wanna give it a try and see what happens?" he asked in a low, alluring whisper. "Can I kiss you, Cedar Dale?"

For a moment, she was certain she was dreaming—she had to be! However, when she realized he really had asked if he could kiss her—when she felt his breath on her cheek as he kissed the bridge of her nose—she shivered, and a wave of euphoria washed over her. She was almost painfully nervous—yet why in the world would she ever deny him permission?

Still, as her nervous and confused state caused her to pause, Tom pressed his forehead to hers.

She reached up and began twisting and untwisting a loose strand of her hair around one index finger, and he said, "I'll go slow if ya like, darlin' . . . but are you gonna let me—"

"Yes!" Cedar interrupted in a breathless whisper.

Tom Evans didn't hesitate. Rather he pressed a tender, almost tentative kiss to her trembling lips. As soft as his kiss was, the powerful effect of it— the knowledge that Tom Evans was kissing her— did indeed cause Cedar's knees to weaken. She stumbled backward, bringing their kiss to an end—to a disappointing end—and far too soon. Tom caught her by the shoulders to steady her, however, gathering her into his arms and holding her against him.

"I-I . . . I'm sorry, Tommy," Cedar whispered. "I just . . ."

Tom inhaled a deep, ragged breath to keep himself from giving into his abrupt, over-whelming desire for the girl in his arms. For some reason, her calling him Tommy had sent his mind spinning like a dust devil. His body flamed with a sudden ravenous hunger and thirst—a physical craving for passion that he knew could only be satisfied by having her.

He pulled her more snuggly against him, nearly crushing her body to his as he fought to maintain his good sense. He'd told her he'd go slowly—yet he was fairly trembling with restraining himself.

"I've just always wanted you to . . . ever since I was a little girl I wanted you to . . ." she stammered. "I guess I was just so overwhelmed that I . . ."

He pressed his face into her hair at the top of her head—toyed with a strand of it with his lips—tugged at it with his teeth. He wanted her in a manner that should be inconceivable, considering their brief association. Every muscle in his body was rigid with restraint. He was half afraid that if he kissed her again, he might damage her somehow.

Cedar felt tears welling in her eyes. She'd ruined her only chance—her one chance to share a kiss with Tom Evans. In truth, it was his fault, not hers—for he was too wonderful, too handsome and alluringly provocative for any woman to manage the maintaining of her wits and composure. Still, the moment had been lost, and Cedar was nearly distraught in knowing it.

"And now I've missed my chance . . . haven't I?" she unknowingly whispered aloud.

Again her words sent a flame blazing through his mind and body. She wanted him to kiss her—and he surely wanted to kiss her. He knew he could restrain himself enough to keep from swooping her up into his arms, carrying her back to the wagon, and ravaging her. But he was fairly certain he couldn't keep his kiss sweet and measured the way he feared she needed him to.

"Can I kiss you again . . . the way I want to, Cedar . . . instead of the way I should?" he mumbled into her hair.

"Yes," she breathed.

Tom held his breath for a moment as the sensation of being liberated washed over him. He ended their embrace, taking her lovely face between his hands and pressing a firm kiss to her lips. This kiss, as well as the three that would follow, would be her summons—her rousing indication that she should prepare herself for something the like she'd never known. Tom knew she'd never been kissed the way he was planning on kissing her, but she was a strong little filly—even for her scars—and he suspected she could weather it well.

His kiss was firm—powerful—driven. Cedar closed her eyes as Tom Evans's lips lingered against hers—as his thumbs caressed her chin, her cheeks—as his hands slid from her face to the back of her neck and into her hair. He kissed her in this manner several times—and then—then something changed in him—in her.

As Tom's mouth began to play at coaxing Cedar's now parted lips into meeting the warm, moist rhythm of his kiss, she melted against him, and the strength of his arms enveloped her. In an instant, she was overcome with a desire to accept, consume, and return his heated kiss. She felt her hands fist the fabric of his shirt on either side of his collar, endeavoring to pull him closer to her—though her body was already held tightly against his. As she felt a tear trickle from the outer corner of one eye, she let her hands find his shoulders, then his neck—lose themselves in the soft hair at the back of his head—all the while his kissing growing more and more demanding, her response growing more and more accepting.

Cedar felt alive—thoroughly alive—more alive than she'd felt in so very, very long! It was as if a small seed had been planted in her bosom—a seed that Tom Evans's kiss had caused to suddenly sprout—erupt into a wonderful and renewing vine spreading through her bosom—through her limbs—through her soul! The alluring scent of him filled her lungs, refreshing her senses like a summer rain rejuvenated wilted crops.

Tom's body quivered as he realized Cedar's kiss was meeting his own with equal aggression and desire. Her now eager response caused his breathing to grow labored and heavy. She tasted like every good thing he'd ever eaten—only better! He kept thinking of how very close the wagon was—about how easily he could carry her to it, lay her down in the wagon bed, and . . .

Her hand slipped beneath his shirt at his neck for a moment, sending goose bumps breaking over his body. It was a warning—a signal that passion would consume them both if they continued to linger in such pleasurable activity. Just a few more minutes and he would release her—take her home to her mother where she'd be safe from his weakening self-restraint.

Tommy Evans! Cedar thought as Tom Evans's mouth continued to mingle kisses with her own. She was struck by how perfectly their lips blended—by the way her mouth moved in unison with his as he endeavored to quench her thirst for his kiss. She ignored the hot sting of fresh tears in her eyes—the result of the overwhelming awareness that Tom Evans held her—kissed her.

She reached up, slowly caressing his cheek and jawline with one soft hand. A low moan rumbled in his throat, and he abruptly broke the seal of their lips, pulling her tight against him.

"You really should slap me, Cedar," he mumbled, his breathing quickened and hot in her hair. "I'm sorry. I'm sure ya weren't expectin' me to be so . . . so . . ."

But Cedar had not had her fill of Tom Evans's kisses. Smiling up at him, she raised herself on the tips of her toes, pressing a soft, lingering kiss to his lips.

"I've waited something close to sixteen years to kiss you, Tommy Evans," she whispered. "One more minute won't matter . . . will it?"

Again Tom's mind was spinning. He tried to look away from Cedar's lovely face—tried to find something else to hold his attention. For pity's sake, he'd nearly mauled the girl—still wanted to maul her. He'd finally managed to regain some breath of self-control and restraint, and now she was tempting him further.

For a brief moment, he wondered if she were so accepting of his affections because she liked him—or was she just missing something she'd lost? Was it Tom Evans she wanted, or was she kissing him because she missed her murdered lover?

The excess moisture of desire flooding his mouth fed his craving for hers, however, and when she pressed a second tender kiss to his lips, whispering his name, "Tommy"—well, she broke him like a worn-out gelding.

"No . . . I don't suppose one more minute will do any harm," Tom whispered.

Cedar smiled, still astonished at her own forward and profoundly inappropriate behavior. Still, in those blissful moments she didn't care— for Tom Evans had been right. Her knees were knocking; her blood was boiling! Passion raced through Cedar's mind and body, rapid and searing like a windswept flame. Even in her most cherished dreams of him, his kisses had not compared to the reality of them—and she wanted more. Oh, she hadn't forgotten it was all a farce— that Tom Evans was not truly courting Cedar Dale. Likewise she knew it would end far too quickly. But Cedar would have his kiss for as long as she could.

But one more minute turned into five—then ten—lingered into thirty. As the temperature of an early spring evening cooled—as Johnny Thornquist finished his hour of fiddle practice— the meadow found Tom Evans and Cedar Dale still wrapped in each other's arms.

The tender flesh surrounding Cedar's mouth throbbed with the abrasiveness of Tom's whiskers, but she didn't care. She didn't notice her feet were cold or that her cheeks stung from the evening frost. Thoughts of Tommy Evans being hers—of cooking his meals, of having his children—all these thoughts raced through her passion-mad mind as he kissed her, caressed her—as standing there in the moon- and starlit meadow, she imagined he loved her. Warm, delicious indulgence was what his kiss was, and Cedar marveled at how she could've walked the earth for nineteen years and been so unaware of such a wonder.

It had to end, however—and it did. Tom broke the seal of their lips, holding her away from him as he studied her face—as his thumb caressed the abused flesh around her mouth.

"That, my purty little filly, was not the proper way for me to behave," he said as he winked at her. "And yer mother would drop of apoplexy if she knew what we'd been up to out here."

"I don't care," Cedar whispered. "You asked me what my dreams were, Tommy Evans," she said. She was thrilled with the way his hands went to her waist, drawing her against him as she spoke. "The dream I've had the longest . . . you just made it come true."

"Well . . . I don't know about that," he said. His smile broadened, and Cedar recognized the mischievous twinkle in his eyes. "But I hope it put ol' Agnes Hollar to eatin' her heart out."

Cedar giggled as he took her hand and began leading her back toward the wagon.

"Come on," he said. "Best I get you home

before yer mama thinks I've been up to no good."

Tom knew he was fairly dragging her toward the wagon—but what else could he do? He deserved a good switching. What in the world had he done? He'd laid his whole hand out on the table the very first time he was secluded with the girl, that's what—and he knew she wasn't ready. He wondered again if she were just in such desperate need of male companionship after losing the boy from the city that her need to replace what she had lost simply mingled with her childhood infatuation with Tom Evans to find her so agreeable in his arms. Did she want *him,* or did she just need someone to help her through the remnants of her grief?

He put his hand to his chest for a moment, somewhat disturbed at the condition of his body. His heart was still racing; his arms and legs felt weak. If he was certain of nothing else, he was certain that Cedar Dale had entirely unwound him.

Once he'd helped her up onto the wagon seat to sit beside him, he reached back into the wagon bed to retrieve the quilt they'd laid on while watching the stars. Placing it around her shoulders, his attention lingered on her face a moment, and he frowned—disturbed by the rather sad, melancholy smile she wore.

"Don't worry, Tom," she said. "I haven't forgotten that it's all just to protect Mama's good name."

"What?" he asked. Surely she didn't think he'd just spent an hour sparking with her simply because he was pretending to be her beau.

"I know it's all only make-believe," she explained. "I don't want you to worry that—"

Cedar was silenced as Tom covered her mouth with one strong hand.

"Darlin' . . . the make-believe part of all this ended long before now," he said. Smiling, he asked, "Or were you too busy with somethin' else to notice?"

Cedar's heart soared as he cupped her chin in his hand, pressing a firm kiss to her mouth. With a wink, he gathered the lines, slapping them at the backs of the horses to send the wagon lurching forward.

"Mama?" Cedar called, closing the front door behind her as she entered the house. "I'm home, Mama."

Hurrying into the parlor, she sighed as the warmth of the fire in the hearth warmed her. Nothing in the world would ever warm her the way being in Tom Evans's arms did—the way his kiss did—but the fire in the parlor hearth felt good all the same.

She heard the kitchen door open and close.

"Cedar?" her mother called. "Is that you?"

"I'm in here," Cedar called.

In another moment her mother was there beside

her. Flora reached toward the fire, rubbing her hands together and then drawing them to her face.

"Were you outside?" Cedar asked as she looked to see her mother shivering the same way she was.

"Mm-hmm," Flora answered. She looked to Cedar, smiling. Cedar felt her own eyes narrow—for her mother's cheeks were quite rosy from the cold, and she wondered why she'd been out in it.

Before she could inquire of her mother, however, Flora asked, "Well? Did you have fun?"

"More than you can possibly imagine," Cedar sighed.

"Oh, I can possibly imagine . . . I promise you that," Flora giggled. She reached up and placed the back of one loving hand to Cedar's cheek. "And he kissed you, I see."

Cedar blushed—couldn't help but smile.

"Yes . . . though I don't know how you could possibly see that," she giggled.

"Oh, I was young once too, sweetheart," Flora said, smiling. "I'm not blind to the evidence of a man's affections."

Cedar thought there was a long-absent shimmering to her mother's blue eyes—something she hadn't seen there for a very long time.

"I was a bit worried though. You didn't take a shawl or a coat or anything," Flora said. She giggled, adding, "Though I'm sure that little devil

Tom Evans found some way to keep you warm."

"Mother!" Cedar exclaimed as her blush intensified.

"Oh, quit scolding, and tell me all about it," Flora giggled. "Was it wonderful?"

"Oh, Mama . . . I never dreamed of such a wonderful evening!"

As Cedar began to tell her about Tom Evans—about how he drove them to a meadow, about watching the stars appear from the bed of the wagon—Flora Dale tucked a loose strand of hair behind one ear. Her own delight was still fluttering inside her, but she wouldn't reveal it—not to Cedar or anyone else.

Only moments after Tom had collected Cedar for the evening, Reno Garrett had appeared on the front porch. He'd told her that he simply wanted to make certain she and Cedar hadn't seen any other animals behaving suspiciously—that nothing had been displaying symptoms of rabies. Of course, his conscience got the better of him later, and he admitted to knowing Tom was going to spend the evening with Cedar—admitted knowing Flora would be alone. All this he'd revealed as they'd sat for hours out on the back porch talking—simply conversing—sharing stories of their individual life experiences, laughing, and speculating about the future.

Reno hadn't kissed her the way Tom had

kissed Cedar—of course he hadn't. He hadn't kissed her at all, though she'd secretly wished he would. But Reno and Flora were just two neighbors sharing a friendly visit—or so Flora tried to convince herself. Still, as her heart swelled with hope and joy for her daughter's obvious delight, she couldn't keep the visions of Reno Garrett from lingering in her mind's eye— couldn't keep the goose bumps from springing up along her arms whenever she thought of the way his leg or arm often brushed hers as they sat on the top step of the back porch in conversation.

"Then I heard fiddle music . . . just floating out over the cool night air," Cedar said. "And we began to waltz . . . right there in the meadow . . . with the stars twinkling overhead and Johnny Thornquist playing 'I'm Floating Down the Pecos' on his fiddle."

Flora smiled. Tom Evans—the little devil was too charming for his own good!

As the parlor fire warmed her—at the knowledge that her daughter's heart might soon be healed and in good hands—Flora sighed. Tragedy had wounded them both, she and Cedar. But they'd weathered it; they hadn't been entirely destroyed by it. They'd endured, survived, and kept living. And now it looked as if Cedar were about to reap the blessings of survival: newfound hope and love.

"Fancy meetin' you out this way at such a time of the night," Tom said as Reno Garrett's horse fell into a slow walk beside the wagon. "You ain't been peepin' through Mrs. Dale's windows now, have ya, Reno?"

Reno chuckled. "Nope," he said. "I did get up on the back porch . . . though keep in mind I didn't try to go in no further. I figured the back porch was a good enough place to start."

Tom smiled. "What did ya use as yer excuse for bein' out her way?" he asked.

"Rabies," Reno answered, a sly smile causing the wrinkles at the corners of his eyes to grin. "I figured I'd best make sure them Dale women hadn't seen any more infected animals out their way."

"That's wise," Tom mumbled. "I shoulda thought of that one."

"Oh, I'm sure you got yer own ways about ya, Tom Evans," Reno said. "I've heard plenty about how charmin' you are."

"From who?"

"From all them lovesick women in town," Reno told him. "I figure you didn't show up at the Dales' house tonight without a plan for winnin' that purty girl over."

Tom smiled, trying not to be too pleased with himself for his clever idea of waltzing in the moonlight to Johnny's fiddle practice.

"Maybe I did," he admitted. He looked to Reno, his knowing smile broadening. "But which road are you takin' where Flora is concerned?"

"The straight and steady, boy . . . the straight and steady," Reno chuckled.

Tom laughed, though he was suddenly very grateful that Reno Garrett had set his eye on Flora Dale instead of Cedar. Reno Garrett would've put up a sight more worrisome competition than poor Lucas Pratt had.

Goose bumps raced over Tom's arms as he thought of the warm, sweet flavor of Cedar's kiss. He about turned the team around to head back to the Dale place, but he knew that wouldn't do. He needed to get home and recover his patience—and his self-control. Straight and steady—that's the way Reno was going about things where Flora was concerned, and Tom knew the same would be what Cedar needed—patient, steady encouragement and reassurance.

"Uncle Tom! Uncle Tom!"

The team startled as Tom's young cousin Johnny Thornquist came riding up from the right.

"Whoa, Dolly! Coaly, hold on there. Whoa . . . whoa," Tom said, pulling the lines tight to halt the team of Clydesdales.

"Johnny! For cryin' in the bucket! You 'bout stopped my heart, boy!" Tom scolded as the boy reined in beside Reno.

"Uncle Tom! Someone's spookin' the cattle out

at our place! Eldon . . . I mean . . . Daddy thinks it's rustlers!"

Tom frowned. He'd heard tell of a band of rustlers up near Limon, but everyone had been hoping they'd move north.

"You think you can handle the team?" Tom asked the boy.

"The Clydes?" the boy gulped.

"You'll be fine, Johnny," Tom said, standing and offering the lines to Johnny. "Let me take yer horse so Reno and I can ride out to yer place and help Eldon." He paused for a moment, remembering the last time Johnny had tried to help in a dangerous situation. "I know that you know that what you can do to help most is to get this team home and let my boys, Pete and Ray, know what's goin' on. Have them ride over to Reno's place and fetch Hadley too. Then you stay put and keep an ear out to make sure nobody comes after my new thoroughbred. You know where the rifles in the house are. All right?"

Tom understood the boy needed to feel helpful—useful and heroic. He hoped what he was asking him to do was enough to keep Johnny safe as well as round up more help.

"Yes, sir," Johnny said, dismounting his horse and handing the reins to Tom.

Tom mounted Johnny's horse as Reno nodded to him.

"Get that team home easy as you can, Johnny . . .

but send the boys over to us as soon as you do," he instructed.

"Yes, sir," Johnny said.

Tom didn't pause any longer but spurred his horse into a gallop alongside Reno's.

"Them damn cattle rustlers," Reno shouted.

Tom ground his teeth and rode hard for Eldon's place, hoping Johnny got back to the ranch fast enough to send the rest of the cowboys out to help. A vision of Cedar flashed into his mind, sending a wave of fear traveling through him. Would she be safe? Yet rustlers wouldn't have any interest in a small farm with no stock—would they? Secretly he was suddenly and sinfully relieved it was Eldon's herd the rustlers were after—for Eldon's herd was nowhere near Cedar Dale.

Chapter Eleven

"That's what Katherine Pickering told me not an hour ago, Flora," Elvira Gunderson said. Dramatically placing a hand to her ample bosom, she added, "Rustlers! Can you imagine it?" Elvira shook her head and exhaled a long, compassionate sigh, adding, "Those poor children of Katherine's . . . and Katherine herself . . . they've all been through so much this past year."

"But everyone's fine . . . aren't they, Elvira?" Flora asked.

"Everyone's fine . . . though Katherine said a bullet grazed Tom Evans's left leg." Instantly, Mrs. Gunderson stretched out a hand, placing it reassuringly on Cedar's arm. "He's just fine though, honey. Don't you worry. Them Evans boys are made of stronger stuff than most men."

"I-I know," Cedar stammered, though her heart hammered with fear and anxiety. She wanted to bolt from the general store—run all the way to the Evans ranch to make certain Tom really was all right.

"And Reno Garrett?" Flora asked.

"Oh, he's fine too," Elvira said. "He was in here this mornin' after some witch hazel for a mighty ugly black eye. But he was fine otherwise."

"Cattle rustlers," Cedar breathed. "Does the sheriff think they'll come back?"

"No . . . at least not for a long while," Mrs. Gunderson sighed. "Anyway, two of 'em are in jail, and a couple of cowboys are plantin' two more out in the boneyard."

Cedar looked to her mother, wincing with worry as her mother shook her head, indicating her own concern.

"The important thing is everybody's fine . . . and them rustlers didn't get away with Eldon Pickering's herd," Elvira said. "Still, it makes me glad I live in town. I wish yer house was a bit closer, Flora."

"I'm sure we're close enough to be safe from cattle rustlers," Flora said, placing a comforting hand on Cedar's arm.

"And anyway, you got Tom Evans lookin' out for ya," Elvira said. She smiled—a broad smile of suspicion mingled with understanding.

"Well, good mornin', ladies!"

Cedar turned to see Tom striding into the general store. Instantly, her heart leapt, goose bumps breaking over her arms, and she sighed—relieved to see he appeared truly unharmed—delighted by his mere appearance in the same room.

"Well, good mornin' there, Tom," Mrs. Gunderson greeted. "I hear there was a little too much excitement in your life last night."

Cedar blushed an even deeper shade of scarlet as Tom looked to her, grinning and with one eyebrow raised.

"Well, I don't think it was too much excitement," he chuckled. "Do you, Miss Cedar?"

A puzzled frown puckered Mrs. Gunderson's brow as she looked to Cedar.

"I thought you all didn't know about the rustlers," she said.

"Oh!" Tom exclaimed. "You meant there was a little too much excitement over them rustlers. I misunderstood ya there for a minute, Elvira."

Flora giggled, and Cedar quietly scolded, "Mother!"

"Yep, I coulda done without them rustlers," Tom sighed. He looked to Elvira Gunderson, adding, "Ol' Eldon lost a couple of head in all the ruckus . . . but that ain't too bad considerin' what could've happened."

"Mrs. Gunderson said you were wounded," Cedar prodded.

"Wounded?" Tom asked, his handsome brow puckered with bewilderment.

"Katherine Thornquist said a bullet grazed yer leg," Mrs. Gunderson offered.

"Oh, that," Tom said, leaning on the counter and smiling as his eyes traveled over Cedar. "Well, that ain't no wound, baby," he said to her. "I've gotten hurt worse just slicin' into apples."

He winked at her, and Cedar smiled, greatly

comforted. After all, he didn't appear to be in pain. In fact, his eyes were as bright and as full of mischief as ever.

"And . . . and Reno Garrett's all right as well?" Flora asked.

"Yes, ma'am," Tom said, nodding to Flora. "That man's tougher than old moose leather."

Cedar saw her mother visibly sigh with relief. Flora Dale liked Reno Garrett, and Cedar was glad.

"Did Cedar tell ya what a nice evenin' me and her had last night, Elvira?" Tom asked. "Before the cattle rustlers caused all that trouble, of course."

Mrs. Gunderson smiled. Her eyes began to dance with amusement.

"Why, no, she didn't, Tom," she said. "Do tell."

"Yep," Tom began, "me and Cedar had us a real nice evenin' last night. Didn't we?"

Cedar look up at him, blushing radish-red as she nodded. He winked at her, coaxing a delighted smile to her lips.

"Did ya now?" Mrs. Gunderson prodded.

"We did indeed," Tom affirmed. "We went waltzin' out there in that meadow, near Eldon Pickering's place." Tom shook his head. "Guess we were too distracted with our own business to hear them rustlers comin'."

"Did ya get any sparkin' done?" Mrs. Gunderson asked.

"Elvira Gunderson!" Flora exclaimed. "Shame on you."

Tom chuckled. "I can't hardly believe you'd think I'd be such a tomcat only a week into courtin', Elvira." He paused, winked at the old woman, lowered his voice, and added, "And besides, you can't expect me to discuss such matters with the girl's mother standin' right here next to me, now can ya?"

Cedar smiled when her mother winked at her and said, "I think I'll just meander on down to Mrs. Jenkins's shop and see if she's still got that pretty lavender dress in the window." Looking to Tom, she added, "Would you mind seeing that Cedar gets home all right, Tom?"

"Of course not, Flora," Tom said. "It'll be my pleasure."

"I'm sure it will be," Flora giggled. Sighing, she tossed a wave to Elvira Gunderson. "I'll see you in a few days, Elvira." She paused, looking to Cedar a moment and adding, "And I'll see you at home before supper, won't I?"

"Supper?" Cedar asked. "It's not even noon, Mama."

"Now, honey . . . when your own mother gives you permission to stay out with your young man 'til supper time . . . you don't argue it," Mrs. Gunderson whispered as Flora winked at her daughter and left the store.

Cedar blushed as Tom nodded and mumbled, "Damn right."

"Tom Evans!" Mrs. Gunderson scolded. "We're ladies and gentlemen in here!"

"My apologies, Elvira," he chuckled. Grinning at Cedar, he added, "And to you too, darlin'."

Cedar smiled, lost in the brown confection of his smoldering gaze. Her entire body warmed— just for the sake of being near him.

"Now that yer mama's gone, Cedar," Elvira began, "let Tom tell me about yer evenin' together."

"Well, good mornin', all."

At the sound of Lucas Pratt's voice, Cedar's delight was somewhat squelched.

"You all seem to be havin' a good chat," he said.

Tom turned to face the young man, but Cedar paused. She felt self-conscious, fearful that Lucas would somehow see through her mother's lie—even if Tom had implied he truly meant to court her now. Still, not wanting to appear ill-mannered, she turned, offering a kind smile.

"Good mornin', Lucas," Tom greeted.

Cedar glanced up to Tom. He didn't appear to be anything but friendly toward the young man.

"And how are ol' Tom and little Miss Cedar doin'?" Lucas asked, glancing around the room as if searching for something. "Did ya have Mrs.

Gunderson order ya in one of the new wheelie chairs, Tom?"

Cedar's jaw dropped, her mouth hanging agape for a moment. She was astonished at Lucas Pratt's obvious resentment toward Tom.

But Tom merely grinned. "I think this boy's got a burr under his saddle, Elvira. Don't you?" he asked.

"Sure sounds like it," Mrs. Gunderson agreed with a nod.

Cedar was dreadfully uncomfortable. Altercations between men had always unsettled and frightened her. But ever since her father and Logan were killed—they terrified her.

"Ain't got no burr under my saddle, Tom," Lucas said, smiling. "I just know yer gettin' on in years, and bein' the good neighbor that I am . . . I worry about yer well-bein'."

Tom's eyes narrowed, though his smile remained. "I think you need a good lickin', boy," he chuckled. "Maybe I oughta turn ya over my knee and give it to ya."

"Ah, Tom," Lucas began, "crippled ol' cowhands like you oughta stick to things they can handle . . . applesauce, rockin' chairs, and the like."

"Don't go tryin' to hide yer envy so hard, boy. It ain't healthy," Tom countered.

Lucas glared at Tom for a long moment. His eyes narrowed, and Cedar could see his jaw was tightly clenched.

"She'll come around, Evans," Lucas growled. "You'll see."

Tom exhaled an impatient sigh, shook his head, and said, "Well, 'she' is named Cedar." Leaning toward Lucas and lowering his voice, he added, "And she's made her choice."

"Only 'cause you got to her mama first," Lucas said. "Come to think of it, I can't see why yer not courtin' Flora Dale instead of Cedar. She's closer to yer age, ain't she?"

"You'd better back it down a step, boy," Tom growled. "I only got so much patience with unruly pups."

Cedar was trembling, awash with anxiety. She was thankful when Mrs. Gunderson lifted the door on the counter and made her way to standing between the two men.

"Now you boys stop this nonsense. Do you hear me?" Mrs. Gunderson scolded. Glaring at Lucas but speaking to Cedar, she said, "Now, Cedar . . . you and Tom go on about your day. Go on and get to sparkin' or whatever yer plannin' on doin'." She took hold of Lucas's arm and, with the scolding demeanor a schoolmistress might offer a disruptive child, said, "And, Lucas . . . you cool that temper and let me know what I can get for ya here in the general store. All righty?"

Desperate for escape, Cedar took hold of Tom's hand and began tugging his arm to urge him toward the door.

"Come on, Mr. Evans," she said. "You told Mama you'd see me home."

Tom and Lucas remained firm in their glaring at one another, however—like two angry wolves ready for a fight.

"She can't call ya nothin' but 'Mr. Evans'?" Lucas said, endeavoring to provoke Tom.

"Oh, she calls me plenty more endearin' things when we're alone, boy," Tom growled.

Cedar could see Tom's patience was spent. Furthermore, she knew if Tom and Lucas decided to start throwing fists, Lucas wouldn't get two raised before Tom laid him out on the general store's floor. She thought of Logan and her father and tugged with more pleading force on Tom's hand.

"You go on with yer girl, Tom," Mrs. Gunderson said. "I don't need Lucas bleedin' out on my nice clean floor."

Tom nodded to Lucas as if to say, *See there? Elvira knows I'd wipe the room with you.*

"Please, Tom," Cedar said. "Let's just go."

Finally, Tom turned, looking down into Cedar's face. His anger seemed to begin diluting, and he smiled at her.

"All right then, sugar," he said, lacing his fingers with hers. "Let's you and me take a little stroll."

Once they were out of the general store, Cedar exhaled the anxious breath she'd been holding.

Having obviously sensed her discomfort, Tom said, "I'm sorry, baby. He just got my dander up. It ain't like I don't know I'm old."

Cedar glanced up to him, frowning, puzzled by his remark.

"You're not old," Cedar said. His hand was strong and warm as it held hers, and she glanced down, delighted by the fact he hadn't released her. "You're just a man . . . and he's a—"

"He's a little pile of . . . he's an unruly little pup," Tom finished. He frowned for a moment then. "Do you think I'm too old for ya, Cedar?" he asked.

Cedar could tell by the deep pucker in his brow he was truly concerned.

"Goodness no!" she exclaimed. However, suddenly suspicious of what thoughts had prompted his question, she asked, "Do you think I'm too young for you?"

His smile returned, and it warmed her heart.

"Probably," he chuckled as Cedar frowned. "But I'm too selfish to care."

Cedar bit her lower lip to try and hide her delight in his confession.

"Come on," he said, turning down the alley between two buildings. "Let's get outta town and find us some privacy."

He led her away from the main buildings. They walked—hand in hand they walked—toward the little schoolhouse not too far from town. It being

Saturday, the place was deserted. At the back side of the schoolhouse sat several benches—seats for the children during warmer days when outside was a better venue for learning.

"Wanna sit a spell?" he asked, nodding to one of the benches.

"Of course," she chimed. Cedar was blissful in his company. In fact, she wondered what had transpired to find her so at ease in that moment. In truth, though they'd spent some time sharing conversation the day he'd come to till the garden and fix the roof, though they'd shared more conversation the night before as they lay in the wagon gazing up at the stars, she really couldn't believe she knew him well enough to feel so comfortable with him. Yet there was the time they'd spent standing in the moonlight waltzing—then kissing. If she was comfortable enough to kiss him the night before, then why shouldn't she be comfortable enough to sit with him on an old bench out behind the schoolhouse?

She wondered if he truly found her interesting. Whatever could he possibly see in her? Yet she sensed in him a protective nature, a deep sincerity, even for the sake of all his teasing and flirtations. On the other hand, she well knew what she found interesting in Tom Evans—everything!

For years she'd wondered about him; for all the years she'd been away, she had wondered. Often she'd worried over his well-being, though she always had to explain to herself that she may never know what became of him. She'd often wondered whether he'd married and whom. She'd never let her mind nest on those thoughts for any length of time at all, for they disturbed her too deeply. Still, through the ten years her family had lived away in St. Louis, she'd always wondered what had become of the handsome man she'd loved as a child.

Her thoughts prompted her to speak before thinking. "Why didn't you ever get married?" Cedar heard herself ask. She was immediately embarrassed—but knew the question couldn't be retracted.

"Well, don't drag yer feet, girl," Tom said, grinning. "Come right on out and ask me anything."

Cedar looked away for a moment, but then her curiosity got the better of her patience, and she prodded, "Well? Why didn't you?" She smiled, teasingly adding, "I'm sure Agnes Hollar would've been happy to oblige."

He laughed, nodding with agreement. "More'n likely."

"So? Why aren't you married?"

Cedar recognized the mischief gleaming in his eyes. Winking at her, he answered, "I was waitin' on you to grow up."

Cedar giggled, shaking her head, delighted by

his flirting. Rolling her eyes with exasperation, she said, "Don't tease me. Tell me the truth."

Tom inhaled a deep breath, and she watched his broad chest rise with it. He removed his hat, setting it on one knee and running his fingers back through his hair. Cedar watched him—all the while enraptured by how blissful it was to be sitting next to him.

"The truth is . . . I just never found any woman I liked hard enough," he said. "That, and the fact me and Slater was busy workin' ourselves into an early grave." He paused for a moment, cocking his head to one side as he seemed to reconsider his response. "Now that I think about it though, Slater was the one always workin' us so hard. Times were when I wanted to just run off and take me a nice nap in the summer sunshine. But Slater always had a list as long as his arm of things needin' doin'."

Cedar smiled. Oh, it was well she remembered Tom's older brother, Slater. "I was always afraid of your brother," Cedar admitted.

"Afraid? Of Slater?" Tom chuckled. "Why's that?" He shrugged, adding, "I mean . . . most folks is afraid of him . . . grown-ups, anyway . . . but not usually children. And you were awful young when you was here."

Cedar shrugged as well. "I think it was that grouchy old frown he always wore." She studied Tom a moment—marveled at his handsome face and pleasant countenance. "But you . . . you were always smiling."

"That's 'cause I was always up to no good," Tom chuckled.

She giggled. "Like what?"

He reached out, tweaking her nose just the way he had when she'd been a child. "Like helpin' little girls steal licorice whips from the general store," he said with a wink.

Cedar's eyes widened, her mouth dropping open. She'd nearly forgotten!

"I'd almost forgotten about that!" she laughed.

"Well, *I* remember," he assured her. "I told you it'd be all right for you to take one of them licorice whips . . . 'cause you was the purtiest little filly in town. A couple a days later, you were sittin' on the steps of the general store lookin' as sour as a lemon drop, thinkin' you were an outlaw."

Cedar laughed. "And then you told me you had paid Mr. Gunderson for it because I *was* the prettiest little filly in town." She sighed and looked at him. "You were always so nice to me."

Tom smiled at her. "That's because you really were the purtiest little filly in town," he said.

"And why are you so nice to me now?"

"'Cause yer still the purtiest little filly in town."

Cedar smiled, whispering, "Well, you're the—"

"Best kisser?" Tom interrupted.

Cedar's giggled, "No!"

"I'm not?" Tom teased.

"No . . . I mean, yes. I mean . . . I meant to say you're still the best man I've ever known," she stammered.

"The best man but not the best kisser?" he laughed.

"You're the best man *and* the best at . . . and you're the best at . . ." Cedar stumbled over her words, too embarrassed to admit to him that she loved the way he'd kissed her the night before—that she'd dreamt of it—that even in that moment she longed for him to kiss her again.

"Fixin' roofs? Tillin' up soil for gardens?" he teased.

"All that too," Cedar said, blushing to her toes.

"And?" he prodded.

Cedar drew in a deep breath, forcing herself to bravery. "And you're the best kisser." Her eyes widened as she realized exactly how misunderstood her words could be. "Not that I've had a whole lot of experience, mind you."

She was relieved when he didn't attempt to tease her about the matter any further. He simply smiled and rubbed at the whiskers on his chin for a moment.

"I can grow a nice full beard too," he said. "Little fellers like that Lucas Pratt . . . they can't get much past peach hairs."

Cedar giggled, and Tom smiled at her, obviously pleased to have amused her.

"Do ya think I'll make a good lover?" he asked next.

Cedar glanced away, still tentative over what appeared to be happening between them.

"I'm not sure I know what you mean," she mumbled. Her thoughts were drawn to Logan and the sadness that would ever linger in her scarred heart.

"Maybe I need to put it more gentle to you," he said. "Do you think I'll make a good *beau?*"

She smiled at him, amused at how awkward the word sounded coming from his mouth.

"Beau?" she giggled. "For some reason, I can't see you as anybody's beau."

He grinned, the impish expression of mischief she adored owning his countenance. "You see? That's why I asked you the way I did the first time. Do you think I'll make a good lover?"

"Thomas Evans!" she scolded, though she was wildly delighted in that moment. "I swear . . . the things that come out of your mouth sometimes. You'd put even Elvira Gunderson to blushing over that one."

"You still haven't answered my question," he mumbled, leaning toward her and brushing her cheek with the tip of his nose. "I know yer still afraid I'm playin' at all this for the sake of yer mother's reputation . . . but I ain't. How can I prove that to you, darlin'? I thought last night mighta give you an idea that I ain't playin'. If you

258

want playin' . . . then I'm sure Lucas Pratt's yer man. After all, his daddy does own the drama house in town." He took her chin in one hand, forcing her to look at him. "But I ain't playin'. All right?"

"Do you really . . . are you sincerely fond of me?" Cedar asked, breathless and trembling with anticipation.

Tom chuckled and brushed the hair from her forehead with the back of one hand.

"Oh, yes, Miss Cedar Dale," he whispered, his head descending toward hers. "Indeed I am."

His kiss was soft at first—warm and teasing. He pressed tender, playful kisses to her lips—then her cheek. He brushed the loose hairs from her neck—pushed the fabric of her collar down with one thumb as he trailed moist kisses from her ear to nearly her shoulder. Every inch of flesh on Cedar's body broke into goose bumps, and she couldn't keep her hand from caressing his neck— being lost in the hair at the back of his head.

"I-I shouldn't be kissing you this way," she whispered.

"You shouldn't be *lettin'* me kiss you this way," he whispered against her mouth a moment before gathering her in his arms.

He'd determined he wouldn't nearly ravage her the way he had the night before—at least not at first. Tom wanted Cedar to know there was something in him besides wanton fervor; he owned a gentle, teasing manner as well. He could savor the soft press of her lips to his as much as he could relish the warm moisture of her mouth. Well, maybe not quite as much, but it was different after all—flirtatious as opposed to passionate—and both were enjoyable where Cedar Dale was concerned.

Still, his resolve to remain composed, to kiss her sweetly, rather innocently the way he'd planned to, was more difficult than he'd thought it would be. She was like ambrosia to him, and his mouth began to water with his ravenous craving to deepen their kiss.

He exhaled a breath of restraint when she took his face between her small hands and whispered, "You're being careful with me."

Tom grinned. "Maybe," he admitted.

The truth of it was all the more endearing— that he would kiss her sweetly—for the sake of what? Of proving he could? Because he didn't think she wanted him to kiss her the way he had the night before?

"Why?" Cedar asked.

"Maybe I'm just bein' a gentleman," he mumbled, placing a soft kiss to the bridge of her nose.

"Or maybe you're worried someone will happen by and my reputation will be tarnished," she suggested.

He chuckled. "Tarnished? Darlin', if someone

happens by, yer reputation would be hell and gone from bein' merely tarnished."

She smiled, but her insecurities wouldn't allow her to giggle.

She dropped her hands from his face—though she didn't want to give up caressing him.

"Maybe you're changing your mind about me, and don't want to . . ."

She was silenced, however, by the fact that Tom Evans simply stood up, taking hold of her arm and pulling her up from the bench.

Before Cedar had even had a moment to catch her breath, she found herself pressed back up against the schoolhouse's back door. As Tom's hands at her waist held her firmly against the schoolhouse door, his face was so close she could feel the warmth of his breath on her lips.

"I was gonna try and be a gentleman, Cedar Dale," he mumbled. "But yer just too damn delicious for your own good."

Cedar gasped as his mouth crushed to hers then. The playful kisses he'd been administering before were abandoned for more driven, impassioned affections—and Cedar was swept away to blissful oblivion.

After several euphoric minutes, however, Tom stepped back, releasing Cedar and shaking his head in disbelief.

"What is it?" she asked—uncomfortably aware of how dangerous it was for them to risk a kiss when townsfolk were milling around so close by.

"Yer gonna think there ain't nothin' to me but some fourteen-year-old kid who can't get enough sparkin'," he said, smiling at her.

Cedar felt her eyes widen with astonishment. "You went sparking when you were fourteen?"

"Well . . . well, not like this, exactly," he stammered. She fancied for a moment that he was actually blushing a little. "But I stole a kiss here and there same as the next fella."

"Tell me," she said, stepping off the threshold. "Tell me about when you were fourteen, Tommy Evans . . . only leave out the part where you went sparking."

She was surprised when he actually stepped back from her.

"All right, I will," he said. Wagging an index finger at her, however, he added, "But you need to leave off callin' me Tommy for a few minutes. Otherwise you might end up pinned back against that door 'til suppertime."

"Very well," she giggled, walking to him—standing directly in front of him. "I told you all about myself last night. Now it's your turn."

"I told you plenty last night too," he countered.

"But you obviously left out a great deal," she said. Playfully frowning, she said, "Fourteen? Why, that's just plain scandalous."

He grinned. "Step back up in that doorway there,

262

and I'll show ya somethin' scandalous, honey."

Cedar giggled and reached out, taking hold of his hand.

"You just tell me about the year you were fourteen," she said. "That sounds to be scandalous enough."

"All right," he agreed. "Sit back down on that bench with me, and I'll tell you some tales . . . but you gotta promise not to run off screamin' into the hills."

"I promise," Cedar said.

She watched him pick his hat up off the ground—adored the way he rather plopped it onto his head, adjusting it with one hand as he sat down next to her on the bench.

"Now, let's see . . . where should I begin? The year I was fourteen . . . fourteen," he mumbled. He was thoughtful for a moment. Then, as his eyes began to sparkle with amusement, he began, "Well, there was the time me and Slater was out swimmin' neked in the crick after brandin' some new calves . . . when who should wander by . . . but Mrs. MaryAnn Watson, the preacher's wife, and all five of her lovely daughters."

Simultaneously gasping and giggling, Cedar scolded, "Tom Evans!"

Tom chuckled, leaned back against the bench, looked at her with smiling eyes, and asked, "Do you wanna hear about the year I was fourteen or not?"

Cedar smiled. Fighting the nearly overwhelming desire to throw herself against him and beg him to kiss her, she nodded. "I do."

Tom winked at her. "Then sit back and listen a spell, sugar . . . 'cause the year I was fourteen? Well, it was somethin' to behold."

Flora sighed as she rather ambled down the road toward the house. It was in sight now, and she studied it a moment, thinking how desperately it needed some fresh paint. The house needed a lot of things—things she and Cedar would have to address soon. She smiled as mingled feelings of joy and melancholy washed over her. It could be that she would soon be addressing things by herself. She was certain Cedar would soon own Tom Evans's heart every bit as wholly as he owned hers. With any luck, there'd be a wedding in town soon—and Cedar would be happy. Yet the knowledge that Cedar would one day leave Flora's company to begin her new life—to start her own family—was something Flora had faced before. She silently scolded herself for thinking it would be easier to give Cedar over to Tom Evans than it had been to think of giving her over to Logan Davies. Logan was a wonderful young man—good, strong, and loving. But Tom Evans was more. Still, when Cedar had been engaged to Logan, Flora had had Jim at her side. She wouldn't have been left all alone when Cedar was gone then—the way she would be now.

Still, she forced a smile, inhaled a deep breath of fresh spring air, and determined that she would bathe in her daughter's happiness. She'd had hers—lived a carefree happy childhood, met the young man of her dreams at an early age, been blessed with many, many years of his loving company and their beautiful daughter. It was Cedar's time now—Cedar's time to love and live. And after all, Tom Evans's ranch wasn't so very far away. No doubt they'd come for Sunday supper once in a while; no doubt she'd still see her daughter several times a week. All would be well—lonesome, perhaps—but well. As long as her daughter was happy, then so would Flora be.

Flora stopped dead in her tracks as she started around to the back door of the house to see Reno Garrett. He was leaning against the outer wall near the rain barrel, his hands shoved in his pockets—looking exactly as if he'd been waiting for her to return.

"Mr. Garrett?" Flora asked. "Is everything all right?" She found her heart was hammering with brutal force inside her chest, not only for the sake of her nearly violent attraction to him but also for the fact that his face was so battered. His left eye was blackened, deep purple and swollen nearly completely shut; a large cut, looking far too fresh and tender, ran parallel to his left brow. His left cheek was swollen and bruised as well, and Flora was instantly irritated with Elvira Gunderson for not telling her of the severity of the reason for Reno's needing the witch hazel.

He hadn't responded to her or even greeted her, but she didn't care. Instantly, she went to him—reached up, allowing her fingertips to press the bruise at his cheek.

"Elvira Gunderson said you were fine!" she exclaimed. "But her thinking of what fine is . . . differs vastly from mine."

He still said nothing, only continued to stare at her—almost glare at her—the piercing blue of his eyes causing her to tremble just a little.

"You come on into the house, and I'll tend to that properly," she said, stepping up onto the porch to open the door. "I cannot believe Elvira . . ."

Flora gasped as Reno Garrett took hold of her arm, spinning her around to face him again. Standing two steps above him, Flora found his eyes were now level with her own. She recognized the expression on his face—not because she'd necessarily seen it there before but because she was a woman of thirty-six and had seen similar expressions on the faces of plenty of other men—including Jim's. Reno Garrett's expression radiated pure, driven desire!

"I guess you heard that some of us went 'round a bit with a gang of cattle thieves last night," he began.

"Y-yes," Flora stammered. Her heart was in her throat! She was certain it was!

"It's times like that when a man ends up thinkin' more about what he didn't do rather than what he's in the middle of," he continued. "And do you know what I was thinkin' last night while the boys and me was tradin' fists and bullets with them rustlers?"

Flora couldn't speak, of course, having been struck mute by the mad pounding of her heart and the moisture of her own desire gathering in her mouth. Thus, she simply shook her head in response.

"I was thinkin' that I'm old enough to know better than to let myself have any more regret than I already do," he explained. His voice was low—purely provocative. "I was thinkin' that if I managed to come outta that fight with my teeth still in my head, I wasn't gonna waste any more time than I already have . . . that I wasn't gonna let what's important slip through my fingers."

Flora's body erupted into goose flesh as Reno Garrett reached up, taking her face in his strong, callused hands.

"And I sure as hell ain't gonna die without havin' kissed you first, Flora Dale," he mumbled a moment before his mouth crushed to hers.

Flora saw no reason to play at being bashful. She'd wanted Reno Garrett to kiss her since the first moment she'd ever seen him! Thus, as his hands left her face to linger at her waist a moment before pulling her into his arms, Flora allowed her own arms to encircle his neck as she returned his kiss with willing exuberance.

Reno's kiss, hungry and driven at first, softened after a few moments—mellowed to a kiss of restrained passion mingled with gently applied affection.

All too soon, he broke the seal of their lips, and though he did not release her—though he continued to hold her against him wrapped tightly in his powerful arms—she saw the worry and guilt lingering in the perfect blue of his eyes.

"I know you loved yer Jim, Flora," he mumbled. "I know I can never be the man he was to you, but—"

"Shh," she breathed, tenderly pressing her fingers to his lips to quiet him. "I did love him. I always will love him. That's true, and it won't ever change. But that doesn't mean I can't ever love anyone else just as much as I did Jim. I can . . . just for different reasons maybe . . . and maybe in a different way. But what frightens me isn't whether or not I can love you as much. What frightens me . . . is that you might not want me when I tell you that . . . that . . ." Flora tried to stop the tears from escaping her eyes, but she couldn't. "What if . . . what if it ends up that . . . what if someday I love you more?"

Burying her face in her hands, Flora sobbed. All

the pain of losing Jim mingled with the fear of loving Reno Garrett—a man she hardly knew. She loved him! She did! And in the quiet, well-guarded heart residing in her bosom, she was afraid—afraid she'd been disloyal to the man she'd loved, to her sweet husband—disloyal to the father of her child and to the man who loved her enough to die to protect her.

"Hey," Reno breathed, taking her face in his hands once more. Gazing at her—the guilt and worry that had been in his eyes only a moment before now replaced with understanding and hope—he said, "You might *not* love me more."

She was touched at his attempt to reassure her. "But I'm afraid I might," she whispered.

He caressed her checks, brushing the tears from them with his thumbs. "Then it'll be what you said. It'll just be different," he told her.

Don't be afraid, Flora, she heard Jim's voice whisper. She didn't turn to look for him this time—for she knew that although his voice would linger in her mind and heart forever, his final whisper of, *He's a good man. Don't be afraid to love him,* was the last thing she would ever truly hear Jim say.

Sniffling, Flora felt a warm, comforting serenity settle in her bosom. She reached out, taking Reno's rugged face in her hands, tracing his strong right brow with the tender caress of her fingertip.

"You hardly know me, Reno Garrett," she whispered. She let her finger trail from his brow down over his cheek to his lips.

"My soul knows yers. That's enough for now, ain't it?" he asked, kissing her finger as it lingered on his lips. "Now why don't ya let my kisser get to know ya a little better?"

Flora giggled, pressing a playful kiss to his lips. "My, my, my!" she whispered. "It's been a long time since a handsome cowboy asked me to go sparking." She reached up, removing his hat and running her fingers through his hair.

"Well? What do ya answer?" he asked. "We gonna give ol' Tom Evans and yer daughter some sparkin' competition or not?"

Smiling, Flora tossed Reno's hat to the porch.

"Kiss me then, handsome cowboy," she said.

"Yes, ma'am," Reno mumbled as his mouth captured hers in a kiss that nearly drowned her in blissful waves of desire.

Chapter Twelve

Cedar watched as Reno Garrett held her mother's hand as they wandered toward the creek. Though it was a little strange to her at times—to see her mother so happy and affectionate with a man other than her father—it likewise caused her heart to leap with the sincerest joy. Though Reno was the precise opposite of Jim Dale in nearly every way, he seemed to have literally been made for her mother. And that was the one thing he shared with her father—the appearance that heaven itself had placed him on the earth purely for her mother's sake.

Cedar sighed, returning her attention to the bread dough she'd been kneading before Reno arrived to take her mother for a stroll. She giggled, rolling her eyes in lingering disbelief that her mother would soon be wrapped in Reno Garrett's arms, the way she was often wrapped in Tom Evans's. Still, if her mother had taught her nothing else (and she'd taught her so very, very much), she'd taught her that, deep within their souls, all women remained young—that their hearts were perpetually sweet sixteen in one regard or the other. And Cedar knew Flora Dale was no exception.

She began to hum as she kneaded the bread

dough on the counter, adding a little more flour, for it was still a bit too sticky. She wondered how long it would be before Reno and her mother married—and she knew they would. Only the day before, Reno had told her he planned to "own" her mother—as he so possessively put it. She figured perhaps he wouldn't wait very long to propose—just long enough to be respectable. After all, it had only been two weeks since her mother had arrived home from town to find a bruised (albeit very handsome) cowboy waiting at the kitchen door to kiss her.

Cedar sighed. How romantic it all was! Her mother being courted by the mysterious and attractive Reno Garrett—Cedar being courted by the "so handsome it should be against the law" (as Mrs. Gunderson put it) Tom Evans. She blushed, trying not to think of her desire that Tom Evans would eventually care for her enough to ask her to marry him. That would be too perfect. And though she knew some perfect things did happen in the world, she couldn't believe something as entirely perfect as finding herself married to Tom Evans could actually occur. She hoped it could—dreamed it would—but the doubt and fear the devil plants in every mind kept her from knowing with any true assurance.

She startled when the kitchen door suddenly swung open—smiled as Tom stepped through it.

"Well, howdy, Miss Dale," he said, tossing his

hat onto the table. Cedar giggled as he stepped up behind her, wrapping his arms around her waist and burying his face against her neck. "I see ol' Reno's takin' yer mama down to the creek for a little scandalous behavior."

"I thought you weren't coming until suppertime," Cedar said. Her stomach was so full of butterflies she thought they might start fluttering up out of her mouth.

"I wasn't," he admitted, his arms still holding her against him. She felt his breath in her hair—felt him kiss the top of her head. "But when Reno seen Amelia Perkins headed out my way and stopped in to warn me, he told me he was comin' over to spend a little time with yer mama . . . so I figured you'd be all alone here. And I wouldn't want you to get lonesome . . . so I rode over as fast as I could. I was careful to avoid Miss Amelia, of course."

"Of course," Cedar said, forcing the smile to stay on her face. The knowledge that Amelia Perkins was once again attempting to visit Tom, however, not only infuriated her but greatly concerned her. "I don't trust a woman who would be so brazen in her attempts to win a man over."

"Amelia?" he asked. He puffed a breath, indicating he saw no reason for distress. "She ain't nothin' to be concerned about. I just keep outta her way. Now, leave that bread dough alone and kiss me."

His strong hands at her waist, he turned her to face him, pressing a firm kiss to her mouth.

"You're gonna make me ruin this bread, Tommy Evans," she sighed as he kissed her again. She couldn't touch him, of course—not with sticky bread dough all over her fingers and hands. And, oh, how she wanted to touch him—to lose her fingers in the softness of his hair.

He chuckled, raising one of her hands to his mouth and biting a piece of dough off her index finger.

"Then finish up so we can talk," he told her. He released her, pulled a chair out from the table, turned its back toward her, and sat himself astride it.

Cedar had noticed the look of excitement in his eyes. Tom Evans was enthused about something—something other than just seeing her.

"Talk about what?" she asked him. "I think you've got something swimming around in your mind that you're itching to share."

He smiled and nodded, and the light in his eyes began to glow.

"I'm gonna have me some fine foals come next spring," he said. Cedar giggled as Tom sighed with pride and continued, "That new stallion thoroughbred? He's gonna prove well worth what I paid for him. I got five mares in season right now . . . and six last week . . . and that stallion ain't shy." Cedar blushed slightly, for she was still getting used to how comfortable Tom was talking about breeding stock. "That new Clydesdale studhorse is takin' good care of Dolly and Coaly too. I'm gonna pull him outta their corral tomorrow though. He's hard to handle when he's loose with 'em." He sighed with contentment, his smile broadening. "Yep! Come next spring, you and me are gonna be helpin' our mares foal for months!"

"Mmm . . . baby horses," Cedar hummed as she separated the bread dough into three pans. "It sounds wonderful!"

"Yeah, it does, don't it?" Tom asked.

Cedar glanced at him as she worked the pump at the sink to wash her hands. She patted them dry with her apron as she walked toward Tom. He pulled a chair out from the table for her, and she sat down next to him.

"I'm glad the stallions are . . . proving their worth," she said, still blushing.

Tom chuckled. "Yer blushin'," he needlessly pointed out. "Now, ain't that sweet?"

Desperate to talk about anything that might cool her blush, Cedar babbled, "Mama says we should hire someone to paint the house for us . . . instead of letting you and Reno do the work."

Tom frowned and shook his head. "Naw. Me and Reno can do it . . . or get some of our boys to help. There ain't no need to get nobody else."

He winked at her and asked, "How long you need to let the bread rise?"

Cedar shrugged. "Twenty minutes maybe. Why?"

" 'Cause since Reno Garrett started comin' over here every night to court yer mama, I ain't hardly had a real taste of you," he said as he reached out, placing one strong hand at her neck and pulling her to meet him in a gentle kiss. "We've done plenty of talkin'," he mumbled against her lips. "But it seems like too long since we . . ."

He was right, and Cedar was instantly impatient, silencing his complaint as she took his face in her hands, applying a famished kiss to his mouth. In truth, Tom Evans had kissed her every day— every day since their first kiss was melded in a meadow under a starry, moonlit sky. Still, it was true that her mother's romance with Reno Garrett had found them with little time alone. Ironically, Reno managed to find quite a bit of free time to come courting Flora at all manner of strange hours. But Tom's situation with his horses and new stallions had been a bit more demanding of late. Most nights he arrived just barely before sundown—just in time for supper—only lingering a few hours before fatigue and the anticipation of sunrise forced him to ride home again. Oh, he'd kissed her every night, but Cedar knew what he meant by not having had a "real taste" of her. They hadn't lingered in savoring brutally passionate kisses in days and days.

Tom was on his feet almost instantly, pulling Cedar from her chair and into his arms. "Come along, darlin'," he mumbled, stepping backwards until he was sitting against the table. Pulling her against him, he kissed her sweetly only twice before saying, "Twenty minutes is twenty minutes . . . whether yer watchin' the bread rise or . . ."

He kissed her—really kissed her. She tasted like heaven—he was certain she did. Tom Evans was sure that if heaven itself had a taste, then Cedar's kiss was it. He let his hands be lost in her hair a moment before caressing her neck and shoulders—before wrapping his arms around her to pull her more tightly against himself. He wondered how long he'd be able to politely court her before his desire to own her won over— before he'd end up hefting her up on one shoulder, hauling her into town to the preacher's house and then back to his place to plunk her down in his own bed.

Midst his efforts to control himself—to keep from mauling her there in her mother's kitchen— he wondered how long a man had to wait before he could marry a girl he'd been courting. After all, that was what he wanted—to marry Cedar Dale. He'd pretty much known it from the night he'd dragged her out into the meadow and nearly hauled her home with him then. But that had only been two weeks before, and what would folks think of a man who married a woman after only courting her two weeks? Of course, he didn't care what people thought of him for falling in love so quickly. He just worried over what it might mean for Cedar. Still, gossip simmered down pretty quick. There was always something new that would come along to perk up people's ears—Flora Dale and Reno Garrett, for instance. The truth was Tom couldn't believe Reno and Flora had managed to keep their little secret as long as they had.

Still, what if Cedar didn't want to marry him? He felt his eyebrows pucker together for a moment as doubt and worry interrupted the smooth rhythm of their kiss.

Cedar sighed, breaking the seal of their kiss a moment. She smiled at him, her eyes bright with emotion. The love he saw shimmering in her eyes as she looked at him assured him she wouldn't refuse his proposal when he did ask. She hadn't told him she loved him, but he knew she did. He could see it in her face—feel it in the way her body trembled when he touched her.

"You're thinking about something else," she whispered.

"Oh, believe me, baby . . . I ain't thinkin' about nothin' but you," he chuckled. He wondered what her reaction would be if he told her their impassioned kisses has put him to being all the more impatient to marry her. "Just you . . . about yer purty eyes," he said, kissing her temple. "About yer purty mouth," he said, pressing a soft kiss to her lips. "About yer purty figure," he said, pulling her to him as she giggled, struggling slightly—but only for the sake that she knew she should. "And I'm thinkin' about how much purtier my bed would be with you in it."

She gasped, and Tom chuckled when her cheeks grew rosy.

"Tommy Evans!" she scolded, though he could see the pure delight in her smile. "You shouldn't say such things!"

He shrugged. "You accused me of thinkin' about somethin' else. So I just thought you oughta know what the somethin' else was."

Cedar sighed, enchanted by his flirting—by his touch—by him. He was so handsome! Tom Evans was so handsome—so smart—so capable. He was amusing and kind, a hard worker, and strong as an ox! She brushed a strand of hair from his forehead, wondering how it was she was there in the kitchen with him—how it was that he had come to care for her.

"Those loaves of bread are almost finished rising," she whispered.

"Then we best make the most of the time we got left," he mumbled.

Cedar giggled as he kissed the bridge of her nose before letting his mouth find hers once more.

• • •

"What're you draggin' yer feet for, boy?" Reno asked as he and Tom rode together under a clear midnight sky.

Somehow instantly understanding what Reno was referring to, Tom frowned, looked to his friend, and countered, "What're you draggin' *yer* feet for?"

Reno chuckled, shaking his head. "Well, I'm just waitin' for you. I'm pretty near certain Flora ain't gonna let me haul her off to the church house to get married until she's sure Cedar's tucked in safe and sound with you."

"Well, I'll tell ya . . . tucked in with me is exactly where I want her," Tom chuckled.

"Oh, I hear ya there," Reno said, smiling with obvious understanding. "So what're ya waitin' for?"

Tom shrugged. "Just tryin' to be proper, I guess . . . and givin' Cedar time to make sure I'm really what she wants . . . and that she's ready. Ya know, that she's past her . . . well, that she's past her past."

"It was an awful thing . . . Flora's husband and the young feller," Reno mumbled, nodding affirmation. "But from my way of seein' it, Cedar Dale's about as wrapped up in you as barbed wire in a tornada."

Tom chuckled. "I hope so."

He heard Reno laugh and looked to the man. Reno rubbed the whiskers on his chin.

"What's got you gigglin'?" Tom asked.

Reno frowned. "I ain't never *giggled* . . . not in all my life."

Tom smiled, amused by Reno's gruff response. "What're you laughin' about then?"

Reno's smile returned as he said, "I can't wait to see the look on that Amelia Perkins's pinched-up face when she's sittin' in the church house, watching you and Cedar gettin' all roped up together."

Though he knew it wasn't necessarily a kind or compassionate way to feel, Tom said, "Me neither. That girl about drives me to tearin' my hair out." He paused, shaking his head in disbelief as he said, "She knows I'm courtin' Cedar. I can't understand why she just won't leave me be."

When Reno didn't promptly respond, Tom looked over to see his expression had darkened—and not because it was midnight. The moonlight was brilliant, and Tom could see that Reno was troubled.

Following a few moments of silence, Reno mumbled, "Some women are plumb loco, Tom Evans, that's all."

A strange anxiety caused an uncomfortable shiver to travel down Tom's spine.

"Well, I ain't meanin' to pick open any old wounds you got there, Reno," Tom began, "but that ain't gonna make me sleep easier tonight."

Inhaling a deep breath and shaking his head

slightly as if to dispel unwanted thoughts, Reno sighed, "Oh, Amelia Perkins ain't nothin' to worry about, Tom. She ain't insane . . . just irritatin' . . . like a skeeter in yer ear when yer tryin' to fall to sleep at night."

"Yeah," Tom agreed. "That's an awful good way to put it."

"Even so," Reno began, "let's neither one of us drag all this out too much longer. We both know what we want . . . so what're we horsin' around about?"

Tom smiled. "Yer right. There ain't no reason to fiddle with it any more." He chuckled. "Besides . . . I'm bound to get a lot more work done 'round my place if Cedar's right there . . . instead of me havin' to ride out to the Dale house every night."

As soon as he heard Reno's laughter, however, he understood why the man was amused.

"Boy, the only reason yer gettin' anything done *now* is 'cause she ain't right there," Reno laughed. "It's more'n likely that both of us will end up goin' plumb near broke for the sake of bein' so distracted by them Dale women."

"More'n likely," Tom agreed. He looked to Reno, grinned, and said, "Well, the way I figure, if we're gonna go broke . . . we might as well go broke with Flora and Cedar to keep us warm at night. Right?"

"That's right," Reno chuckled. "So quit draggin' yer feet."

"Yes, sir," Tom said. Winking at Reno, he added, "That would be, yes, sir . . . Daddy."

"Oh, yer plumb hilarious, Tom Evans," Reno laughed.

"Just call me son. That'll do me just fine."

"Oh, have mercy," Reno chuckled. "Ain't all this gonna be somethin'?"

Tom nodded, smiling as he thought of Elvira Gunderson. "Ol' Elvira Gunderson's gonna be talkin' herself hoarse for a year."

"More'n likely," Reno agreed. "More'n likely."

Cedar couldn't sleep. She was restless—more restless than usual. Furthermore, the restlessness keeping her awake wasn't the sort caused by the lingering bliss Tom Evans always drizzled over her. It was something else—an odd discomfort—an indeterminable anxiety. In that moment, she wished Tom and Reno hadn't lingered so late. She wished she could somehow know they were both safe at home. She thought about the cattle rustlers they'd encountered that night two weeks before. The sheriff had assured everyone that the rustlers that hadn't been killed or jailed wouldn't be returning. Still, she worried. She thought of the bullet that had grazed Tom's leg—thought how it could've easily inflicted a more serious injury—or even killed him! Oh, how she wished there were some way she could know he was safe. In truth, she simply wished she were there with him—in his house—in his bed. She knew she probably shouldn't think such things, but she couldn't help it, for they were her true desires—her greatest wishes—what she dreamed of.

Closing her eyes, she tried to concentrate on the sweet whisper of the night's spring breeze outside her window. The sound caused her thoughts to drift to memories of the night Tom had taken her waltzing in the meadow. If she stayed very still—keeping her eyes closed and her breathing shallow—she could just barely hear his voice echoing in her mind.

"Oh, I'm floatin' down the Pecos on a moon-beam," she whispered as Tom Evans's voice sang in her waking dreams. *"Dreamin' dreams of comin' back to you . . . where I know that you'll be waitin' at the millstream . . . and I'll drift into your pretty eyes so blue."*

Gently, Cedar rolled to one side, snuggling beneath the quilt that was not nearly so warm as Tom's embrace.

"Oh, a cowboy, he knows where each lonely river flows," she mumbled as fatigue finally began to overtake her. *"And the Pecos roams the desert to you. Oh, I'm floatin' down the Pecos on a moonbeam . . . dreamin' dreams of comin' back to you."*

The moment before Cedar Dale drifted to sleep, she whispered, "Oh, I love you, Tommy Evans. I love you."

Chapter Thirteen

"Well, hey there, stranger," Amelia Perkins greeted as Tom opened the front door.

"Amelia?" Tom mumbled. He wasn't quite as awake as he normally would've been by sunup. After getting home so late, he'd been up half the night figuring when and how he could ask Cedar to marry him.

Tom rubbed his eyes, still not sure whether Amelia Perkins was really standing at his front door or whether he was still asleep and having a nightmare.

Amelia's smile broadened as she studied him from head to toe. Putting a hand to his chest—his bare chest—Tom realized he hadn't finished dressing. He'd pulled on his blue jeans, socks, and boots before staggering down the stairs to fry up some eggs, but that was it. Glancing to the hat rack behind the door—glad he'd stripped his shirt off and tossed it there the night before—he snatched yesterday's shirt, slipping his arms through the sleeves and struggling with the buttons as his mind fought for clarity of thought.

"What're you doin' out here so early?" Tom asked the girl. Frowning, he added, "What're you doin' out here at all?"

He didn't try to mask his irritation. He was irritated—and he wanted her to know it.

Amelia, however, seemed to ignore his lack of manners and welcoming nature.

Stepping across the threshold and rather pushing past him into the house, she smiled, asking, "Why is it you never will call me Milly like everyone else does?"

"Because you're Amelia," Tom grumbled. "Now, what can I do for you?" he asked, immediately wishing he hadn't sounded so polite.

Smiling at him, Amelia tugged at one glove to remove it—then the other.

"Oh, not much," she said. "Mama and I just worry so about you . . . livin' out here all alone."

"Well, I won't be livin' out here all alone much longer, so you and yer mama can quit yer worryin'."

Tom knew he should've been more guarded, for Amelia's eyes narrowed, and he could see the jealousy in them—the hate.

She seemed to recover quickly, however. "So I guess you'll be hirin' on some more hands now that you're runnin' so many horses then?" she asked.

Tom was uncomfortable—miserably uncomfortable. The woman shouldn't be in his house alone with him. It was far too likely to cause gossip. He had a vision of Elvira Gunderson telling Cedar that Amelia Perkins had been seen out with Tom Evans at his place—alone. The thought nearly panicked him. Still, he hoped Cedar knew him better than to think anything scandalous was going on.

"Amelia . . . I've got to get to my chores," he grumbled. "So you best be on yer way. You can assure yer mama that I'm just fine. Thank her for her concern for me, will ya?" Again he'd been more polite than he'd intended. But it was his nature, after all.

"Why, Tom Evans! Can't you spare a minute for an old friend?" she asked, pushing her lower lip out to pout.

"I got work to do, Amelia," he told her.

"Oh, work can wait, can't it?"

Tom inhaled a deep breath in an effort to calm his temper and patience. "You know I'm courtin' Cedar Dale, Amelia," he told her. "I'm courtin' her, and I'm courtin' her with a serious mind in me. So you just need to understand that—"

"Oh, what Cedar Dale doesn't know won't hurt her," Amelia interrupted.

Tom's eyes widened, his heart hammering with sudden anxiety as Amelia suddenly threw her arms around his neck and tried to kiss him.

"What in the hell are ya doin', girl?" he growled, trying to pry her arms loose. "Back off me, Amelia."

At that very moment, Carl Perkins stepped into the house behind his daughter. Instantly, Tom knew trouble was after him—knew that Amelia had figured a way to cause difficulty.

"Carl," Tom began, "now this ain't nothin', Carl . . . and you know it."

But Carl Perkins wore a face like a prune—wrinkled up and purple with anger.

Glaring at Tom, he growled, "Milly told me you been meetin' with her in secret, Evans. I thought she was just tryin' to get my temper up . . . but now I've seen it for myself."

"Now, hold on, Carl," Tom began. He looked down into Amelia's poisonously sweet face. In that moment, he figured Satan himself owned the same smile.

"I don't know what yer girl has told ya, Carl . . . but I ain't had nothin' to do with her. I'm courtin' Cedar Dale, and you and everyone else knows it."

"Milly explained all that to me," Carl growled. "How you was courtin' Cedar Dale 'cause ya felt sorry for her and her mama . . . and how you and Milly meet up before you ride over to the Dale place every day. Well, it won't wash no more, Evans!"

"Damn right it won't wash!" Tom shouted. "You get yer girl outta here, Carl. And while yer at it . . . ya better get a better handle on her character, 'cause she's been lyin' like the devil."

"You better watch how ya speak to me, boy," Carl shouted. Tom shook his head, infuriated as Carl Perkins drew a pistol from the holster at his hip. "My Milly ain't never told a lie in her life, and she sure as hell wouldn't lie 'bout somethin' like this!"

Tom ground his teeth. Why hadn't he put his gun belt on before coming down the stairs? Because he hadn't expected to have some angry father, with a liar for a daughter, show up first thing in the morning, that's why. He couldn't believe what was happening. Had Carl Perkins lost his mind?

He looked to Amelia, hate and disgust rolling in his stomach.

"What are you doin' here, Amelia?" Tom growled. "What in the hell are you up to?"

Amelia dabbed at her now tear-stained cheeks with a handkerchief she produced from inside her sleeve. She looked to her father, her eyes filled with pleading and feigned innocence. Tom had never seen a more repulsive display of acting—not even at Tillman Pratt's drama house.

"Go on, Milly," Carl urged his daughter. "Go on. Don't be afraid. The truth will always set you free, darlin'."

Amelia sniffed, brushing conjured tears from her cheeks.

"I-I had to tell Daddy, Tom," she sniffled. "I had to. I mean, don't you care at all? Don't you care about the baby?"

"What?" Tom breathed. "What are you talkin' about, Amelia? What baby?" He was tired—

hadn't slept a wink. Still, in that moment, his mind began to fit the pieces of Amelia's heinous puzzle together.

As he looked from Amelia to her father and back, he said, "Oh, no, no, no. No you don't! Yer not gonna hang *me* for this! I have had nothin' to do with yer daughter, Carl . . . not one livin' thing to do with her. And I think you know it!"

"She says yer the pa, Evans," Carl growled. "She says you two have been meetin' for months . . . in secret. Now, I won't have my family name drug through the mud! And I certain won't see my daughter bearin' a bastard neither!"

"Well, then ya best get her to fess up to who the daddy really is!" Tom shouted. "If there's even a baby to consider at all."

"You're gonna make an honest woman of my girl, Evans!" Carl growled, leveling his pistol at Tom. "Or else I'll blow a hole clean through yer head."

Tom was enraged with fury. He glared at Amelia, never having known his soul could own such hatred and resentment.

"Go on and blow a hole through my head then, Perkins," he shouted, " 'cause yer daughter's lyin' to you, and I ain't about to let her get away with it."

"What's goin' on?" Reno Garrett growled, reining in his horse near the front porch.

"I'm about to kill yer neighbor here, Reno," Carl snarled. "So ya best keep yer distance."

Reno dismounted and leapt up onto the porch. "Carl Perkins, you idiot," he grumbled. "Holster that pistol!"

But Carl simply cocked the Colt in his hand, leveling it at Tom's head. "I'll kill him if he don't make it right, Garrett. I will."

Frowning, Reno looked to Tom for explanation.

"You were right, Reno," Tom said. "I shouldn'ta drug my feet this long."

"You'll marry Amelia today, Tom Evans," Carl barked. "You'll marry her today, or I'll blow a hole right between yer eyes."

But Tom shook his head. He wouldn't marry anybody but Cedar Dale—not even if he had to die to keep from it. Furthermore, he didn't think Carl Perkins was the murdering type—not even for the sake of his daughter.

"Then you might as well pull the trigger," Tom growled.

"Daddy! Make him marry me!" Amelia cried. "But don't kill him! I don't want my baby growin' up without a father!"

"Baby?" Reno mumbled, looking to Tom.

"Remember them women you was tellin' me about on the way home last night, Reno? Them plumb loco ones?" Tom asked, nodding toward Amelia.

"Shut yer mouth, boy!" Carl bellowed, stepping closer to Tom.

"Lower that pistol, Perkins," Reno growled.

"You mind yer own business, Reno Garrett," Carl said, turning to level the pistol at Reno.

Although he'd been thinking only of Cedar—wishing he'd asked to her marry him the first time he'd kissed her out in the meadow with Johnny Thornquist's fiddle tickling the breeze—although he'd determined to let Carl Perkins shoot him, to die before he allowed Amelia's lies to plant any doubt in Cedar's mind—something else about the woman he loved whispered to him. As Tom stood in literal horrified disbelief at what was transpiring—as he saw Carl's pistol now leveled at Reno, the man Flora Dale loved—as he watched Carl return his attention and the pistol's aim back to him—he thought of Jim Dale and of Logan Davies. He thought of the pain Cedar had endured because of the loss of her father and her lover—of the nightmarish hell his death would return her to—of what Reno's death would do to Flora and thereby Cedar. He'd die for Cedar all right—without hesitation, he'd die for her. But he wouldn't die and send her to certain, perhaps unendurable misery and pain, all for the sake of a hateful girl's sinful lie.

"I ain't lyin' to you, Carl," Tom said. Though he was careful not to again accuse Amelia out loud, he added, "I ain't. I swear to heaven, I ain't." Pausing a moment, exchanging glances of understanding with Reno, Tom said, "So let's settle it now."

"That's all I'm askin'," Carl said, lowering his weapon's aim to Tom's chest. "I'm near angry to murder, Tom Evans. But all I'm askin' is for you to make an honest woman of my daughter."

"All right," Tom said. "Then let's get to town."

"To the preacher's house," Carl added.

"No. To Doctor Prichard's place," Tom suggested.

"Doc Prichard?" Carl asked, obviously too overcome with rage to think any rational thought.

"Yep," Tom said. "We'll let Doc Prichard take a look . . . have a talk with Amelia." Glaring at Amelia, he added, "You ain't been in to see the doc yet, I'm guessin'."

"Daddy!" Amelia sobbed. "Doc Prichard is only gonna tell you the same thing I've told you. I'm havin' a baby, and Tom Evans is the one who—"

"What if Doc Prichard says my daughter's tellin' me the truth?" Carl asked Tom. "What then?"

"It still don't prove I done anything," Tom said. But as Carl raised the level of his pistol again, he added, "But you know me, Carl . . . and I ain't lyin' to you. I'm willin' to go into town with you and see the doctor. Just give me that. After all these years . . . just give me that."

"But I don't wanna see Doc Prichard, Daddy!" Amelia pleaded, sobbing, sniffling, and wiping her tears with her wadded-up hanky.

"How long have you known Tom Evans, Perkins?" Reno asked. "Do you know him to meddle with women?"

Tom watched as a flicker of doubt crossed Carl Perkins's face.

"Let's all get over to the doctor's place and sort this out," Reno said.

"All right," Carl agreed at last. "But if she's in the family way . . . yer gonna make sure it's a family she's in, Tom Evans."

Tom breathed a sigh of relief as Carl lowered his weapon.

"Get back in the buggy, Milly," Carl told his daughter.

"But, Daddy!" Amelia pleaded.

"Get in the buggy," Carl growled. Still glaring at Tom, he said, "I'll give ya five minutes to saddle yer horse, Evans. Then we're all headin' to town . . . together."

"All right," Tom agreed. He watched as Carl took hold of Amelia's arm and began leading her back toward the buggy—his teeth grinding with disgust as she glanced back over her shoulder, triumphantly winking at him.

"Boy, you got yerself in a pickle now," Reno mumbled.

"I ain't in no pickle," Tom told him. "She ain't pregnant."

"Well, I know you didn't do nothin' . . . but what if somebody else did?" Reno asked.

But Tom shook his head. "Nope. She's lyin' . . . and she's lyin' all the way around it."

"Well, ya best get yer horse saddled," Reno said. "Carl Perkins will have a slow enough time drivin' his lyin' daughter and that buggy back to town. It'll give me time to ride over to Flora's and . . . and . . ." Reno paused, frowning. "What do you want me to tell Flora and Cedar . . . exactly?"

The burning sensation caused by mingled anger and fear raced through Tom's veins. Would Cedar believe Amelia Perkins's lies? No—he was sure she wouldn't. She knew him, she loved him, and she'd know who the liar was.

"Tell them the truth," he said. "All of it." He glared at Carl Perkins as he watched him help Amelia into the buggy. "Bring Cedar and Flora to town . . . to Doc Prichard's place."

"All right," Reno said. He turned, rumbled down the porch, and mounted his horse. "Best take a moment and fetch yer gun, boy . . . just in case."

"Yep," Tom said.

He took the stairs three at a time, retrieving his gun belt and pistol before heading out to saddle a horse. If Carl Perkins still wanted to shoot him once Doc Prichard had seen Amelia—well, he wouldn't let anything keep him from marrying Cedar Dale—not anything.

• • •

Cedar frowned as she watched Reno talking with her mother. Being that they were outside near the back porch, she couldn't hear what they were saying from her viewpoint at the kitchen window, but something was wrong. She could see it in Reno's face and in the way her mother kept shaking her head and covering her mouth with one hand as if restraining strong emotion.

As her stomach began to churn with trepidation, her thoughts reeled back to the night before— when she'd been lying in bed attempting to go to sleep and too worried about whether Tom and Reno had returned home safely. Had something happened to Tom? Was he hurt?

She couldn't endure the anxiety welling up in her—the sudden memories of pain and loss flooding her body. Untying her apron, she tossed it on the counter and left the kitchen by way of the back door.

"What's wrong?" she asked. Both Reno and her mother looked at her, worry and concern having caused her mother's face to grow pallid and what appeared to be anger furrowing Reno's brow. "Is it Tom?" she ventured. "Has something happened to him?"

"He's fine," Reno said. "At least he ain't been shot or hurt or nothin'."

Tom was alive and apparently unharmed. The knowledge soothed Cedar, but only somewhat—

for she felt in her soul that whatever had sent Reno Garrett riding up to the house at a full gallop, fairly yanking her mother out the back door and into serious conversation, concerned Tom.

"What is it?" she asked, barely able to breathe.

Swallowing hard—as if she were struggling for courage to speak—Flora began, "It's Amelia Perkins, Cedar."

"Amelia Perkins?" Cedar mumbled. The name sat in her mouth like bitter, rancid meat.

"She's accused Tom of . . . oh dear," Flora stammered.

"Accused Tom of what?" Cedar asked, though somehow she already knew what.

Reno didn't waltz around the subject, however.

"She's sayin' she's expectin' a baby and that Tom's the father," he stated.

"What?" Cedar gasped.

"Flora . . . let's just all of us head into town and see what Doc Prichard has to say," Reno said. "Amelia Perkins is a liar if she's anything at all, and you girls well know it. I told Tom I'd have you two there by the time he comes in with Amelia and her daddy."

"Amelia and her daddy?" Cedar asked. She felt cold and sick inside. She knew Tom would never trifle with any woman, let alone Amelia Perkins. At least she thought she knew it.

"Here," Reno said, taking hold of the reins of

his horse. "We can walk there faster than the time it'll take me to hitch the buggy."

"Mama?" Cedar breathed. She felt tears welling in her eyes. It was as if she could feel the life draining from her body.

Reno took her chin in hand. The intensity of his gaze was more intimidating than almost anything Cedar had ever experienced.

"Now you listen to me, honey," he said. "I was there. Tom Evans was ready to let Carl Perkins shoot him in the head before he was gonna agree to marry Amelia."

"Marry her?" she gasped, feeling as if the contents of her stomach might lurch up into her mouth and out onto Reno's shirt.

"Listen to me now, Cedar," Reno said. His voice was firm but gentle. "Ol' Carl Perkins had his pistol leveled right between Tom's eyes . . . and Tom told him to pull the trigger. But then I seen Tom thinkin' on you . . . and he wasn't about to die and leave you wonderin' if he'd done something the like she's sayin' he done. He wasn't about to die no matter what . . . for yer sake. So you just come on into town with me now. Everything's gonna be fine. All right?"

"All right," Cedar breathed.

"That's my girl," Reno said, pulling her into his arms a moment. "That's my girl."

Cedar felt him kiss the top of her head before he released her.

"Let's go then, Flora," he said, taking her mother's hand as her mother took Cedar's. "And when this mess is cleaned up . . . I was gonna wait. I was tryin' to do things in a timely manner . . . all proper the way you'd most likely prefer. But the longer I live, the longer I think the only good that comes of waitin' for propriety's sake is calamity." Looking to Flora, he asked, "You wanna walk to the preacher's house to marry me of yer own free will, Flora? Or am I gonna have to heft you up on one shoulder and haul you there?"

"I'll walk," Flora said, wiping tears from her cheeks. "But I'd rather run."

Reno nodded, and even for the seriousness of the situation, he smiled, bending down to kiss Flora hard and long on the mouth.

"Then let's get on into town and make sure Tom don't lose his temper just to find himself in more trouble."

"It'll be all right, sweetheart," Flora told Cedar as they hurried toward town. "It'll be fine."

Cedar nodded—but though she desperately clung to hope, the familiar chill of fear raced through her like a frigid winter river.

Reno had insisted on fetching Amelia's mother to Doctor Prichard's house. Cora Perkins dabbed at her tears with her handkerchief as Cedar sat across from her, reminding herself the woman's daughter was lying—Amelia was lying. Yet one thought kept haunting her—the fact that her own mother had lied the night Lucas Pratt had appeared at the threshold to ask permission to come courting Cedar. If Flora Dale could lie, then couldn't anyone? Even Tom?

Cedar shook her head in trying to dispel the thought. Tom Evans loved her; Cedar was certain he did. Perhaps he hadn't said the words aloud, but his eyes told her—his actions, his attention, his affections. Other things he said told her he loved her. She thought about the day before—just the very day before when he'd been telling her about his horses—when he'd said he and she would be busy birthing foals the next spring.

Come next spring, you and me are gonna be helpin' our mares foal for months! he'd said.

Hadn't his words implied he meant to keep her? She was positive they had. Cedar was certain Tom Evans loved her. Furthermore, she was certain he was a man above others—that there could be no way he would ever have trifled with Amelia Perkins to even the smallest degree. At least that's what her heart told her. Still, the tiny flicker of doubt the devil made sure everyone owned whispered in her mind.

"You're mistaken, Cora," Flora said. "Tom is a good, honest man. He would never take advantage of a young woman in this manner."

Cedar's attention was drawn back to the

strained conversation between her mother and Amelia's then. Furthermore, Cedar could tell by the quiver in her mother's voice that she wasn't so certain of her spoken convictions in Tom's defense.

"And he certainly would not be so disrespectful to Cedar," Flora finished.

"I know how hard this must be for ya, Flora," Cora said, sniffling. Glancing to Cedar, she added, "And for Cedar. But my Amelia would never lie. Never. From what she's told me, we figure the baby's due to come in the fall. This obviously happened before . . . well, before Tom started pretendin' to court Cedar."

Cedar felt sick—literally ill—as if the very hand of death were at her throat poised to choke the life from her. It was true. Tom had agreed to *pretend* to court Cedar—he had agreed to pretend. Though she tried to shield herself from them, thoughts of the worst being true flashed into her mind. Suddenly, she thought of how willing Tom had been to make-believe he was courting her, of how quickly she had fallen into his arms—believed him when he claimed he truly wanted to court her. She felt sick—she felt so sick! She covered her hand with her mouth in an attempt to keep from heaving.

From his place leaning up against one wall across the way of Doctor Prichard's parlor, Reno said, "Yer girl's lyin', Mrs. Perkins. You best start askin' yerself as to how yer gonna go about beggin' Tom Evans's forgiveness . . . and Flora's and Cedar's."

"And what business is all this of yers, Reno Garrett?" Cora spat.

"It's my business on account of I've been there . . . in the very boots Tom's wearin' now," Reno answered. "It seems to me vindictive, connivin' women are near as common as violent, evil-doin' men these days." Reno straightened, and Cedar could see the furious indignation in his eyes even though he was on the other side of the room. "Furthermore, it's my business as much as it is yers because yer daughter's tryin' to ruin that girl's happiness," he said, pointing to Cedar. "And that girl, Mrs. Perkins, is about to become my daughter. That's what makes it my business."

As Cora Perkins's mouth gaped open in astonishment—as she looked from Reno to Flora and back—she stammered, "Flora Dale! Yer gonna marry this man? Why, you Dale women are as easy as—"

Cedar gasped when she saw her mother slap Cora Perkins solidly across one cheek. Never in all her life had Cedar seen her mother react in such a manner. She looked to Reno, still astonished at what her mother had done. Reno, however, simply nodded his encouragement to Cedar that her mother had acted as she should have.

"Your daughter is going in that room because she's lying, Cora," Flora growled, pointing to a closed door to a room off the parlor. "Lying about sharing intimacy with a man she is not married to. And yet you're going to sit there and accuse me and my daughter of inappropriate behavior? You're pitiful . . . sorely blind to who your daughter is . . . to what she is. Sore blind and pitiful."

At that moment, the front door of Doctor Prichard's house burst open, revealing an infuriated Tom Evans. He did not enter immediately but was preceded by Doctor Prichard, a sobbing Amelia Perkins, and her prune-faced father.

"My apologies, Mrs. Perkins . . . Mrs. Dale," Doctor Prichard greeted, stepping into his own parlor as if he expected something to jump out and devour him.

Mrs. Prichard appeared from the kitchen. She'd disappeared into the bowels of the house after Reno, Flora, and Cedar had arrived with Cora Perkins and explained the reason for their visit.

"I've prepared the examination room, Henry," she said, disappearing into another room.

"It's a lie, Cedar, and you know it!" Tom growled, charging into the room like an enraged bull.

"I-I know," Cedar said. She wanted to cry as an expression of relief washed over Tom's handsome yet haggard face. Striding to where she sat, he dropped to his knees and took her hands in his.

"She's lyin'. Doc Prichard's gonna prove it," he said.

"I know," Cedar whispered. Yet in the back of her mind—in that nagging, miserable part of the human mind that exists only to breed doubt—she doubted.

She gazed into Tom's beautiful, saddened, warm-brown eyes, willing herself to believe him—trying to convince herself that a girl could be so desperate as to conjure such a lie as Amelia had in trying to own a man.

"Come with me, Miss Perkins . . . Mrs. Perkins," Doctor Prichard said.

As Tom collapsed into the chair beside her, the reassuring squeeze from her mother's hand on hers did little to comfort Cedar as she watched Amelia and her mother follow Doctor Prichard through a door leading from the parlor.

Tom removed his hat, raking a trembling hand through his hair.

"Could be she ain't far enough to tell for sure," Carl grumbled.

"Then we'll have the preacher and his wife board her for a couple a months until it's proven," Tom growled.

Cedar covered her mouth with one hand for a moment as the contents of her stomach lurched upward into her throat. It couldn't be true! Amelia was lying! She had to be lying!

Cedar thought of her days with Tom—the honest, true, and valiant character she knew him to own. She didn't want to believe it—wouldn't believe it. And yet terrible things did happen. For whatever reason, they did happen—and often to good people. Weren't the deaths of her father and Logan, the deaths of two good men, the very example of terrible things happening to good people? The two situations were dissimilar in moral fiber perhaps, but if Cedar knew anything, she knew the most unthinkable things could happen.

Tom looked at Cedar, nodding with reassurance. Yet she saw the worry—the pain in his eyes. She removed her hand from her mouth, willing the contents of her stomach to remain where they were, and forced a smile in return.

Tom's eyes narrowed, however. He studied her for a moment—intently studied her—gazed into her eyes for a measurable time.

"Yer doubtin' me," he mumbled.

Cedar saw visible rage and anger rise to his countenance again.

"No . . . no, not at all," she whispered.

"Cedar," he began, "do ya really think I would do this? Do ya think I would do somethin' like this to you . . . to anybody?" he growled.

"No, of course not, Tom. Of course not," Cedar

told him. But it was too late. He'd read her doubt—her lack of faith in him.

Nearly bolting up from his chair, he crushed his hat onto his head, striding toward the front door.

"Tom," Reno began.

But Tom Evans just shook his head, holding up a hand to stay Reno.

As he opened the front door, however—as he started to leave—Cedar cried, "Wait!"

Tom turned, glaring at her as Carl Perkins shouted, "Where the hell do ya think yer goin'?"

Tom continued to glare at Cedar for just a moment—then turned to face Carl Perkins.

"If you wanna waste yer time seein' how this comes out . . . go right ahead," he growled. "I already know everythin' I need to."

"Tom," Cedar cried in an agonized whisper. He was telling the truth—she knew he was! In that moment, all her doubts were rinsed away, but she knew the wrong she had done to him—the damage she had inflicted. He'd seen her doubt—her distrust—and he hated her for it.

"Sit down, Tom," Reno said, placing a hand on Tom's shoulder.

But Tom pushed Reno's hand away.

"Do as he says, boy. Sit down," Carl Perkins growled. "Unless ya wanna die," he added, drawing the pistol at his hip.

"Go ahead, Carl. Shoot me!" Tom shouted.

"Then yer wife and lyin' daughter can watch you rot in jail for murderin' an innocent man."

He didn't pause to see whether Carl Perkins meant his threat of shooting him. He simply stormed out of the house, leaving the door open in his wake.

Instantly, Cedar leapt to her feet. Racing from the house, stumbling down the front porch steps, she called, "Wait! Tom! Wait!"

Tom halted, but he did not turn to face her.

"Don't say anythin' else, Cedar," he said. "Yer eyes said plenty."

"Please, Tom . . . please," she pleaded, tears streaming down her face. "I know she's lying. I truly know she's lying. I know she is. I just . . . I just . . ."

He turned to face her then, and the look of pain and anger in his eyes was like a knife through her heart.

"You just what, Cedar?" he asked. "If ya know she's lyin' . . . then why are ya doubtin' me? Why are you doubtin' my character? If ya know she's lyin' . . . then why do ya look so scared?"

"Because I am scared," she sobbed. "You wouldn't be the first good man who . . . who's faltered when a beautiful woman wanted him . . . offered herself to him."

Tom was silent. She could see his jaw clenching and unclenching with restrained emotion. Finally, he shook his head, exhaling a heavy sigh.

"No, I wouldn't. That's true," he mumbled. She saw the excess moisture brimming in his eyes. "But the good man we're talkin' about here is *me,* Cedar," he said. "And I wanted *you.*"

Again an overwhelming wave of nausea engulfed her. She thought she might die from the pain in her chest. For a moment, she even wished that she would. He'd said he'd wanted her—not that he still did want her—and his words felt like a bullet had pierced her brain, her heart, her very soul.

"I wanted *you* . . . not her," he growled. Then he turned—and walked away.

Cedar was paralyzed with disbelief—with agony and illness. She couldn't move—knew that it wouldn't matter if she could. If she knew anything about Tom Evans, it was that he valued honesty, trust, and good faith. She'd failed him.

"Cedar! Cedar, honey!"

It was her mother's voice calling through the fog of pain and despair. Cedar turned to see her mother rushing out of Doctor Prichard's house and toward her.

"It's proven, darling! It's proven!" The smile and tears on her mother's cheeks told Cedar just what had been proven—exactly what shouldn't have needed proving.

Collapsing into her mother's embrace, Cedar sobbed as her mother wept, "She lied, sweetheart! Amelia lied. When Doctor Prichard started questioning her, she realized he'd know the truth . . . and she confessed to lying. Everything's fine, sweetheart . . . just fine."

Shoving herself from her mother's arms, Cedar fell to her knees as the contents of her stomach escaped at last. Sobbing as Reno Garret hunkered down beside her—as he joined her mother in promises of everything being righted once more—Cedar prayed she'd lose consciousness—prayed for the black nothing of oblivion. But oblivion didn't come. The sun hung high in the morning sky—and Tom Evans was gone.

Chapter Fourteen

The days were gray following the "incident" with Amelia Perkins and Tom Evans—and the gray days grew into a week. It seemed spring had changed its mind about bursting into bright bloom—or that winter was determined to heap one final breath of gloom and despair over the world before slinking away.

To Cedar, it didn't matter whether the sun were shining, whether winter gave way to spring, whether the weather were warm or cold. To Cedar, nothing would ever be warm again. Oh, she went about her daily tasks well enough. She slept, ate, cooked, washed, dusted, fed the chickens—but there was no light in her eyes—no spark in her soul.

The one tiny light of anything close to happiness that she knew flickered from the fact that, true to his word, Reno Garrett had taken hold of her mother's hand and led her to the preacher's house almost the moment Amelia Perkins had been proven a liar. Naturally, he'd seen to Cedar's well-being first. After Tom had left, unknowingly leaving Cedar in a heap on the ground outside Doctor Prichard's house, Reno had scooped Cedar up in his arms and carried her back inside. He'd asked Doctor Prichard to give Cedar something to calm her stomach, driven a fist into Carl Perkins's face (which Doctor Prichard discovered had broken the man's nose), and led her mother off to the preacher's house. They'd returned not fifteen minutes later, and the three of them—Cedar, Flora, and Reno—had returned home.

Though Cedar knew her own misery had made it impossible for her mother to find any joy in having wed the man she loved, both her mother and Reno assured her that the wedding didn't matter. It was their life together that would be beautiful.

"Married folks weather misery and joy together their whole lives," Reno had told her. "And sometimes they weather 'em when they're tangled up like this. I love yer mama . . . and I want her through the good and the bad. So don't you worry none if we ain't startin' out rolled in sugar." He'd chuckled and brushed a tear from Cedar's face, adding, " 'Cause we sure will end up that way. All righty?"

Even now, as Cedar ambled toward the creek, she thought of how wonderful Reno had been through it all. She'd nearly forgotten what it was like to have a father—someone big and warm to love and protect her in the manner only a father could. But now, even though she was no longer a child and he was very different from her true father, Cedar had already begun to love Reno.

She could see how desperately he loved her mother, and she could feel that he already loved her as well. Reno's having married her mother, it was the one flicker of light in her soul—would be the only glad thing she ever knew again. Cedar knew that without Tom Evans, she would exist only as an empty, wounded being. She would exist without him, she'd live without him, but she'd never feel joy and hope again—only pain, regret, and anger.

It was everything Cedar could do those first few days after Tom had walked away from her—everything she could do to keep from running to the Perkins farm and tearing Amelia's hair out, gouging out her eyes, screaming at her, spitting at her, and slapping her. When she'd risen above the agonizing initial shock and despair of what had happened, Cedar had nearly run off to the Perkins farm to fly into a fitful rage at the girl who had ruined her life—stripped her one true love from her.

But Reno had stopped her. "That girl deserves it," he'd said. "I ain't sayin' she don't . . . but it ain't gonna fix nothin' between you and Tom. That Perkins girl dug her own grave with all that lyin'," he'd said. "She'll pay for it . . . and with a lot more pain than you diggin' her eyes out would cause."

Cedar knew Reno was right, and she'd almost smiled when he'd given her permission to slap

Amelia soundly across the face if their paths ever did cross again. He's almost gotten a smile out of her with that—almost.

No one but Reno had seen Tom Evans since the day he'd been accused by Amelia Perkins of wrongdoing. Reno had ridden out to the Evans place to check in on Tom the afternoon following the incident with Amelia. He'd found Tom angry, weathering pain and splitting wood. Reno assured Cedar that all he needed was time—that he'd forgive her for her moment of doubt. Tom Evans was a good man, and good men always came around. At least that's what Reno said.

Yet it had been more than a week, and Tom still hadn't come to see Cedar. He hadn't been into town either, and folks began to speculate that he'd taken off up north to visit his brother. The gossip in town spread that Tom Evans planned to sell his horses and land and move up north for good. Reno assured Cedar that Tom would never run, however—that he loved his horses too much—and that he loved Cedar even more.

But Cedar knew she'd lost his love—lost it the day her faith in him wavered. The pain caused by the knowledge she would never be in his arms again, never again see his smile appear because of her, never know his laughter, his kiss, it was not only unbearable but debilitating. Though she'd never thought it possible—though she felt guilty for it—the truth was that her misery over losing Tom Evans was more destructive and more painful than Logan's death had been.

She ate very little, and when she did, it didn't stay in her stomach long. Each night she sobbed herself to sleep—bitter, bitter tears drenching her pillow. Each day she stayed alive, but she didn't live. Over and over and over she silently tortured herself for that terrible moment she doubted Tom—the moment that found her now hopeless and alone.

Cedar didn't even have the determination or strength to fend off Lucas Pratt's ridiculous persistence in wanting to court her. She was bathed in guilt whenever she saw him—guilt borne of not only the lie her mother had told when he'd come to ask permission the first time but also the fact that he'd watched her spurn him and still wanted her afterward. Furthermore, she was obliged not to spurn him again, for her wounded heart wondered if perhaps it was better not to be madly in love with the one man who fulfilled her every need and desire. Perhaps then, when death or tragedy stole a man away, perhaps then the pain wouldn't be so wholly destructive.

It was this line of thinking that gave Cedar cause to consider accepting Lucas's second request at courtship. She hadn't accepted him, of course, but she had considered it. After all, her mother had a chance at happiness. Cedar knew that until Reno could whisk her mother away to his cattle ranch—until they could be alone instead of living at the Dale house with a daughter awash with misery and heartbreak—her mother could never truly be happy. And she wanted her mother to be happy; she wanted Reno to be happy. Thus, she'd begun to consider Lucas's proposal of courtship, for she wouldn't have her mother's happiness snatched away because of her. If Cedar couldn't have Tom Evans, then she didn't really care what man ended up saddled with her.

Glancing down to a tuft of daffodils growing along the creek bank, she winced. At once, tears began spilling from her eyes.

"Tom," she breathed. "I'm sorry. Oh, please, I'm so sorry!"

She dropped to her knees then, burying her face in her hands as sobbing wracked her very soul. She knew then that no matter how she tried to convince herself that she would keep living without Tom Evans and his love, her life without them would be nothing—empty and miserable. Again she begged for oblivion—for respite from her pain—but none came.

"Her very soul's dying, Reno," Flora said as she saw her daughter collapse to her knees beside the creek.

"I know it," Reno mumbled, gathering Flora into his strong embrace.

She sighed as she melted against him—as the

comforting scent of his shirt and skin filled her lungs.

"You've been so patient with us," Flora mumbled, letting his shirt soak the tears from her cheeks. Looking up into his handsome face, she added, "You've been so patient with me."

Reno grinned. "I've waited a lifetime for you, Flora Dale," he mumbled. "I think I can wait a little longer to have you all to my lonesome. Though it is takin' a might longer for Tom Evans to pull his head out of the mud than I thought it would."

"Flora Garrett," Flora corrected him, smiling.

Reno's smile broadened. "That's right . . . Flora Garrett," he chuckled.

"I know that because of all this with Cedar . . . well, I know I haven't been a ray of sunshine since we got married, Reno," she said. "But will you kiss me anyway?"

"You bet, baby," Reno said, pressing a kiss to her lips. "And when this mess gets sorted out," he mumbled against her mouth, "you and me ain't leavin' the ranch house for a month of Sundays."

"Promise?" Flora flirted.

"Yes, ma'am," Reno said. "And when we're finished here . . . I'm gonna ride over to Tom's place and beat some sense into that thick head of his."

His mouth captured hers in such a wanton, impassioned kiss that Flora Garrett was ready to ride over to Tom Evans's place and beat some sense into him herself! She wanted to linger in Reno's arms forever—wanted to see her daughter happily tucked in Tom's arms so that she could bask in the love she and Reno had found with a clear head and a fully blissful heart.

"I love you," Flora whispered when Reno broke the seal of their lips for a moment.

"I love *you*," Reno breathed as he brushed a strand of hair from her forehead. "That's why I ain't gonna let this go on any longer."

With one final kiss, Reno released her, winked, and headed to the barn to saddle his horse.

Flora smiled as she watched him go—as her attention fell to the seat of his pants. His blue jeans needed mending. A large worn patch just under his right hip was beginning to tear. She smiled, thinking she'd leave them alone—wouldn't mend them yet—because she liked the way his underwear was peeking through the place.

She glanced back to the creek to see Cedar still on her knees in the grass—still weeping. Closing her eyes, she began to whisper a prayer.

"Oh, please," she breathed. "Please take a hand in this, Lord. Don't let her soul wither and die. Don't let their love be lost over one foolish thing."

Tom sat watching the fire in the hearth die. It had been three days since he'd had a bath. There were chores to be done, but he didn't have the heart to do them. He figured his stock was lucky to be alive considering the neglect they'd endured since Amelia Perkins had ruined his life.

Squeezing his eyes tightly shut, he thought instead, *Until I ruined my life.*

Every day and every night since he'd left Cedar crying outside Doc Prichard's, he'd lingered in self-hatred. His guilt over his treatment of his beautiful Cedar had eaten at his gut like rancid meat. What else could he have expected of her? He'd seen the love in her eyes as she'd looked at him that day. He'd seen her struggle, her pain—and, yes, he'd seen the little flicker of doubt and fear. For all of it, the doubt had been the least of what he'd seen. And yet what had he done? He'd allowed his rage—his anger and disgust with Amelia Perkins and her ignorant parents—he'd allowed something so foolish as an idiot woman's lie to overpower him. Instead of falling at Cedar's feet, thanking her for the fact that she loved and trusted him enough to even let Reno drag her to Doctor Prichard's house in order to endure the horror and humiliation with him, he'd let the anger and pain of the situation control him. He'd been selfish, so selfish that he'd lost sight of the very reason he'd demanded Doc Prichard see Amelia in the first place—Cedar! He didn't care what the folks in town thought. Reno Garrett was right. Many a man found himself accused of just what Amelia had accused Tom of. Some were guilty, and some weren't. He knew Amelia was lying, but he'd wanted Cedar to believe she was lying before it was proved, and she'd had one moment of doubt—one moment. And had he given her his heart—his understanding? Had he owned a moment of patience and sympathy for her? No! He'd let his pain and his pride take control. His stupidity had walked him away from the one thing in his life he'd loved more than anything, including his own life—Cedar.

He thought of what a fool he'd been. He'd been willing to let Carl Perkins shoot him in the head—willing to die before he'd let someone force him into marrying any woman other than Cedar Dale. He'd die for her, but he couldn't instantly forgive her for a moment of doubt?

The truth was, even if she'd done anything that warranted forgiving (and she hadn't), Tom's rage over Amelia's lies and her father's stupidity had owned him—had gripped him like the devil's own fist—and he'd lost his mind for a time. He hadn't been thinking straight, not since the minute he'd opened the door to find Amelia standing on his porch. He hadn't started thinking straight until he'd ridden home, cussing and swearing under his breath the whole way. But the moment his mind had cleared even just a little, he knew he might as well have let Carl Perkins shoot him before they ever got to town. That would've hurt Cedar less than what he'd done had hurt her.

He'd almost turned his horse right around and ridden hell-bent for the Dale place. But he'd paused, wondering how he could ask Cedar to forgive him when he hadn't instantly understood and forgiven such a lesser failing as her moment of doubt.

Sighing, Tom let his head fall back against the chair. He tried to will away the excess moisture in his eyes, but each time he closed them, he saw nothing but Cedar. If he held very still, he could almost feel the warmth of her breath on his cheek—almost sense her beautiful form resting in his arms—almost taste the passion of her kiss. He was miserable—hopeless—knowing she could never forgive him. He would simply have to live out the remainder of his wretched life without her.

"Cedar," he whispered aloud. Though the word sat on his tongue like pure confection, the emotional anguish washing over him at the sound of it felt as if someone had pressed a shotgun to his chest and pulled the trigger.

Tom was so lost in the pain and misery of what he'd done to Cedar that he didn't hear the pounding on the door at first.

When he finally did realize someone was standing on his porch, hammering on the front door, he simply shouted, "Go away! I ain't here!"

The pounding stopped, but Tom startled,

jumping up from his chair when he heard glass breaking. Instantly, visions of the vile outlaw who had come gunning months before leapt to his mind, and he grabbed the shotgun he'd kept over the parlor door ever since.

A moment later, a hand reached in through the broken front window, unlatching the door.

Tom leveled his shotgun, growling as the front door burst open to reveal an irate-looking Reno Garrett.

Tom lowered his weapon, sighed, and said, "Yer lucky I paused, Reno. I 'bout blew yer head off."

Reno scowled, studying Tom from head to toe a moment.

"You drunk, boy?" he asked.

Tom sighed, still frowning, and shook his head. "No. I ain't drunk."

"Well, you look like hell," Reno noted.

"Well, thank you, Reno," Tom said. "That makes me feel a whole world of better."

Tom reached up, placing the shotgun back on the rack over the door in the parlor. "I suppose you come to chew me out," he said.

"No, no. I just come over to see why it is yer willin' to forgive that sorry ol' bull of yers for hornin' ya two or three times a week but ya ain't willin' to forgive poor little Cedar for one moment of weakness."

"Forgive Cedar?" Tom exclaimed. "I ain't got

nothin' to forgive her for . . . but I ain't ignorant enough to think she'd ever forgive me."

Reno inhaled a deep breath—exhaled it slowly. It was just as he thought. Tom Evans was near as ignorant as he was. He figured it was Tom's pride, self-hatred, or both that was keeping the man from riding over to see Cedar. Still, he'd worried that Tom really had been holding a grudge against the woman he loved, for it had been over a week since the whole mess erupted.

Still, he was encouraged now. It was obvious the man was a wreck—that he'd been sitting in the house stewing and regretting since the day it all happened. He grinned a little. It wouldn't be long now, and he'd have his sweet Flora all to himself—and Cedar would be warm in her own new bed too.

Tom sighed. He looked to Reno—rubbed the more than a week's growth of whiskers at his chin.

"I heard you broke Carl Perkins's nose and married Flora Dale all within five minutes," he mumbled.

"How'd ya hear that?" Reno asked. "You ain't been in town since the mess happened."

"Ray told me. I sent my boys into town a few days ago for supplies," Tom explained. "You feel that cold front comin' in?"

"Yep."

"Well, good for you for marryin' Flora . . .

though I wouldn't have stopped at breakin' Carl's nose. I'd have busted him up a might more thorough than that," Tom grumbled as the very thought of Carl Perkins caused him to feel overheated with rage. "I can only pray that when I have children, I ain't the blind fool that man is."

"So yer gonna have yerself some children?" Reno asked. Tom shrugged, and Reno continued, "How you plannin' on doin' that when yer hidin' out here and Cedar's over at Flora's place?"

"Is she all right?" Tom asked.

"Hell no, she ain't all right!" Reno barked. "Pull yer head outta the trough and go get her."

"She ain't gonna wanna see me," Tom said, "not after the way I treated her."

"If you can forgive her for doubtin' you . . . then I'm sure she can forgive you for bein' a man," Reno said. "Ain't a man on this earth that ain't let his temper get the better of his thinkin' at one time or another . . . exceptin' maybe them sissy sorts. What separates the good men from the bad is the strength to go crawlin' back with yer tail between yer legs when you've hurt someone you love."

Tom grinned—breathed a weak chuckle. "Somehow I have a hard time imaginin' you with yer tail between yer legs."

Reno smiled. "Oh, I been beat down by humility and desperation plenty of times." He chuckled. "I figure with the way Flora's got me wrapped around her little finger, I'll be scootin' back beggin' for a pat on the head more often than I care to admit."

"I've let this drag on too long," Tom mumbled.

"Yes, you have," Reno agreed. "Now don't let it go on any longer."

Tom sighed. "I feel like I'm fifteen and gettin' a talkin'-to from my daddy," he said.

"Well, yer actin' it . . . and you are," Reno teased.

Tom nodded. Reno was right. He'd just been so lost in despair and misery he hadn't come up long enough to think straight.

"Now, Flora's sendin' Cedar to town to fetch some things this afternoon," Reno began. "We thought it might do her good to see ol' Elvira Gunderson and face her worries about runnin' into Amelia Perkins."

"She'll be terrified," Tom mumbled, frowning. He was a little irritated at Flora's forcing Cedar to town—even though he understood the reason for it.

"Yes, she will," Reno agreed.

"So yer sayin' I oughta clean up and ride to town."

"Yep."

"You know," Tom began, smiling at his friend, "there might come a time when yer the idiot and I'm the daddy."

"Ain't a question of if . . . just when," Reno chuckled. "Now, get into town, haul that girl off somewhere, and kiss her 'til she forgives you. I got me a brand-new wife that I wanna have all to myself for a while."

"I'm sure you do," Tom said. The smallest glimmer of hope had begun to burn in his heart. Though he was awash anew with self-disgust— this time with his own stupidity—he felt the familiar power of determination to conquer welling up inside him.

Cedar might not want him now; he knew that was a very real possibility. Still, whether or not she wanted him anymore—whether or not she'd be able to forgive him if she did want him— Cedar Dale was worth fighting for.

"Go on now," Reno said. "Lick yer wounds, clean yerself up, tuck yer tail between yer legs, and get on with it."

"All right, all right. Quit yer naggin', you old woman," Tom chuckled.

Twenty minutes later, Tom Evans was slicked up, mounted on his fastest horse, and riding out for town. Glancing up to the dark, heavy clouds hanging low and threatening, he hoped he could get Cedar to talk to him before the snow started falling and he had to see her home. He knew empathy for Reno Garrett in that moment, wondering how the man had managed

325

to remain so patient when there couldn't be anything he wanted more than time alone with Flora.

Fastening the top button of his coat, Tom spurred the horse to a gallop. Suddenly, he felt an even greater urgency, as if time were running out—and not just because of the storm looming on the horizon.

"I ain't seen him in here since . . . since it all happened," Mrs. Gunderson said.

Cedar nodded and looked away from the old woman as tears filled her eyes. She'd been determined not to ask Mrs. Gunderson about Tom Evans. When her mother had begged her to go into town to fetch a few things, Cedar had agreed only because she knew Reno and her mother were desperate for some time alone in each other's company. She knew that though they understood she was happy for them, they couldn't be comfortable in each other's arms when Cedar was there, bathed in constant misery.

Thus, she'd agreed to go—even though she knew Mrs. Gunderson would have questions about the entire Amelia Perkins–Tom Evans–Cedar Dale triangle. Still, she'd surprised herself when she'd found that she was the one who introduced the subject to Mrs. Gunderson. Yet she couldn't keep from asking about Tom—asking

Mrs. Gunderson if she'd seen him or if the rumors were true and he'd really headed up north to his brother's place.

"But I don't think he went on up to Slater and Lark's place," the old woman continued. "Ray Kirby was in here just a day or two ago and said Tom had sent him." Mrs. Gunderson paused, and Cedar was touched by the compassion in her eyes when she said, "I'm sorry I don't have more to tell you, honey."

"That's all right. I-I was just wondering how he . . . if he's well and . . . and happy," Cedar stammered.

Mrs. Gunderson reached out, cupping Cedar's cheek.

"I doubt he's either, honey," she said. "I know Tom about as well as anyone does. He'll come around. He's just angry and hurt, that's all. That mess with Amelia Perkins . . . things like that don't set easy with a man like Tom. He'll come around. You'll see."

"I don't give myself any false hope, you know . . . where he's concerned, Mrs. Gunderson," Cedar explained. "I don't give myself any hope at all . . . but I do want to know he's well."

"There's always hope, sweetie. Always."

Elvira Gunderson paused a moment, and Cedar watched a puzzled frown wrinkle her already wrinkled brow.

"But what I don't understand is why yer givin' up so easy," she said. "Why have you given up on Tom?"

"I've never given up on Tom," Cedar said. "I just know . . . he's doesn't want me now. So what else can I do?"

"You can ride on out there to his place, throw yerself in his arms, and tell him you love him, girl!" Mrs. Gunderson exclaimed. "Quit mopin' around like a sick calf and go out and get what you want." She inhaled and sighed. "Anyway, men . . . they just got too much temper about them. I'm guessin' Tom wasn't even angry with you. He was just angry with Amelia and didn't have his wits about him."

Cedar smiled, and for a moment, hope sparked in her bosom. Maybe Tom could forgive her—maybe he could still love her. Maybe if she ran to him, dropped to her knees, and begged . . .

"Them clouds is lookin' a bit dangerous this afternoon," Lucas Pratt said as he entered the general store. "Snow's startin' up too."

Cedar's stomach churned with anxiety as he smiled at her.

"Ya might not want to linger in town too long, Cedar," Mrs. Gunderson warned. "Whiteout can come up and bury ya before ya turn all the way around once." Cedar wasn't sure whether Mrs. Gunderson was truly warning her about the weather or offering her a venue of escape before

Lucas Pratt attempted to draw her into too much conversation.

"But you remember what I said, ya hear?" the old woman added.

Cedar smiled as the tiny spark of hope in her heart flickered a little.

"Do you want me to see ya home, Miss Cedar?" Lucas asked.

"No," Cedar answered far too abruptly. "But thank you," she added, forcing a smile. "It's not far. I'll just hurry along."

Handing her the basket she'd filled with several eggs and a few pieces of candy, Mrs. Gunderson smiled and said, "You run on home now, honey. But as soon as this storm blows itself out . . . you do what I told you to do."

"Yes, ma'am," Cedar said—though her hope had already been vanquished. For a brief moment, she actually considered that running to Tom and begging his forgiveness might make a difference. But the truth was she'd considered it every time her mother had suggested it as well. Each time her heart would leap a little with hope, only to come crashing back down to the pit of her stomach, beaten by despair.

As Cedar left the general store, she brushed a tear from her cheek, pulled on her gloves, and fastened her top coat button. Snow had indeed begun to fall—and already much heavier than she'd expected. Still, she wasn't worried. Home was just down the road—just past the school-house a ways. At the thought of the schoolhouse, Cedar's body erupted with goose bumps—warmed by the memory of the day Tom Evans had kissed her there. She felt perspiration beading at her temples, even for the cold, for any memory of Tom's arms around her—of his moist, heated kiss—caused her to tremble.

She wanted to get home—past the schoolhouse and the memory it bathed her in. Quickly Cedar made her way down the boardwalk and into the street. She fancied the snow was falling heavier—that she was having difficulty making out the trees and road beyond the buildings in town. Yet surely she had time to safely make the short walk home. After all, it wasn't very far.

"I hope you've got an extra bed in the back for one more idiot cowboy, Elvira," Tom Evans said as he blew into the general store. "I come in for . . . for supplies," he lied, glancing around the room in search of Cedar. "But I don't see no way I'm gettin' home in this. A couple more minutes and it'll be a whiteout."

"Oh, Tom!" Elvira exclaimed. It was only then he noticed the worried expression on her face. "I'm so glad to see you! Cedar was just in here, and I sent her runnin' home before the storm got too bad . . . alone! How bad is it? Do you think she'll make it to the house?"

Tom frowned, hoping he'd misunderstood Elvira's babble.

"You ain't tellin' me Cedar's out in this, are ya?" he asked.

Elvira glared at him. Wagging a scolding index finger, she answered, "Yes! That's what I'm tellin' you! And if ya had half the sense given a skunk . . . you'd have understood that girl's predicament, and she'd be married to you and home safe in yer bed by now, instead of out in this storm."

"Don't waste my time tellin' me things I already know, Elvira," Tom grumbled. "How long ago did she leave?"

"Five or ten minutes maybe."

Tom nodded. "All right. But if it turns out she comes back for some reason . . . don't let her leave again."

"Oh, I won't, Tom," Elvira agreed as worry overtook her scolding expression. "I shouldn't have let her go in the first of it."

"I'll ride out to the Dale place and make sure she got there all right," Tom said. He turned then and, without another word, stepped out of the general store and into the beginnings of a whiteout.

Chapter Fifteen

The storm was worsening with each passing moment! Cedar was frightened—worried she wouldn't make it home. She kept thinking of the children caught in the spring storm sixteen years before. Already the wind was blowing the heavily falling snow to swirling so thick she could only see a few feet in front of her. The white curtain of weather hid the outlines of the buildings in town behind her. Although she couldn't see the schoolhouse or her house beyond, she knew she had to be closer to them than to town. She dared not turn back. If she were going the right direction, the schoolhouse should be just ahead. When she reached it—if she reached it—she'd stop there, wouldn't try to press on home, though it was not much farther. She couldn't remember the storm of sixteen years before, but she did remember standing in the graveyard as small coffins were lowered into the ground.

She sighed with relief when she caught a glimpse of a structure just ahead of her—the schoolhouse! Barely visible through the thick, blowing snow, in one more moment the building would be undetectable—completely hidden by the malice of the spring storm. Cedar knew she would need to weather the blizzard inside the schoolhouse. She prayed Tom Evans was safe in his ranch house—that her mother and Reno were warm in front of the parlor fire.

The wind at her back helped to blow the schoolhouse door open. As she struggled to close the door in order to shut out the storm, a violent gust of wind thwarted her efforts, and she found herself hurtled to the floor as the door swung open with tremendous force.

Wind and ice stung her face, but she knew she must close the door. Wiping the snow from her eyes, she stood, blinking several times as she watched Tom Evans stride into the room leading a horse. He loosely tied the reins around a small desk nearby and then pushed the schoolhouse door closed, bolting it behind him.

"Tommy?" Cedar gasped. It hadn't been the wind that had kept her from closing the door.

"What in tarnation are ya doin' out in this storm, Cedar?" he growled as he stomped the snow from his boots.

"I-I lingered too long at Mrs. Gunderson's store, I suppose," she stammered. She was trembling—violently trembling—but she didn't know whether she trembled from the cold or with the emotional upheaval now coursing through her.

She wanted to cry! She wanted to throw herself into his arms and beg his forgiveness—beg him to hold her, to kiss her—to love her. But she didn't. She only stood staring at him in witless astonishment.

Tom frowned, pulling his gloves from his hands. Moving past her, he strode to the wood-stove in one corner, mumbling, "Ya coulda frozen to death out there." He hunkered down and opened the stove door.

She watched—still unable to speak—as Tom tossed kindling from the kindling box into the stove. He drew a match from the match tin hanging on the wall and lit the kindling—waiting for it to catch strong before adding more wood.

He stood then, returning to Cedar and taking her by the shoulders. Tears began to fill her eyes as she looked up at him. Oh, how she loved him! With every inch of her flesh—with every drop of her blood—with every breath that was her soul she loved him!

His eyes were smoldering, even for the cold in the room—smoldering warm and brown—dark and enticing. His lips parted, and he inhaled a slight breath as if he'd meant to say something and then changed his mind.

"Come on over here by the fire," he said— though she was certain he'd begun to say something else. "We could be here awhile . . . so let's get warmed up."

Cedar nodded. She found herself unable to speak, for she was awed to silence—awed by his presence and the emotions racing through her mind and body. She followed him across the room to the stove that was already giving off live-saving heat. Its warm glow brightened the dark room, casting shadows on the walls that eerily danced to the tumultuous refrain of the storm outside. It was only then—as the fire began to warm her—that her teeth began to chatter and she realized her fingers were numb.

"Yer coat is soaked through," Tom mumbled as he rather roughly stripped her coat from her body. He took her gloves too, hanging everything over a chair near the stove. "Here," he said, removing his own coat and draping it over her shoulders. It was heavy and warm with the comforting heat of his body. Cedar inhaled the familiar, consoling scents of leather and smoked ham. She pulled the collar up around her face—breathed heavily—savored the essence of the man she loved.

"I can't believe Elvira let you go out in this," Tom grumbled. He exhaled a heavy sigh, shaking his head. "Cedar . . . I know—"

He was interrupted by a loud beating on the schoolhouse door, however—and the frantic voices of children crying out for help.

Instantly Tom was across the room to the door. He lifted the bolt, and three snow-covered children tumbled into the room.

"Mr. Evans!" It was a boy of about ten who Cedar had seen in town on occasion. She

335

remembered his name was Percy Buckets, and he had his two little sisters with him. Cedar dropped to her knees, gathering the young girls into her arms as they shivered and sobbed.

"We got lost goin' home from the crick," Percy explained. "It's so white out . . . we couldn't see nothin'!"

"It's all right," Tom told the boy. Looking to Cedar, he nodded to her, repeating, "It's all right." Cedar wasn't sure whether he wanted her to reassure the sobbing little girls in her arms or if there were some other implication in his words.

"Come over by the fire, and let's get them wet coats off," he told Percy.

Cedar stood, leading the little girls to the stove before gently removing their coats and mittens.

"It's warm here by the fire," she said softly. Tenderly, she brushed the tears from their cheeks with her fingertips. "And here." She removed Tom's coat from her shoulders, snuggly wrapping the girls together in its masculine warmth. "This is already warm. You'll be fine now."

Percy's teeth were chattering, and Cedar was sorry her own coat was too wet to be useful. She glanced to Tom and knew he was concerned for the boy as well.

"Here, boy," he said, unbuttoning his shirt and stripping it off. "Take that wet shirt off and wrap up in this. It'll help a bit."

"Yes, sir," the boy said, stripping off his own

shirt. Cedar could see Percy's entire torso was riddled with goose bumps. She sighed, slightly relieved as the boy wrapped up in Tom's warm shirt and nodded. "It's better," the boy mumbled. "But won't you be cold, Mr. Evans?"

Cedar's gaze lingered on Tom's bare, muscular torso a moment. She blushed when she glanced up to see him studying her with just as much intensity as she had no doubt been studying him.

"Our pa says it ain't proper to run around in yer birthday suit after ya turn three," the littlest Buckets girl offered.

"Well, yer pa's right, sweetheart," Tom said, hunkering down in front of her. "But in situations like this . . . sometimes stayin' warm is the most important thing. Do you understand?"

The little girl nodded, and Tom reached out, tweaking her nose.

Cedar could not take her eyes from Tom—and not simply because of his state of undress. How desperately she wanted to own him—to belong to him! She thought of Amelia Perkins, of her malicious, harmful lie. Yet for a moment, she understood such reckless desperation. Still, as much as Cedar loved Tom Evans, she could never have done such a thing as Amelia did.

"You best linger by the fire too, Cedar," Tom said.

Cedar nodded. She pulled a chair away from its

place against the wall and positioned it near the stove.

"I'm Fanny Buckets," the eldest of the two girls said, offering her hand to Tom.

Tom smiled, accepting her tiny hand and quietly chuckling. "Your name's Fanny, and you all are worried 'bout me bein' in my birthday suit?"

"Yes, sir," the little girl said, a bewildered frown puckering her tiny brow.

Cedar bit her lip to keep from smiling.

"Yer Tom Evans," the girl added. "Our mama told us she used to be sweet on you. She used to be Agnes Hollar . . . before she married our pa."

"Hush, Fanny!" Percy scolded. "Mama would skin you alive if she knew you told him that."

Tom chuckled. "Well, it's nice to meet ya, Miss Fanny Buckets." Cedar smiled when the younger of the two girls stepped in front of her sister, smiling at Tom. She curtsied and offered her hand as well.

"I'm Petunia," she said.

"My pleasure, Miss Petunia," Tom said, accepting Petunia's hand. "Fanny and Petunia," Tom chuckled as he looked at the two little girls. Cedar could see the amusement in his eyes— noticed the way a smile played at the corners of his delicious mouth. She likewise noticed that neither of the two girls had thought to introduce themselves to Cedar. She smiled, recognizing the expressions of pure and instant infatuation on the faces of the two Buckets girls—knowing her face must have held just such an expression in Tom Evans's presence when she was as young.

"Pa said he named me," Percy whispered aside to Tom. "I've always been mighty glad it was him that named me and not Mama."

Tom chuckled and tweaked the tiny noses of each little girl. "Well, let's keep you all nice and warm. Miss Cedar too." He winked at the children and said, "I think Mrs. Gunderson can hear her teeth chatterin' all the way over to the general store."

"Here," Cedar said, positioning the children at a safe distance from the stove. "Mind you don't get too close."

She looked to Tom, her smile fading when she saw his smile vanish as he studied her. As her anxieties, fear, and pain began to return, she reached up, twisting a long stand of hair around one index finger.

"I got somethin' to say to you," he said. "But it'll have to wait." He nodded toward the children, and she understood. She understood that whatever Tom Evans was going to say to her couldn't be said in front of children.

Instantly tears filled Cedar's eyes as she tried to keep from throwing herself at his feet and begging him to forgive her. But she knew the children were frightened. They needed to be cared for—reassured that everything would be all right. A sobbing woman wouldn't offer any reassurance. She thought for a moment of the children of Lamar who had been lost sixteen years before—frozen to death in a late spring storm. She'd never liked Agnes Hollar much, but she wouldn't have wished the agony she must be enduring with her children missing on anyone—not even Amelia Perkins.

"We'll be fine in here, children," she said. "Mr. Evans is a very capable man. He knows just what to do in times like these."

"I'd feel better if you'd sit by me awhile, Miss Cedar," Petunia said.

Cedar pasted on a courageous smile and nodded. Leaving the comfort of her chair, she sat down on the floor in front of the stove, gathering the two girls into her arms.

"Everything will be just fine, girls," she told them. "Just fine."

But as the afternoon waned into evening and the evening into night, the wind continued to howl and blow the heavy snow into drifts. There was nothing that could be done but to wait out the storm.

Every time Cedar chanced a glance at Tom, it was to find him staring at her—studying her as if he were trying to read her thoughts. His eyes seemed to burn with—something. Anger? Hatred? Desire? She wasn't certain which.

Hours passed. Cedar and Tom attempted to keep the children's minds off the storm. When Tom would grow weary of storytelling, Cedar would sing songs with them. At last the children drifted asleep, lulled by the steady moan of the wind. They rested in rather a lump—all together— and Cedar smiled, thinking they resembled a litter of pups piled up in a basket.

Tom sat astride a chair near the stove. Cedar had noticed he'd been sitting in the same position for some time, staring at the wall, seemingly deep in thought. If there was going to be a time to talk to him—to beg his forgiveness—to hope—this was it. She almost moved—almost lunged toward him. Yet her courage failed as she continued to study him. The deep frown puckering his brow intimidated her, as did the sight of his bare, broad chest and muscular arms. Unable to muster her courage, Cedar simply lay over on the floor herself, watched the fire burn in the stove, and listened to the wind howling outside like some mournful beast.

She was tired—oh, so very tired. She was tired of storms, tired of pain and fear—tired of being tired. As tears escaped her eyes and traveled over the bridge of her nose and temple, she allowed her eyes to close—allowed herself to daydream for a moment. She dreamt of the warmth of Tom Evans's arms, the resplendence of his smile, the joy of his laughter—and she dreamt of his kiss—his moist, hot, healing, impassioned kiss.

"I'm sorry."

Cedar thought she was still dreaming. But when warm breath tickled her ear, she opened her eyes to see Tom bending over her.

"I'm sorry," he repeated in a whisper, gazing at her with pain-filled eyes. "I woulda doubted me too," he said. "Can you forgive me, Cedar? Do you even wanna forgive me?"

It was as if the moment weren't a moment at all, but rather an hour—a day—a year. As Cedar sat stunned into silence at Tom Evans asking her for forgiveness—asking *her,* when she had been the one to let fear and doubt come between them—as she sat staring up into the inviting warmth of his eyes, an unexpected revelation washed over her—a vision in her mind that served as a rare epiphany to her soul.

Every hope of every dream of happiness she'd ever owned coming true was paraded before her in a vision—a vision of horses playfully bounding through vast pastures of sweet green grass—a memory.

Cedar was drenched in remembering—lost for a moment in enlightening reverie. In May of the year she'd been thirteen, she'd traveled with her father and mother to Louisville, Kentucky. The purpose for the trip was to fulfill her father's decade-old dream to witness the famed Kentucky Derby. Cedar well remembered the race, the atmosphere of excitement at the track, the exhilaration of the crowd—the little more than two minutes and thirty-seven seconds it took the chestnut thoroughbred Joe Cotton to win the race. However, what Cedar remembered most were the vast fields of emerald grass—the pastures of Kentucky where beautiful thoroughbred horses frolicked, shaking their heads with apparent giddiness as the breeze created by their running feathered long manes and tails in the wind.

She remembered how the family had paused before entering the city—paused to watch the stunning horses romp through the deep green Kentucky grasses. As Cedar had stepped up onto a fence to watch the horses, her father had sighed, and she looked to him to see a broad smile spread across his handsome face—the smile one only smiles when a dream has just come true.

"You like the horses, Daddy?" she asked.

"I do," he whispered, seeming almost reverenced by the sight of the horses before him. He looked at her then, his eyes warm and filled with hope and love—love for her.

"Moments like this are rare, Cedar," he told her then. He looked back to the horses. "Moments when something you've waited for your whole life is offered to you . . . and you have one chance to claim it." He'd paused, and she remembered the way his eyes had narrowed. "You can't be afraid to reach out and take hold of the moment when it's offered, angel. You've got to take it . . . reach out and snatch it before something pulls it away." He made a gesture of reaching out, fisting the air, and pulling it back to his chest.

In that instant—standing there on the fence watching the beautiful chestnut and black horses frolic in the field—Cedar had understood that her father was realizing a dream. She'd understood that, although he was trying to teach her something, the thing he was trying to teach her was something she couldn't truly comprehend—not yet. At that moment, the elegant thorough-breds had only put Cedar in mind of Tom Evans—the man she'd been dreamy-eyed over and calf-loved as a child. Horses always reminded young Cedar of Tom Evans, for she remembered how the young cowboy loved horses more than anything. Thus, in that long-ago moment shared with her father, Cedar hadn't truly comprehended the message he'd planted in her heart. She'd only thought he'd simply been overcome with joy at realizing his own dream.

Now, however—now the full meaning of her father's counsel that day swelled in her heart. She felt tears streaming down her face as she also recognized the irony of it all—that she'd actually been thinking of Tom Evans in those moments—

thinking of Tom as her father told her to reach out and take hold when chance itself presented a thing offered only once in a lifetime.

"Don't pause when that one chance in a lifetime is offered to you, Cedar," her father's words echoed in her mind. "Reach out, take hold, and never let go!"

"I'm sorry, Cedar," Tom was saying. "Please, I—"

But his plea was muffled into silence as Cedar reached out, taking hold of his face with both trembling hands, pulling him to meet her fervent kiss.

Tom didn't pause but gathered Cedar into the trembling strength of his arms. He was ravenous for the taste of her kiss, desperate to hold her—to feel her body against his and savor the warmth of her mouth. He'd felt it the instant she'd touched him—her release of timidity borne of pain and fear. Her kiss was void of any doubt. She owned no lingering doubt in him—no lingering doubt in herself.

The memory of a herd of wild mustangs he'd once seen as a boy flittered through his mind—the vision of the beautiful chestnut mare that had paused to study him for a long, lingering moment before racing off to the horizon. That moment with the beautiful mustang had branded his heart—and Tom Evans had been a horseman ever since. He knew he sensed the same wild freedom rising in Cedar as they kissed. He imagined they were not trapped in a snowbound schoolhouse with three frightened children nestled nearby but rather that they were standing in a green pasture—the summer sun warming their faces and limbs as the balmy wind played with Cedar's hair just the way it had feathered the mane of the wild mustang so many years before.

She was his! She was his! He could taste it in her kiss—feel it in the way her body molded to his. He'd won her. For all his stupidity and manly weakness, he'd won her heart.

He pulled them both to their feet as he continued to make love to her, for he was ravenous with wanting as passion swirled around them—consuming them like a windswept flame consumed the prairie.

Suddenly, aware that the wild fervor of his affections might actually be causing her discomfort, Tom abruptly broke the seal of their lips, pulling her against him as he struggled to regulate his breathing.

"I didn't doubt you . . . not really," she whispered.

"It don't matter," he breathed—almost panted for the sake of restricting passion. "None of it matters."

Cedar didn't worry about the tears on her cheeks, the tears Tom Evans brushed away with his thumbs as he took her face between his strong hands. As he gazed at her, she smiled—for she knew what he would say next.

"I love you," he whispered. His voice was low and breathy at first. But then the deep, masculine boom of determination and confidence she so loved rumbled in his throat as he said, "I love you, Cedar Dale . . . and when this storm finally blows itself out, I'm gonna haul you home, and I'm gonna . . . I'm gonna . . . well, I guess I'd better haul ya on over to the preacher's house first."

"Promise?" Cedar breathed, caressing his face with her hands before running her fingers up through his hair.

"Do I promise to haul you home . . . or do I promise to haul you on over to the preacher's house first?" he teased.

She smiled, delighted by the playful mischief that mingled with the desire smoldering in his molasses-colored eyes. "Both," she giggled.

"Yes," he said.

"Do you know that I've loved you for as long as I can remember, Tommy Evans?" she asked.

He chuckled warmly. "You keep callin' me Tommy, and we might not make it over to the preacher's house first," he teased.

Her smile broadened, for she loved his teasing—loved that he would tease her about such a thing when she knew he would never haul her home without marrying her first.

"I love you," she whispered. "And you and I . . . we're gonna raise the best horses this side of Kentucky."

"And babies too," Tom added.

"Yes," Cedar giggled, a thrill of anticipation racing through her. "Though I don't know much about horses," she admitted. Remembering then the moment of reverie—the epiphany she'd experienced over her father's beloved, and now fully comprehended, counsel years before—she added, "Though I did see the famous thorough-bred Joe Cotton win the Kentucky Derby when I was thirteen." A puzzled expression slightly puckered Tom's brow as she added, "And I was thinkin' of you . . . at the very moment Joe Cotton won the race. I've been thinking of you my whole life, Tommy Evans."

"A-are you tellin' me you saw Joe Cotton . . . the chestnut bred outta Woodburn Stud . . . you saw that horse win the Derby?" he asked.

Cedar giggled again, delighted by his obvious awe.

"Yes," she told him. "The year I was thirteen, Joe Cotton won the Kentucky Derby with a time just over two minutes and thirty-seven seconds." She caressed the pucker from his brow. "Why? Don't you believe me when I say I was thinking of you at that moment?"

"I-I believe you," he rather stammered. "It's just . . ." He shook his head, as if stunned by residual disbelief. "Baby, you know that new stallion breedin' my mares?"

"Yes," she prodded.

"I bought him from Woodburn Stud in Kentucky almost three months ago. Joe Cotton was his sire."

Cedar understood the expression of astonishment on Tom's face then. It was extraordinary, the thread connecting Cedar's moment of understanding with Tom's stallion's siring. But to Cedar, all of it was extraordinary. Thus she wasn't as astonished as he was—though she did delight in his astonishment.

"See?" she whispered. "I was meant to come back here and marry you . . . raise horses with you."

"And babies," he added.

"Yes," she giggled as his mouth descended to hers again.

She bathed in the bliss of his affections then. As his mouth rained a wonderment of passion-borne ecstasy over her, Cedar Dale was delirious with a sense of blessed attainment—a knowledge that in reaching out and taking hold of the dream when it was offered to her, she would know true, exhilarating, and fulfilling happiness. And she would know it in entwining her life with Tom Evans's.

"I ain't never seen kissin' the likes of that before!"

Percy Buckets's exclamation caused Tom to break the seal of the impassioned kiss he and Cedar had been sharing.

He chuckled as Fanny whispered, "Me neither!"

Cedar glanced to see little Petunia nodding her head in wide-eyed wonder.

"Then you ain't never seen kissin' done right," Tom chuckled.

"Are you gonna marry her or somethin', Mr. Evans?" Fanny asked.

"Yes, ma'am, I am. As soon as this snow stops."

"Well, the snow did stop," Percy said. "And it's mornin' to boot."

Glancing past Tom to the window, Cedar saw that indeed the snow no longer fell—that the wind had died as well—that the sun was just breaking over the horizon in the east.

"Mr. Evans?" Petunia began.

"Yes, darlin'?" Tom said, unwillingly releasing Cedar and hunkering down before the small girl.

"Yer horse," she began, pointing to the horse standing in one corner at the back of the room. "He doin' his outside business inside."

Cedar giggled as she looked to see that the horse had indeed lifted his tail and was dropping horse apples on the floor.

"Well, that's what horses do when ya bring 'em to school, Petunia," Tom chuckled. "I guess I'll have to clean up after him good before I ride him home, huh?"

"Yes, sir," Petunia nodded.

"Percy? Fanny? Petunia?" called a frantic female voice from the other side of the school-house door.

"It's Mama!" Fanny cried, racing toward the door with her brother and sister.

Cedar sighed as she watched Percy lift the bolt. Tom smiled when Agnes Hollar Buckets stumbled into the room, gathering her children in her arms as she sobbed her gratitude to heaven for their safety.

The children's father, Willard Buckets, stumbled in after her. He looked up to Tom, nodding his head and saying, "Mornin', Tom." Looking to Cedar, he added, "Ma'am."

"Mornin', Willard," Tom said. Leaning toward Cedar, he whispered, "I best go explain why I'm standin' here in my birthday suit. Especially since Agnes don't approve of birthday suits past the age of three."

Cedar giggled and followed him as he strode across the room toward the reunited family. She bit her lip, restraining her own amusement as she saw Agnes Hollar Buckets look up to Tom, blushing to the very core of her soul as her eyes lingered on the bareness of his chest.

"The kids said they was down by the crick when the storm come in," Tom began.

"We've been worried near to death!" Agnes exclaimed, brushing tears from her cheeks as her eyes traveled the length of Tom Evans's body once more.

"We thought they'd been caught out in it," Willard exclaimed. "I thank ya, Tom. I thank ya for takin' care of 'em for us."

Willard offered a hand to Tom, and Tom accepted it.

"I'm just glad we were here and could help 'em out," Tom said.

"Cedar?" Cedar heard her mother's voice and looked up to see her mother and Reno stepping into the schoolhouse.

The moment her mother caught sight of her, she burst into sobbing.

"Oh, Cedar!" Flora cried, racing forward and flinging her arms around her daughter. "Oh, my baby! I've been so worried! I've been torturing myself over sending you to town."

"Darlin'," Reno said, hugging them both. "I was hopin' Tom found ya and that you two were holed up safe and sound somewhere together."

"Thank you again, Tom," Willard said, gratefully shaking Tom's hand again. "I guess we best get the children home."

"But we want to go to the weddin'!" Fanny whined.

"What weddin'?" Agnes asked, looking from Tom to Cedar and back.

"I heard Mr. Evans say he was gonna haul Miss Cedar to the preacher before he hauled her home," Fanny explained.

Cedar blushed as Agnes's eyes widened—as Reno chuckled—and Fanny continued, "And then Miss Cedar said she was meant to come back and marry Mr. Evans and raise horses with him."

"And babies," Petunia put in.

"Oh, my!" Agnes gasped. She stood, hurrying to where Tom had placed the children's coats to dry near the stove.

"Well, I guess I oughta say congratulations, Tom," Willard offered.

"Help me get the children dressed, Will," Agnes ordered her husband. "We need to get 'em home."

Cedar saw Agnes blush as she looked to Tom again. Tom nodded and winked at the woman, sending her into nervous smiles and giggling.

As Flora wiped tears from her eyes, Reno slapped Tom on the back with approval.

"It don't do no good to drag yer feet," Reno said.

"Amen," Tom sighed.

"I suppose you might be needin' yer shirt back, Mr. Evans," Percy said, "if'n yer plannin' on goin' to the preacher's house and such."

"Thank you, Percy," Tom chuckled as Percy pulled the shirt off over his head, offering it to Tom.

"Thank you, Tom," Agnes said as she ushered

her children out the door. She paused, looking to Cedar and offering a sincere smile. "And congratulations, Miss Dale. I'm sure you'll be very happy."

"Thank you," Cedar said.

Once the Buckets family was gone—the children whining all the way about wanting to go to the preacher's house for the wedding—Flora hugged Cedar once more.

"My darling!" she breathed. "I was so worried. Reno said Tom had gone into town after you . . . that you'd be fine . . . but I was so worried."

"I know, Mama," Cedar said. "I'm sorry."

Brushing more tears from her cheeks, Flora smiled at her daughter. "But you're fine, and it seems things are all better between you two."

"Yes," Cedar said.

"I ain't really gone about this the proper way, Flora," Tom began, "but I was wantin' to ask you if I can have yer permission to—"

"Oh, quit babbling on, Tom," Flora interrupted. "Let's all just get over to the preacher's house," she said, reaching out to pinch his cheek as if he were no older than Percy Buckets. "I don't want anything else getting in the way of my daughter's happiness."

"And I don't want anything else gettin' in the way of me and my wife finally havin' some time to spend a couple of days in—" Reno began. He was hushed, however, by Flora's hand covering his mouth.

"You just get that horse out of here and help me over to the preacher's house," she scolded, though she smiled at him with more love and desire than all the world could hold.

Looking to Tom, she said, "We'll expect you to be right behind us, so put your shirt on . . . and your coat." With a wink, she added, "Then you can take Cedar home and keep her warm for the rest of your days, Tom Evans."

"Yes, ma'am," Tom chuckled.

Cedar watched her mother and Reno lead Tom's horse from the schoolhouse. Reaching back, Reno pinched her mother's sitter, and Cedar giggled when her mother playfully scolded him.

Tom slipped his arms into the now well-used and wrinkled shirt.

"It's hard tellin' what them children heard us talkin' about . . . or what they saw goin' on when we thought they were still sleepin'," Tom said, resting his hands at Cedar's waist as she endeavored to fasten the buttons at the front of his shirt.

Cedar shrugged. "It doesn't matter," she said. "In half an hour, I'll be your wife . . . and it won't matter what anyone says." She paused, trailing her finger from the hollow of his throat, down over his chest, until she came to the next button in need of fastening.

Tom caught her hand in his, drawing it to his mouth and placing a firm kiss to the inside of her wrist. He pulled her head to his, driving one ravenous kiss to her mouth before releasing her.

"Get yer coat, darlin'," he said. "We need to get us to the preacher's house so we can start raisin' babies and horses."

"Babies and horses," Cedar breathed. "It sounds like a dream."

"It will be," Tom said, brushing a strand of hair from her face. "I promise."

He kissed her once more, sealing his promise—the promise of a life abundant with horses, babies, and love.

Epilogue

"Grampa," Jimmy asked, tugging on Reno's shirttail. "When will the cousins be here?"

"Oh, 'bout suppertime, I expect, Jimmy," Reno chuckled, tousling Jimmy's dark hair. Jimmy smiled, and Reno shook his head—astounded at how much the little boy looked like his daddy, Tom Evans.

"Daddy," Raina said, tugging on Reno's arm.

"What, honey?" Reno asked his young daughter. He smiled, instantly enchanted by the little girl with Flora's chestnut hair and his own blue eyes.

"Tom says I can go out and see Solomon if you come with me," she answered. "Oh, please, Daddy. Can we?"

Reno looked to Tom, who simply shrugged. "She sure likes that Clydesdale colt, Reno."

"Don't I know it," Reno sighed, shaking his head. He had the dangedest time refusing Raina anything. Flora was forever accusing him of spoiling their daughter.

"Can I go out too, Daddy?" Jimmy asked Tom.

"If it's all right with Grandpa," Tom said, smiling.

"Can I come, Grampa?" Jimmy asked.

Reno shook his head again. The fact was

he couldn't refuse his grandchildren anything either—and Tom knew it.

"Of course, son," Reno answered. "We might as well see if yer grandma wants to come along."

Raina squealed with delight. Taking hold of Jimmy's hand, she chirped, "Let's go get my mama. Daddy never tells her no . . . and she'll let us play with the puppies in the barn after we see Solomon."

Reno heard Tom chuckle as Raina and Jimmy ran off hand in hand in search of Flora.

"I remember when you weren't such a big, soft, fluffy bunny, Reno Garrett," Tom teased.

Reno chuckled, nodding his agreement. "I can't tell none of the kids no. And now Slater and Lark will be ridin' up at any moment, and there'll be three more to run me around."

"It's good for ya, Reno," Tom said, slapping his father-in-law soundly on the back. "They keep ya young."

"They wear me out," Reno laughed. He sighed, secretly thinking he was just as impatient as Jimmy was for Tom's brother, his wife, and their three kids to arrive. He liked when both litters of Evans children were together. It was fun for Raina—and for himself.

"Mama," Mittie began as Cedar shelled peas into the bowl in her lap.

"Mm-hmm?" Cedar prodded.

"Is it true that cousin Sue is named after a cow?" Mittie asked.

Cedar giggled, handed Mittie a handful of peas, and answered, "Cousin Sue is named after a bull, Mittie . . . not a cow."

"Well, I think it's awful mean to name a pretty little baby girl after a cow," Mittie mumbled. "You and Daddy didn't name me after a cow, did ya, Mama?"

Cedar smiled. "No, sweetie. You're named after a horse."

"Really, Mama?" Mittie asked. "A horse? One of Daddy's horses?"

Cedar handed Mittie a few more peas, smiling as the little girl popped them into her mouth one by one.

"No, honey," Cedar giggled. "I'm just teasing. Daddy and I just heard your name somewhere before you were born. We thought it was pretty, and it is . . . just like you."

Mittie smiled. "I like that story. Though, if I had to choose, I'd rather be named after one of Daddy's horses than after one of Uncle Slater's ol' cows."

"It's a bull Sue's named for, honey," Cedar corrected.

"We're goin' out with Gramma and Grampa to see Solomon, Mittie," Jimmy exclaimed as he tumbled up onto the front porch holding hands with Raina. "Do ya wanna come along?"

"Are we now?" Flora Garrett asked as she stepped up onto the porch.

"Daddy says we can go, Mama," Raina told her. "But I can tell he wants you to come too."

Cedar bit her lip, restraining her giggle as Jimmy nudged Raina with one arm and whispered, "Yer daddy just wants to go sparkin' with yer mama."

"I know it," Raina said, rolling her eyes with exasperation. She smiled, however, adding, "But they won't start into sparkin' until we get to the barn . . . and then we can play with the puppies longer."

As Cedar's mother winked at her, affirming that what the children expected would be exactly what would happen, she smiled. Cedar could never have imagined her own life being so full and wonderful—let alone her mother's. A familiar twinge of remembered pain and loss pricked her heart as she thought of her father. But the pain subsided nearly as quickly as it had come, and her heart fluttered as Tom stepped up onto the porch then. The sight of him thrilled her as much as it ever had—even more perhaps.

"Hey, baby," he said, leaning down to kiss her where she sat in her chair shelling peas.

Jimmy rolled his eyes. "See, Raina . . . my folks are as much sparkin' fools as yers," he mumbled. "Come on, Gramma," he said, taking Flora's hand. "Grampa might change his mind if we don't hurry." He paused, looking back to his mother and father. "You'll come and get us when the cousins get here, won't ya?"

"Yes, son," Tom said. "You all just have fun with Grampa and Gramma. But you keep away from that new stallion's stall out in the new barn, all right?"

"Yes, Daddy," Jimmy said. "Come on, Gramma," he said, tugging on Flora's arm.

"Have fun, Mama," Cedar giggled as she watched her mother being dragged away by the three children.

She looked to Tom when she heard him chuckling.

"What?" she asked.

"Reno and yer mama are gonna be plumb wore out by the time Slater and Lark head home with their litter next week," he said.

"I know," Cedar giggled. "But they love it."

"Yes, they do," he said.

He hunkered down in front of her then, removing the bowl of peas from her lap and setting it aside on the porch. Cedar smiled, recognizing the mischief in his eyes—delighted by it.

"I figure Reno and yer mama will keep the kids busy for near to half an hour at least," he said. "So we can either shell peas or do some mean kissin'. What'll it be, Mrs. Evans?"

Cedar smiled, sighed, and leaned forward, lacing her fingers at the back of Tom's neck. He was so handsome! Even more handsome than he'd been the day she'd married him. She liked the sifted silver at his temples—the wrinkles at the corners of his eyes that were evidence of a life lived with a happy countenance. He was a wonderful, caring, protective father—a faithful, loving husband—everything she'd always known he would be.

"Well, you know I'd rather spend half an hour kissing you than shelling peas any day, Tommy Evans," Cedar giggled.

Tom Evans smiled—pressed a warm, firm kiss to Cedar's mouth. He pulled away, gazing at her for a long moment—chuckling as she began twisting and untwisting a loose strand of hair around one index finger. It was a lure she always cast for him—a gesture she wasn't even aware she made most of the time—an invitation for him to take her in his arms and sweep her away into an impassioned exchange of affections, whether trifling or intimate. And as was ever the outcome of her casting her lure, he was willingly and gladly hooked.

"Then come on, Mrs. Evans," he said, rising and pulling her to her feet. "Time's a-wastin'."

Cedar giggled as Tom gently pushed her back against the outer wall of the ranch house.

"Do you still love me, Cedar?" he asked, placing a teasing kiss at one corner of her mouth.

"Yes," she whispered. "More than ever." She kissed his cheek.

"More than ya did that first night we kissed out there in the moonlight with Johnny Thornquist's fiddle singin' across the meadow?" he asked, kissing her neck.

"Yes," Cedar whispered, kissing his lips.

"More than ya did that night we spent in the schoolhouse with Percy Buckets and his little sisters, Fanny and Petunia?" he whispered, kissing her other cheek.

"Yes," Cedar giggled.

"More than ya did on our weddin' night when we—"

"Hush, Tommy!" Cedar scolded, covering his mouth with her hand.

"Well, do ya?" he asked, brushing her hand from his face and pressing his mouth to hers.

"Yes," she breathed.

"Well, I love you more too," he said, the deep rumble of his voice thick with emotion.

Cedar wrapped her arms tightly around her husband—hugging him—holding him—never wanting to release him again. Sometimes she still wondered if it were all a dream—if being married to Tom Evans and having his children to love and cherish was real. But it was real—and it was wonderful.

"Hurry up and kiss me, Tommy," Cedar said, gazing up at him with tears brimming in her eyes.

"Kiss me the way you did that night in the meadow . . . the way you did that night in the schoolhouse . . . the way you always do."

"My pleasure, ma'am," he whispered. "It'll surely be my pleasure."

*If you wanna have a *really* sentimental and syrupy experience while reading this Author's Note for *The Windswept Flame*, download the old sentimental song "Run for the Roses" by Dan Fogelberg first and then play it on repeat as you read. You'll see why. I'm *so* sappy!
~Marcia Lynn McClure

Author's Note

Sometimes a moment in life will offer an epiphany that we didn't fully appreciate, understand, or even recognize while we were experiencing it. Sometimes we don't even realize, until much later, that it *was* an epiphany—a literal, true, life-altering epiphany. Often it isn't until we drift away into sentimental reverie decades later that we realize a certain moment factually changed our life—set us on a different path—was instrumental in molding us into the person we became. One of those moments—one of those late-recognized, life-changing moments, one of my treasured flashes of epiphany—is woven through this book. Like a cherished secret I've only shared a few times, only let myself linger in remembering once in a while, one night—one moment I lived so long ago, and many of its beloved, melancholy details—wind through *The Windswept Flame* like the Pecos roams the desert. Though this moment from my past has always been a profound and tender memory for me—though I've always known I should've appreciated it more when it happened—it wasn't until I extended *The Windswept Flame* into a novel that I consciously realized just how deeply that seemingly simple moment had touched me—changed me—and in many regards actually saved me.

By the time I turned sixteen, I'd been weathered. Not by anything so terrible as losing a loved one, serious illness, or transgression—simply by heartbreak—thorough, devastating, debilitating heartbreak. The experience had left me broken—not visibly of course, but emotionally and physically. My heart ached with agony almost constantly for months. Any thoughts of the thing that had so thoroughly destroyed me would literally send me into violent vomiting and tears. I was unhappier than I'd ever imagined a person could be. Everything felt dark and hopeless for a time. Yet I was sixteen, resilient, and obviously a fabulous actress, for very few people knew I was struggling to eat, to sleep, and to find joy. My mother knew, and one good friend, but no one else. I kept it all secreted to myself and went about making certain no one else I knew was as unhappy as I was. It was literally the most miserable, despairing time of my life to this point.

Still, a year passed, and I'd begun to recover—or at least I thought I had. I'd made some new friends that were wonderful! They were fun, energetic, and silly, and I could lose myself in their company and escape the scars and lingering pain of heartache. I turned seventeen and went on with my life. I was fine. I mean, at least I wasn't throwing up too often anymore. So along I went—la-dee-da—doing tons of fun stuff with friends and keeping very, very, very busy—and thinking I was fine. After all, I had only been sixteen. How bad could the damage have been, right?

So there I was, la-dee-da-ing my way through my senior year in high school. Some great stuff happened too. A boy I'd been in love with in the fourth and seventh grades moved back to Albuquerque, and we were hanging out a lot. (He'd actually proposed to me during the fourth grade incident. It was wildly romantic—a ring and everything!) I was doing a lot of singing (especially duets with a boy I just adored), I had a job as a secretary with a fancy corporation, and I was looking ahead to getting out of high school and into real life. I'd even (rather unknowingly) met the dream-borne man who would one day be my perfect, wonderful husband (though it would still be some time yet before things got going there). Everything was wonderful! Wasn't it? No—it wasn't. Fear, pain, and the brutal weathering I'd endured had hardened me—though I didn't know how much. Thus, when what was probably one of the most thoughtful and sweet, beautiful and romantic, fairy-tale evenings of my life was sort of thrust upon me, I didn't recognize it until it was coming to an end. Furthermore, I didn't fully appreciate it for years and years—not until my heart had healed and I was finally blessed with that wonderful thing we all call hindsight.

One of my closest and most cherished friends at this time was named (for all intents and purposes) "Phil." Phil was a handsome, kind, fun, outgoing, multitalented young man, and I literally adored him. He'd been blessed with a very matured, very masculine singing voice that was pretty stunning for his age. He and I occasionally practiced and performed duets together—sometimes in rather romantic situations such as wedding receptions. (This often prompted questions from audience members as to whether we were engaged—how funny!) Now, in addition to being an absolutely dreamy singer, Phil owned another rare talent— Phil could dance! Oh, sure, lots of guys could dance, but Phil knew how to really dance! Dance—as in all-the-girls-at-the-dances-wanted-to-dance-with-him. Phil would powerfully and capably hold you in perfect ballroom dance position, swirl you around the room until you felt just like Ginger Rogers (in a way that made you look down to see if you were literally floating on a cloud), all the while making it seem completely effortless for you and himself. Now, the clincher is this: as Phil swirled you around the dance floor in some low-lit, streamer-strewn room to a slow, romantic song that everyone else could only sway back and forth to, he was totally manly! I mean really masculine! Furthermore, he didn't have to concentrate. He could hold entire conversations, sing along to whatever song was playing, and really sweep you off your feet in every way imaginable. My darlings—ladies—girlfriends—chicas . . . Phil was one of those boys we girls only dream of! And as I adored him, I began to realize how truly damaged I was—how broken and in pieces my heart remained. What girl in her right mind wouldn't hitch up her skirts and take out after Phil like a bee to honey? A heartbroken one, that's who—one who'd been hurt and had lost who she was along the way.

So life went along, and I graduated. I did the regular summer stuff—worked, dated, hung out with friends, saw Bryan Adams open for Journey—you know, the same old same old.

Phil and I had been hanging out a lot at parties and dances and singing together. Then it happened: he asked me out. Terror rippled through me, of course—because I adored him, loved him, and valued his friendship so much. I knew I wasn't in any state of mind or heart to have anything to offer above intimate friendship, and it frightened me. How many guy friends do we lose along the way because dating makes stuff weird? That was what I was afraid of where Phil was concerned. Furthermore, I was struggling with the fact that I was about ready to leave for college and would be leaving my good friends behind—the friends who had so unknowingly helped carry me through the most monstrous storm of my life—and I was feeling insecure, afraid, and weak. However, I adored Phil and couldn't possibly have told him all my secrets—but could never have spurned his request. So I accepted his offer, and the night of our official "date" was planned. Phil planned it—and, boy, did he plan it!

I don't remember what night of the week it was; I don't remember what time he arrived to collect me. I do, however, remember opening the door to see Phil standing on my front porch. He was sharp-dressed, not in tuxedo or suit, but in dress pants, dress shoes, a white shirt, a classy tie, and a sports coat. (Why do they call it a "sports coat" anyway? Guys never play sports in them.) He offered me a dozen roses (which, believe me, in 1983 must've cost a mint!), and I was instantly and entirely overwhelmed—overwhelmed with anxiety! All the agony of heartbreak, all my fear and self-doubt, came flooding back, and I can remember hoping that I wouldn't throw up and ruin Phil's evening—or the carpeting in his parents' van.

I forced on my happy face, and we left to experience literally the dream date of my life—of any girl's! I'm going to leave out some of the details of my feelings during the first part of that night because I want to focus on the sweet, romantic beauty of it. Suffice it to say, the entire time I was worried about my stomach and whether Phil could tell I was a nervous wreck. In knowing Phil wasn't "the one," I likewise felt overwhelmed with guilt because, believe me, he really dropped a wad that night—and I felt guilty for it.

After he picked me up, Phil drove us to what was (at the time) one of the most hoity-toity restaurants in town, the original Gardunos—when it was awesome instead of iffy like it is now. Even though I was already seventeen, no boy or man had every taken me to such a nice place. The ambiance was awesome! Beautiful flowering plants were everywhere—low-lighting and soft music. Soft music, that is, until Phil asked a musician to serenade us. Yes, there we sat, in one of the best restaurants in town, sharing a giant bowl of guacamole as our appetizer, with a finely dressed, handsome, older Hispanic man serenading us with his guitar and voice. The guilt and anxiety I was experiencing was crushing!

My stomach was in knots—and I still needed to pile a large plate of enchiladas on top of it!

I remember sitting there in the restaurant across from Phil thinking, *Marcia! What is wrong with you? This guy is your friend! There's no pressure. He doesn't want anything from you other than to have a wonderful evening. So why can't you just have a wonderful evening?*

I don't even want to talk about how much Phil paid for dinner. If I did, I'd feel a wild urgency to Facebook him and ask him if he wanted me to write him a check for what I should've pitched in twenty-seven years ago. However, I figure the accumulated interest would make my ability to fit that many numbers on a check space impossible—and no one has that much money anyway. So Phil paid for dinner (I hope he had a job—I can't remember if he did), and we left the restaurant.

The enchiladas were staying down, and I began to relax. We'd been at the restaurant for a long time, and I figured with what he spent for flowers and dinner, he'd take me home so he could run downtown, open his guitar case, and start singing in hopes of making a few hundred handfuls of change in an effort to recoup the vast expenses of the evening.

He didn't take me home immediately following dinner, however. Instead, we went for a drive. It was a warm summer night, and the enchiladas had really settled in, so I didn't mind at all. Phil was a rare jewel, and I was always comfortable and happy in his company. We drove for a little while—wound through the city of Albuquerque—from somewhere up near the east side, down toward the north valley, to eventually end up meandering along a street called Rio Grande Boulevard. (I love that street. Even now, I occasionally go out of my way to wind down its familiar curves.)

Unexpectedly, Phil turned off Rio Grande Boulevard, onto Rio Grande Lane, and then took a right onto Los Poblanos Lane. This place was very familiar to me, so I wasn't surprised to see the empty field at the corner. I *was* surprised, however, when Phil pulled the van intentionally—albeit slowly—off the road and into the center of the grassy field.

"What are you doing?" I asked. Having had too many other boys try to, shall we say, "sequester" me in order to (to use a painfully archaic term) "put the moves on me," I was a little unsettled. Still, this was Phil—and Phil was a good guy.

"You'll see," was his only answer, however.

He parked the van, and I watched as he got out and came around to my side. Opening my door, he offered me his hand and said, "Come on."

I was still puzzled and tired, and my anxiety was renewed. But again, Phil was a wonderful boy, and I trusted him.

He leaned into the van for a moment and turned on the stereo. Then he took my hand, led me out into the middle of the field, and as Dan Fogelberg began to sing "Run for the Roses," he gathered me into his arms, and we began to dance. We danced—there in the sweet summer grass—with a cool evening breeze to kiss our skin—under a moon hanging like a perfect opal among twinkling stars that were scattered like sifted diamonds over a canopy of indigo velvet. We danced—really danced. (Seriously—the moon was an opal, and the stars looked like diamonds.)

I remember being nervous—like, giddy-nervous. As Phil held me—slowly led me in a dreamy slow dance to such a beautiful, senti-mental, rather melancholy song—the truth, the magic of the entire evening, finally rinsed over me. What a wonderful boy this was! I was so lucky—so blessed to know him—to have him as a friend. How romantic the evening had been, the stuff of dreams, and he'd planned it all—for me!

As the song played—as Phil sang along to it—the lyrics began to seep into my conscious thoughts—into my heart and soul. The song is about a horse, a racehorse, and the "run for the roses"—the Kentucky Derby. However, the lyrics hold infinitely more meaning—I'm sure Dan Fogelberg intended for them to—and they did for me that night—and for the rest of my life.

In my heart, "Run for the Roses" is a song

about growing up—about the innocence and easy joy of childhood—about recognizing our own strength and endurance so that we can weather the storms of life to come. It's about not letting those storms keep us from the "home" that is ourselves. It's about savoring life no matter what, reaching out, and grabbing hold of the moments that are opportunities of a lifetime—opportunities of knowing joy—opportunities to truly live life instead of just allowing it to pass by.

The moments spent with Phil dancing beneath a moon- and starlit sky while "Run for the Roses" floated out over the field were beautiful. However, it was in that moment that I realized I'd lost myself. Hurt and pain had caused me to despair, and in despairing, I'd lost not only my joy but my true self. I realized I'd been moving through life without recognizing or appreciating the beautiful people and things around me. I'd lost my zest for enjoying the simple things and moments that make life so wonderful and exciting—moments like the one I was living in that instant. I'd lost my hope in ever being truly happy again. It was then that I missed myself and wanted myself back—and in the next instant, dancing there with Phil under a starry sky, I began to find myself again.

I relaxed all at once—enjoyed my moonlit waltzing with Phil—sweetly kissed him as we stood on my front porch sometime later—

watched him stride to his car and drive away. He'd picked a girl up at her house that night, but he left *me* standing on the porch.

To be honest, I can't remember if I even ever saw Phil again after that night. I left for college shortly thereafter, and I never saw him after that, I know. I'm thinking that it *was* the last time I saw him—because the feeling that it was lingers in me with a deep sense of regret and melancholy.

That night with Phil in the field that helped me remember myself also taught me something else—that no matter how brief an evening, an hour, a minute, or even a moment seems, it's the *moments* in life that affect us the most. Those are the brief breaths of time that scar or heal our hearts—the instances that teach us the most important lessons of life—the moments that mold who we become, who we are. Those sweet, tender mere minutes spent waltzing in the field with Phil was one of those moments for me. Of all the moments in my life—of all the brief breaths of life that taught me great lessons—that moment was one of the most profound. And twenty-seven years later, it was rewriting *The Windswept Flame* that made me suddenly so perfectly conscious of it.

I now know that an entire book can be inspired by one breathed memory. I know that an author can subconsciously mirror her own pain in her heroine's struggle—mirror her own healing.

Furthermore, you now know that heroes have always drifted in and out of my life, just as they do yours. Find them; recognize and appreciate them. They give you strength.

Ever since that night in the field with Phil, the song "Run for the Roses" has lingered in me as a profound, meaningful metaphor. The memory of that night and the metaphor of the song are so powerful that I can never listen to it without excess moisture brimming in my eyes. If I do listen to it more than once in succession, I'm reduced to weeping and undone for hours. For my gratitude to, and for, Phil—that unknowing hero lingering in my heart—is inexpressible.

Not too long ago I was coming home from downtown Albuquerque, winding along Rio Grande Boulevard, enjoying the sunshine, dry air, and old adobe houses along the way. As I approached the turnoff leading to Los Poblanos Lane, the memory of dancing with Phil in that sweet, grassy field under a beautiful and romantic night sky washed over me, and I turned on my left blinker. There's a big house where that empty field once was—a big house surrounded by tall hedges. The field is gone, and it makes me sad. But I cherish and own the memory. I still have the sweet, tender feelings tucked away in my heart— and no one can build a house over that.

I want you to know that it was only after I was well into the book that I realized the reason for

Tom Evans's breeding horses instead of raising cattle, and it's this simple—Dan Fogelberg's "Run for the Roses." Just like the moment when Cedar and Tom share a waltz in the moonlight was inspired by Phil's successful attempts at romancing me, Tom's love for horses was inspired by that oh-so-meaningful song. It's crazy, isn't it?—what your mind does when you're not paying attention.

I have to tell you that when I first began writing this Author's Note for *The Windswept Flame*, I felt it was too melancholy—that you might not enjoy it. So I went back and took out a few details and adjectives—hoping to lighten it up a bit. I've had so many readers write and tell me that they enjoy the Author's Notes in my books—that they enjoy hearing about where my inspiration comes from. I hope this Author's Note is one you can enjoy as well. If nothing else, you now know how completely sappy I am. But I *love* sappy—though I'm sure you already knew that.

Thus, I'm off—to run for the roses so that I don't ever miss "the dance" again! And thank you, Phil.

~Marcia Lynn McClure

The Windswept Flame Trivia Snippets

Snippet #1—Second only to violets and pansies, the daffodil is my favorite flower.

Snippet #2—After I'd finished this book, I was popping around on the Internet and came across a photo of "Phil" and his good friend that I thought I'd forgotten about—until I remembered Phil's friend's last name was Davies, just like Logan's.

Snippet #3—You know my friend Sandy? Yep, she's a hair twister! I used to (and still do) get a kick out of sitting in often hilarious conversation with her and watching her take hold of a strand of her hair (usually at the back of her head) and begin twisting. My daughter (named Sandy after my hair-twisting friend, Sandy) is also a hair-twister. She used to twist knots into her hair when she was little. Fortunately, I could usually untangle them and only ever had to cut one out. I hair-twist as well—though not as habitually as Sandy the Younger and Sandy the Elder.

Snippet #4—When I was growing up (actually, my entire life), in the months anywhere between Labor Day and mid-May, my mother would insist that I have a sweater or jacket with me at all times. Naturally, this often aggravated me, especially growing up in Albuquerque, where in mid-May the afternoon temperatures were usually in the 80s and I was forced into having to drag a coat home with me, along with all my books in the years before backpacks were a cool or standard school supply. I can remember whining at my mom about it—to which she would always say, "I remember a story my mom used to tell me . . . about a school bus full of children who died in a spring storm out in Holly before I was born. My mother always said that if those children had even had a light coat on, they wouldn't have died." Of course, I would roll my eyes, snatch up a jacket, and head off to whatever adventure or misery I was heading off to.

However, we all grow up and get a clue—eventually. I grew up, got married, had my children, and got a clue so that I nagged them anytime between Labor Day and mid-May about taking a sweatshirt with them when they went out to play or before I dropped them off for school. Then, in 1996, my mother, my daughter, and I attended a States family reunion in Holly, Colorado (about thirty miles from Lamar, Colorado, where my mother was born—where her mother used to nag her about taking a sweater with her every time she left the house between Labor Day and mid-May). Naturally, as part of our trip, we headed out to the old cemetery in

Holly to see where those who had gone before us were resting.

While wandering among the tombstones (awash in mingled melancholy and appreciation as I always am in cemeteries), I glanced up and noticed a tall, monolithic stone marker some ways off in the distance. I meandered over, curious as to who the rich guy was, buried out in this humble, rural cemetery belonging to a tiny town where my Grandpa States had played high school football in the early 1930s. I noticed there were several small tombstones placed in rows in front of the large granite marker. Here's what's inscribed on that large marker:

IN MEMORY OF
those children and the bus driver
of the Pleasant Hill School District
No. 17 Kiowa County, Colorado
who gave their lives during the
blizzard of March 27th, 1931.
Mary Louise Stonebraker
Kenneth E. Johnson
Robert G. Brown
Arlo D. Untiedt
Mary Louise Miller
Carl E. Miller

Life lesson from Mom number seven million and thirty-five: always take a sweater or sweatshirt with you anytime you're going to leave the house between Labor Day and mid-May—even if you live in Albuquerque.

Thus, Cedar's mother was forever telling her to take a coat with her the spring Cedar and Tom were reunited and fell in love to finally spend forever together—in a blissful "run for the roses."

About the Author

Marcia Lynn McClure's intoxicating succession of novels, novellas, and e-books—including *The Visions of Ransom Lake*, *A Crimson Frost*, *Shackles of Honor*, and *The Whispered Kiss*—has established her as one of the most favored and engaging authors of true romance. Her unprecedented forte in weaving captivating stories of western, medieval, regency, and contemporary amour void of brusque intimacy has earned her the title "The Queen of Kissing."

Marcia, who was born in Albuquerque, New Mexico, has spent her life intrigued with people, history, love, and romance. A wife, mother, grand-mother, family historian, poet, and author, Marcia Lynn McClure spins her tales of splendor for the sake of offering respite through the beauty, mirth, and delight of a worthwhile and wonderful story.

Center Point Large Print
600 Brooks Road / PO Box 1
Thorndike, ME 04986-0001 USA

(207) 568-3717

US & Canada:
1 800 929-9108
www.centerpointlargeprint.com